Death's Midwife

by

Karen Eisenbrey

Published in the United States by
Not a Pipe Publishing, Independence, Oregon.
www.NotAPipePublishing.com

Paperback Edition

ISBN-13: 978-1-948120-76-0

Cover art by Michaela Thorn
Cover design by Benjamin Gorman
Map by Steve Scribner

Dedication

In memory of my late writing buddy
Anne Gilbert,
the first person other than me
to get acquainted with Luskell.
I hope she has been
reading along from the Other Side.

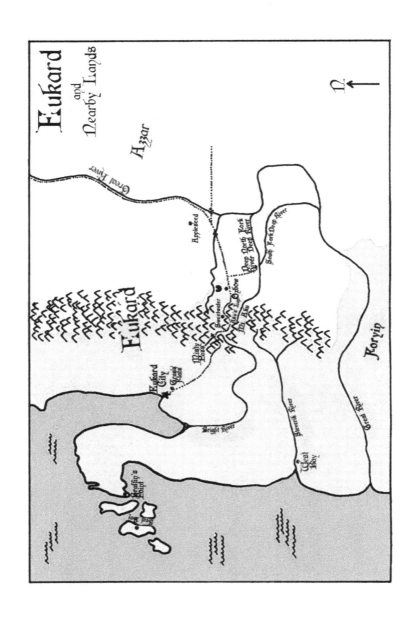

Death's Midwife

Chapter 1

Luskell plunged into the mountain lake. The frigid water shocked the breath from her lungs. She surfaced, gasping. Her bones ached with cold. Soon she couldn't feel anything. She forced her limbs to move and swam with clumsy strokes toward the bleached trunk of a half-submerged fallen tree.

That was the problem with accepting a dare from a dead man — it wouldn't occur to him it might kill her.

Luskell dragged her numb body onto the log and lay shivering, exhausted ... and exhilarated. She had waded before, but this was her first real swim. And maybe her last. Although late in the season, it was the first hot day at this elevation. Snow might fall any day, and in a few weeks, her time in Knot's Valley would end. She didn't have to return to shore the same way she'd come, though. Once she'd rested, she could become a bird and fly back, skipping the water altogether. Or be an otter, which would enjoy the swim more. Luskell smiled as she imagined playing in the water, then frolicking up the bank.

She stretched out on the log and closed her eyes. A light breeze carried the honey scent of lupines from the surrounding meadow. Sensation returned as Luskell's bare skin dried in the heat of the sun. It was almost worth braving the icy water for that delicious warmth alone, and one of the few benefits of complete solitude. This valley was, at least temporarily, her sole domain. No one except the mosquitoes cared whether she wore clothes or not.

Other than a brief visit from a supply party around Long Day, Luskell hadn't seen or spoken to another living person since Spring Balance, not even through mind-talking. She needed the time apart to master her skills ... and herself.

Fatigued by the swim and lulled by the warmth and quiet, Luskell slipped into a daydream: mostly sensation at first, relief from all pain buoyed by euphoria, warm as the sun on her skin; then the face associated with the feeling. Light hair, hazel eyes, gentle smile ... No. It wouldn't do to indulge such thoughts yet. Better to devote attention to family. With them, she knew where she stood.

Relaxation became sleep and daydream a real dream. Luskell found herself approaching a sunless but equally warm and bright place, the grassy meadow of the Other Side.

No flowers bloomed, but the living world's lupine scent accompanied her. Her grandfather Knot waited for her, shaking his head, waving her off. She was eager to see him, to brag about her swim, but his dark face looked stern, almost angry. What had she done now? But he was right — she should turn back. This was not her place.

Staying too long was a danger. She should wait for him to come to her dreams. But it was such a comfort to be near him.

Luskell?

The dream scattered as she jerked awake at the call. She hadn't heard it with her ears, which would have been odd enough in this remote place. This voice was in her mind, and it spoke her name with an Aklaka accent — the voice of one of the few living men she would rather see than Knot.

Laki? Where are you?

Just coming over the ridge.

He was *here*? With a squawk, she flopped back into the water and regretted it all over again. The cold and the effort to not drown robbed her of the focus necessary for transformation to bird or otter. She would have to reach the shore in her own form.

She crawled out on the muddy bank and shivered into her shirt. She stood and had one leg into her trousers as her oldest friend jogged toward her. He had the good grace to turn his back while she struggled to drag the other trouser leg over her damp skin without losing her balance. The problem wasn't that he'd never seen her naked, but that he had, with her enthusiastic consent. Those days were over, though. She hoped they could go on as friends.

"May I turn around now?" Laki glanced over his shoulder and seeing her dressed, faced her but kept his distance.

Luskell closed her damaged right eye to see him clearly, always a sight she enjoyed. Laki stood at least a head taller than Luskell, though she was considered tall and not only for a woman. His skin was several shades darker, his eyes nearly black. He wore his dappled deerskin "forest clothes" and had his long straight hair tied back. Her damaged eye saw Laki as a bright blob, flaming with strange colors. All living things appeared that way, a change since she had arrived in the spring. Rocks and dead things stood out as dark silhouettes. Luskell had only the beginnings of a theory about what it might mean.

Luskell put on her eyepatch. "I went s-swimming."

"Cold?"

Luskell shivered and nodded. "Mm-hm." She reached out to Laki's feelings, but he knew her too well. Thoughts and emotions alike were shielded.

He grinned and gazed out over the water. "I've never seen this lake without ice. It's pretty in summer."

"Not much warmer, though. Knot must have been tougher than I am, to swim every day."

"Or he was having a joke at your expense."

"I'm not sure he has — *had* a sense of humor."

Laki smiled. "You're allowed to say *has* for someone you talk to regularly, even if he's past and gone for most of us."

"Thanks. I'm never sure if it makes people uncomfortable." She sat on the grass to pull on her socks and boots. The ground was too rocky, the plant life too prickly, for bare feet.

"You're growing your hair out," Laki observed.

"No, I just haven't cut it since I've been here. No scissors, and I don't trust magic for that kind of task. Maybe Jagryn could do it, but I might end up bald or scalped." She stretched one curl out to its full length. She'd cut her hair short before coming to the Valley. It curled more tightly as it grew so it didn't look longer, though she could tell there was more of it. Especially wet. She shook her head vigorously, spattering droplets over Laki. "What are you doing here, anyway? Supply party's not due for weeks."

"We're finished in the city for the summer." Laki assisted his father, the Aklaka Ambassador, as translator and Listener. "Dadad and I were on our way to join the rest of the band, and I wanted to ... see the valley in a different season."

"You wanted to see the valley."

"All right, and see my best friend. Check how you were getting along. I thought I'd camp with you tonight, if you don't mind."

Luskell met his gaze. He was an easy man to look at, with his dark, sculpted features and laughing eyes. "I appreciate the company." She didn't have to force the smile to her face, though it conflicted with the pang in her heart. "But I haven't changed my mind."

He nodded. "I didn't think you would. I'll sleep outside."

The previous winter, when he'd been Aku's Keeper, they had enjoyed a brief love affair in this place. When he'd asked her to marry him, she'd told him no. Laki deserved better.

And Luskell didn't want to be Laki's wife. She didn't want to be anything but a wizard.

They walked together from the lakeshore up to the lodge at the head of the little valley. A typical Aklaka shelter, from outside it looked like a big mound growing with grass and shrubs. Under this disguised dome, a dug-out space provided room for cooking, sleeping, and supply storage. A tall Aklaka man could stand upright in the lodge. Tall as she was, Luskell never felt crowded. Still, she was glad for the warm summer day that allowed them to eat in the open air.

She prepared a simple meal of cold smoked fish, wild greens, and a bowl of ripe salmonberries, gathered before her swim. Laki contributed half a loaf of bread, purchased two days before in Eukard City. Even slightly stale, it was a treat for Luskell, who hadn't eaten bakery bread in months. They sat together with their backs to the lodge and watched the twilight deepen.

Laki sighed with contentment. "It's so much easier here in summer!"

Luskell smacked the back of her neck. "But in winter, you didn't have to deal with the mosquitoes." She pushed back her sleeve to display a collection of welts on her wrist. "I have bug bites on my bug bites."

He threw back his head and laughed. "The mighty wizard has no protection against tiny insects?"

"Nothing but herbal remedies that wear off too soon. The little monsters are apparently immune to magic."

Laki grew serious again. "I suppose if you don't have to spend every moment keeping warm, there's more time to feel lonely, too. It wasn't bad for me, but I know you thrive in company."

"The solitude was challenging, especially at first. It helped to have the responsibility of being Aku's Keeper."

"Something to do every day," Laki agreed.

"And there's a kind of company in Listening," Luskell said. The voices of trees, streams, and the Mountain, though they didn't speak to her, filled the empty days. "It was refreshing, too, not having to shield myself from other people's thoughts and feelings. And I haven't had to apologize in months! Sometimes I wish I could stay."

"I felt the same way, both winters I was here. Everything is clearer and simpler without other people. But you know why you can't."

"I do, but I also understand why Knot couldn't stay away. I see him or Ketwyn almost every night. Knot suggested ways to challenge my power and told me stories about when he lived in the valley." Laki turned to her with a concerned frown. "I thought you weren't supposed to go there."

"I didn't! Not once." Her near-visit before Laki's interruption didn't count. "They come to me in dreams. It's safe."

Departed souls could visit the dreams of anyone with power, but Luskell was better than most at remembering afterward. She had learned on her own how to deliberately visit them on the Other Side. Luskell didn't know anyone who could do that as easily as she could. A living soul who spent too much time on the Other Side risked a shortened life, or some other physical loss. Knot or Ketwyn could visit her dreams without any danger to her, though, which made it easier to keep her promise not to go to them. Still, the temptation lingered.

"Anyway, I wasn't completely alone. I had Aku." Luskell glanced up at the snow-capped peak, rosy in the last of the sunset light. "I played my fiddle and sang for her every day — every song I know, and things I made up. She must have liked it. She's been quiet all summer."

"I hope you haven't spoiled her. Not everyone is as talented as you." Laki grinned. "Will you play for me?"

In answer, Luskell climbed down into the lodge for her fiddle. She tuned up, then played her repertoire of dance tunes and ballads. To finish, she played the Aklaka lullaby known to soothe restless volcanoes.

Laki yawned. "That made me sleepy even without the words."

Luskell flopped down beside him. "Me, too."

He wrapped an arm around her shoulders and drew her in to lean against him. "You've done well here," he said. "I've always admired your fearlessness and spirit, but this ... no one should doubt you now."

"They shouldn't but they will."

His laughter vibrated through her. "Did I ever tell you the vision I had about you?"

"You still get those?"

"Not many. I channel most of that energy into Listening. But three years ago, before I joined you in Deep River, I saw ... us. You and me, together, grown up, with a little curly-haired child I guessed was our daughter."

"You didn't tell me about it. You said you hoped you'd have a daughter who was like me."

"That hasn't changed," he said. "But you weren't even fifteen. I didn't want to scare you or coerce you. It had to be your choice. But it was easy to imagine making a life with someone I'd known for so long. Save the trouble of starting a conversation with someone new."

"What's hard about that?" Luskell asked. "Anyway, you grew up with more girls than just me."

"And they always started the conversations, not me. I didn't have visions about them. Besides, the elders advised me to choose someone from outside our band. And there you were."

He felt warm and solid, a comfort in the gathering dark. Not for the first time, Luskell almost regretted her decision, though she was sure it was right. Wasn't it? After a decent interval, she ducked out of his embrace, but held his hand a moment longer. "You're my best friend, Laki. You know that, right? I'll always love you. But you should find someone else."

"That's what I'm trying to tell you. My vision wasn't about our daughter. It was about a new person who would be important to both of us: your baby brother."

Laki'd had a vision of Crett? Before he was even conceived? Luskell sat up and looked straight at him. "I didn't interfere with your destiny by turning you down?"

"You set me free to look in a new direction."

"And you've already found someone? Good for you." Luskell tried without much success to stamp out flames of jealousy. "Anyone I know?"

"I don't think so. She's been working at Embassy House for a few years, but it was probably after your time when she started."

Luskell had lived several summers at Embassy House, when her parents had assisted the Aklaka ambassador before Laki grew into the job. She tried to remember who worked there. Mostly domestic servants — cooks, chambermaids, and the like — but it was hard to picture Laki getting involved with any of them. As an official member of a delegation, he probably dealt with administrative staff that she, as a child, would never have met.

"Someone from the city. Well, that's outside your band," Luskell said. "What does your mother think?"

"I'm on my way to ask her. But ... I'd welcome your blessing, too."

Luskell released his hand. "Your mother might approve someone she hasn't met. I'm sorry, I can't."

"I should've guessed you'd be difficult."

"No, I'm being sensible. If you love this woman, anything you tell me about her is slanted by your feelings. Besides, does my opinion really matter?"

"It does. I trust your judgment, Luskell."

"Then don't ask me not to use it."

"Fair enough. I want you to meet her, anyway. If Mamam says yes, I'll see what I can arrange. But I think you'll like her. She can carry on a conversation with anyone and make them feel at home."

"So not one of us difficult magic folk?"

He laughed but didn't answer. He unrolled his bedding

and made camp in the shelter of the lodge.

"A spell tent might help with bugs," Luskell said. "Do you remember how?"

"Yes, it's one of the most useful spells I know." He worked the magic that would keep off bugs and hold in warmth. "I need to make an early start. Good night, Luskell."

Luskell would have liked to watch the stars awhile, but he was right. It was getting late. She wasn't sure she would be able to sleep, knowing someone else was in the valley. Especially him. But the fatigue from swimming wouldn't let her lie awake. In no time, she woke to the sounds of Laki packing up. Her dreams scattered before she could dwell on them, but an empty feeling lingered, even before Laki waved goodbye and left her alone once more.

Chapter 2

Six weeks later

On Fall Balance, Luskell welcomed the Aklaka supply party to Knot's Valley: her relief, Kiraknat, and Chakalan, one of Laki's friends. And Laki? What was he doing back?

Before she could ask, he grinned. "Mamam approved my choice. I'll travel to the city with you so you can meet my intended."

Luskell felt like she was falling, though she stood on solid ground. "That's ... good. I'm happy for you." She forced herself to smile. She had let him go. It was the right thing to do. But now it was really happening. Every step of the way, she had to keep on letting him go.

The presence of the others, and work to do, forced

Luskell to put her feelings aside to be dealt with later. The men brought fresh supplies, intended to last Kiraknat till mid-winter. He would supplement them with whatever he could hunt, trap, or gather.

They also provided a string of trout they'd caught along the way. That was Aklaka hospitality: guests never arrived empty-handed and hosts shared freely. Luskell rolled up her sleeves and tied her hair up to keep it from flopping into her face. It wasn't long enough for the braid she used to wear. She settled for a puff of curls on top of her head. She cooked the fish and served them with foraged berries, roots, and mushrooms from her stores. After her solitary half-year, she enjoyed playing host and eating a meal that included conversation. She didn't even realize the conversation had been conducted entirely in Aklaka until she and Laki were cleaning up after the meal, and he spoke to her in Eukardian.

"You do want to meet her, don't you?"

"Do you want me to?" Luskell countered.

"Of course I do! You're family."

"Don't ever forget it. And yes, I do."

That night, the men slept under the stars (and a spell tent — it was chilly now that summer was past). Luskell slept alone in the lodge, ready for solitude again. A whole afternoon with people, novel and entertaining as that might be, had worn her out. She slept deeply and didn't remember her dreams on waking.

But something felt not quite right. She quieted her mind and Listened to Aku. The Mountain dozed contentedly. No imminent eruption threatened. It didn't feel like danger so much as something missing. Someone shouted outside. Maybe that was it — not something missing, but three other people filling the valley.

After breakfast, Luskell hiked with Kiraknat out of the

valley so she could formally introduce him to Aku. He was older than Luskell, older even than Laki, a competent Listener but not as skilled as either of them. This was his first time as Aku's Keeper, partly because the Uklak had let Luskell go ahead of him. With her ability to read emotions, Luskell knew he resented her, but he worked hard to be mature about it. She couldn't imagine he was pleased to serve in winter, though.

Luskell would have preferred to hike with all of them, or to let Laki go with Kiraknat. But tradition — a tradition not much older than Luskell, but tradition, nonetheless — dictated that only Aku's current Keeper accompany the newly arrived relief to the special place where it was easiest to Listen to and soothe Aku.

They passed through the stand of trees behind the lodge. A few asters bloomed in the mountain meadow beyond, but most of the flowers had gone to seed already. The warm air carried a pungent scent of herbs and fir trees. A well-marked trail crossed a steep, rocky talus slope, dropped into a draw that even now held a snowfield, then climbed, steep and stair-like, to a broad ledge at the base of a rough cliff face. Although she sometimes flew here as an eagle, Luskell had been making this climb frequently for months. It no longer felt difficult. Kiraknat breathed hard in the thin air.

"Put your hands on the rock face, there." Luskell placed her hands beside his. "Aku? This is Kiraknat, your new keeper. Kiraknat, meet Aku."

"You can call me Rakni," he said, not to Luskell but to the Mountain. He hadn't acted as Keeper before but already recognized the intimacy of the relationship.

Encouraged, Luskell spoke the ritual words and stepped back. "You can Listen from anywhere, of course; Aku's hard to miss. But in this spot, she knows you're here. She's more likely to Listen to you."

He scowled. "What if she's working up an eruption and I don't happen to be in this spot?"

"If you Listen to her all the time, you'll pick up her warnings early enough to come here before there's trouble. Well, usually."

"Usually?"

"Once last winter, she got worked up in a hurry, and Laki had to calm her from the lodge. During a blizzard." Luskell had been there, too, but she didn't care to go into it with Kiraknat.

"He told me that story, too."

"Good, you need to know it's possible. But if you hike up here every day the weather allows and sing to her, that probably won't happen."

"Probably won't?"

"We're talking about a volcano. She's unpredictable. But mostly, she sleeps."

Upon their return, they joined the others in the task of making the lodge ready for winter. They pulled out all the skins and blankets to air, replacing the worn ones with new. The old bed of fir boughs became kindling, and springy new bedding was cut and laid in place. Food supplies had to be packed into boxes and baskets. Gaps were plugged, and Laki fashioned a new snow shed to go over the smoke hole so it wouldn't be blocked in a winter storm. That evening, they cooked together, and Luskell turned the lodge over to Kiraknat.

Long after the others slept, Luskell lay and gazed at the stars, thicker and brighter than anywhere else she'd been. At this elevation, they filled the sky. Or not the sky. Luskell had flown as an owl above the treetops — in the sky — but no closer to the stars.

She Listened. Laki had taught her to Listen to trees,

rocks, and rivers, but not to stars. She had discovered on her own how to Listen past the trees, which were so much closer they nearly drowned out anything else. When she concentrated, there was something beyond the trees. The stars were more numerous, and probably much bigger if they were as far away as she guessed. Bigger even than Aku. Luskell heard what she could only describe as Song. No words, and unlike any music she knew. It was daunting and reassuring at once. She was a tiny part of something vast.

Eventually, she dozed off and dreamed of hiking to Aku's summit and away into the singing stars.

When she woke in the freezing half-light of dawn, she had the same sense of something awry, but now she knew what it was. Knot had failed to visit her dreams at least two nights in a row. She wasn't sure she'd seen him since her accidental near-visit weeks ago. She didn't remember every dream, so she might have been wrong. But that time, he had seemed angry. With her? The whole time in this valley — Knot's Valley — she'd looked forward to their time together when she slept. Now she was leaving, and he hadn't even wished her well or said goodbye. She had half a mind to go to the Other Side herself. She wasn't supposed to; hadn't needed to in all those months.

Before she gave in to temptation and went back to sleep, Laki sat up and grinned. "Who wants breakfast?"

She continued to mull the question while they ate. Had she done something wrong? Why wouldn't Knot tell her? Or maybe he had and she didn't remember, so —

"Is something wrong?" Laki asked in Eukardian.

Karen Eisenbrey

"What? No, it's just that Knot hasn't visited my dreams lately. I miss him."

He squeezed her shoulder. "It is time you returned to the land of the living."

She carried her empty dish into the lodge. She came back out and tucked her fiddle into the special pocket sewn inside her cloak. "I'm going to see Aku."

The men laughed — the Mountain was right there, all the time. But they knew what she meant.

Laki started to get up. "I'll come with you."

"I want to go alone."

Luskell walked into the fringe of trees behind the lodge. When she was out of sight of the Aklaka, she stopped and removed her eyepatch, then pictured a mighty eagle. With an inaudible incantation, she transformed and flew the rest of the way to the spot where she and Aku touched. Anything she wore or carried in her pockets transformed with her. The eyepatch would not be lost if she transformed without removing it. Earlier experiments, though, had shown whatever she transformed to had a sightless eye. If she removed the patch, the creature had two working eyes. It was not only for flight that she loved transformation.

As soon as her talons touched stone, she resumed her own form and leaned her back against the bare rock of the cliff face. She drew out her fiddle, tuned up, and played a few songs.

"Well, my friend, I'm leaving you today. I wish I didn't have to. I don't know what I'm going to do after this. But your new Keeper is here, so I have to go." Luskell closed her eyes and Listened to the Mountain. The first thing she sensed was a distant, steady vibration, what she thought of as Aku breathing. Beyond that was a vast mind of sorts, remembering innumerable seasons of growth and change. Under it all, the familiar, soothing song, in many voices …

one of them Luskell's. "Don't be too hard on Kiraknat, all right? He's wanted to come here for a long time, and he gave up his turn for me. He's not a great Listener yet, but he loves you." She leaned and Listened. Was that a moment of agitation? Luskell liked to think Aku would miss her, but it didn't do for the Mountain to grow too attached to one keeper, as she had with Knot. No, Aku was calm again.

To be sure, Luskell played and sang Aku's Lullaby, one last time. Then she transformed and flew back down to the lodge. She resumed her own form while still out of sight. Chakalan's voice reached her as she walked out of the trees.

"I'm relieved this little stunt is finally over. Luskell was lucky to catch Aku in a quiet period, but it'll be good to get back to normal and have a man up here the way we should."

Luskell halted on the path, too shocked to move out of the tree cover. In her experience, Aklaka society had always displayed far greater equality between the sexes than the Eukardian culture in which she spent most of her life. Leadership passed from mother to son, father to daughter; Laki would inherit the role of Uklak from his mother. Aku's Keeper had always been a man, though. Luskell had considered that more of an accident than tradition, but maybe she was wrong.

Kiraknat laughed. "An Aklaka man."

This attitude was less surprising. There had been grumbling from some quarters throughout Knot's long service — he was less than half Aklaka, and hadn't spent time among them until he was an adult. Although Luskell had lifelong experience of the community, her heritage was even more diluted than Knot's. She wasn't considered Aklaka. And she was not a man. Aku didn't seem to mind.

Laki cleared his throat as Luskell came around the end of the lodge. "I wonder if she overheard." He fought a smile.

Luskell stepped into view of the other two. "Every word. Now I'm kind of sorry I told Aku to take it easy on you."

Kiraknat and Chakalan exchanged an uncomfortable glance.

"But maybe you'll be lucky and she'll stay quiet."

"They know you have the right skills." Laki said. "Kiraknat was just talking big to bolster his confidence. Right?"

Kiraknat scowled, then nodded. "We'll say that."

"It doesn't matter. I should get used to doubters before I go back to Eukard City." Eukard City, where she would be the first woman in recorded history to earn a wizard's staff. The grumbling of the Aklaka was nothing compared to what she'd already faced from Eukardian wizards.

Chapter 3

Luskell packed her few belongings into the pockets of her cloak: spare socks and underclothes, a clean shirt, her fiddle and bow still in their own special pocket. Laki made up a parcel of food for the two of them. They left the valley with Chakalan, who was returning to the rest of the Aklaka band. They parted from him at the top of the ridge.

Laki watched until Chakalan was out of sight, then turned to Luskell. "So, keep hiking or fly from here?"

Transformation bothered or even offended many Aklaka. Although Chakalan knew Laki and Luskell were both capable of it, they avoided doing it in front of him out of simple politeness. Luskell had planned to fly. It was a good day's hike to Misty Pass but only a couple of hours on the wing. She reached up to remove her eyepatch but dropped her hand to her side. "Let's walk. I'm not in a hurry."

"And with your feet on the ground, you're still touching Aku. Still Listening."

So he knew. "It's hard to leave."

"I felt the same way. Twice."

Luskell sighed and looked back, not for the first time. "Do you ever get over it?"

"No, but it gets easier. You learn to hold the solitude inside you."

"Huh." Luskell nodded and kept hiking. She wasn't in the mood to talk much, but it was good to be with someone who understood.

They took a lunch break in the forest. Luskell lifted her eyepatch and gazed around. It was the same down here as in Knot's Valley. Living things flared with unexpected colors, dizzying in the profusion of a thick forest. She replaced the patch after only a short time.

"Is your eye getting better?" Laki asked.

"Better, or different. I'm not sure what it shows me. At first it was only light leaking in, but it's changed. Now I can make out forms, blurry but brighter and more colorful than they should be."

Laki leaned forward eagerly. "Do you see power, the way your mother and I do?"

"That was my first thought, but now I don't think so. Every living thing shows up, at least a little. But I think it does show me something real, something my good eye can't see."

They packed up again and hiked through the afternoon. Luskell sneaked glimpses with what she had decided to call her *wizard eye*. She had a guess about what it showed her. She wasn't sure what use it could be, but she was glad it wasn't entirely lost. Some mistakes could be redeemed.

They arrived in Misty Pass just before sunset. Luskell was eager for supper at the Fogbank, her grandparents' inn. Laki held her back before she opened the door.

"Prepare yourself," he said.

"For what?"

"You've lived in another world this last half year," he reminded her. "A world of you and Aku and no one else but the dead. Remember what you said about not having to shield yourself?"

Luskell laughed. "And remember what you said about me thriving in company? These are my people."

She shook him off and walked into the long common room, already about half-filled with supper guests. She was eager to see Grandpa Eslo and Grandma Nari, but at the sight of so many other people, her greeting died unspoken. Their feelings and thoughts crashed over her like a wave. She had never minded crowds, but this ... She froze, unable to take another step. Laki gently nudged her forward and closed the door behind them. Luskell shielded herself. How foolish not to think of it on her own! She really was out of practice.

Grandpa Eslo turned from pouring a mug of ale. "Find a seat wherever you like. I'll — " A startled grin lit his face. He stopped pouring just before the mug ran over. "Nari! Luskell's back!" He set down the mug and pitcher so he could wrap Luskell in his arms. He felt smaller than she remembered. "And young Nalaklak. We didn't expect to see you again so soon."

Laki shook Grandpa's hand. "I have ... business in the city. I will ride down with Luskell."

Grandma Nari hurried from the kitchen and greeted both of them with warm hugs. "So good to see you safe, Luskell. I guess the Mountain treated you all right. You're a little skinny, but we'll fix you up."

Luskell struggled to find words. "I ... I'm fine. I ate well."

"And worked hard," Laki filled in for her. "One of your good suppers is just what she needs, ma'am." He steered Luskell toward two open seats at the end of the table nearest the kitchen, away from the crowd.

Luskell sneaked another glance at Grandpa Eslo. He'd always been old to her, but now he looked it. He was greatly reduced from the robust man he used to be; how she still thought of him when she was away. She lifted her eyepatch for a peek. She wasn't happy with what she saw, but it confirmed her guess about that eye. Grandpa didn't blaze and flare the way Laki did. He flickered. In her mother's care, he'd survived a dangerous case of the wobbles the previous winter, but he wasn't well. He wouldn't die tonight or next week or probably even next year, but Luskell doubted it would be much longer.

Grandma Nari brought them bowls of hearty stew. "Your folks went back to the city already, weeks ago."

Luskell accepted a bowl and blew on a spoonful to cool it. "I know. Mamam told me. Balsam needed her help with something. She didn't share details, but it's not another outbreak." She swallowed the bite of stew. It would have been good under any circumstances. After a day of hiking, it was the most delicious food ever cooked.

Nari shook her head and smiled. "You two and your mind-talking. I always forget you can do that. Will you stay awhile, or do you have to go on right away?"

Luskell glanced at Laki. "I shouldn't put it off too long. And Laki has important matters to take care of. Unless you need help with Grandpa?" Luskell wasn't the healer her mother was, but she might do some good.

"No, he's much better," Grandma Nari said. "Ketty got rid of the infection. She couldn't fix all the lung damage, so he still has a bad cough at times. She left some drops for it."

"Do they help?"

"One drop in a warm drink and he sleeps the whole night."

"That's good," Luskell said. "But should he be working?"

Grandma cast a fond glance at her husband. "It makes him happy. Ketty gave her blessing, as long as he doesn't overdo it. We're getting along all right. I promise to take good care of him."

"All right, if you're sure. We'll leave on the morning coach."

"I'll pack a good lunch for you. Oh, and I almost forgot. This is for you." Grandma Nari took a letter from her apron pocket.

Luskell's name was written on it, but no indication who it was from. She opened it and read:

Dear Luskell,
I hope your time on the Mountain was good.

There's no way to say this but to say it. Ruvhonn and I were married on Long Day. We came to an agreement after you left and it felt right to make it official. We're taking a belated wedding trip to Eukard City this fall. I'm not sure I want to see you. I'm not sure you'll want to see me. But if you're there, I think we should. It might be hard to avoid.

Love,
Jagryn

"Grandma, when was this delivered?"

"It wasn't. The young man left it for you himself, this morning."

"This morning? Then they're already ..." Luskell leaned her head on her hands.

"What is wrong?" Laki asked, thoughtfully speaking Eukardian so no one would think they were telling secrets.

"Nothing, but ..." Luskell had feared she might cry, but didn't anticipate the laughter that burst from her. "Oh, it's too ridiculous! Jagryn beat you to it. He got married first."

"It is ridiculous to get married?"

"No, I'm saying it wrong. I'm getting what I asked for, all at once, like someone is playing a joke on me."

"And you are not upset?"

"I am." Luskell sniffed and wiped her eyes. "And I'm not. I should have known. But it gets better — they're on a trip to Eukard City. They left here this morning."

"Oh! I will be pleased to see Jagryn again, and to meet his wife."

"Yes, you'll like her. I like her. I'm not sure she likes me, but ..." Luskell folded the letter with deliberate care. "It might be awkward."

"You met someone else yourself, though. Right?"

"Maybe." Luskell allowed herself a wistful smile as she recalled the feeling and the face and how they'd left things. "I don't know yet."

After supper, Luskell told her grandparents more about her experience on the Mountain, the tale interrupted whenever they needed to serve another guest. The room had filled up, a noisy, sociable crowd. She wasn't entirely used to so many people yet, but no longer overwhelmed. Both of her parents were innkeepers' children; this was what she'd grown up with.

"I could help serve if you need it," Luskell offered.

Grandma Nari smiled and patted Luskell's shoulder. "You walked all day. It's all right to rest a bit." She nodded toward the crowd. "Besides, in your way, you are helping."

Luskell glanced around. Part of the crowd had gathered closer to hear her story. A few drew back at the sight of her eyepatch, but others leaned in. Most of these people had finished eating, but they ordered extra mugs of ale to sip while listening.

Luskell was glad her story was good for business and enjoyed the attention. As Nari had pointed out, though, she had walked all day. She finished her tale with a massive yawn.

"I think I need to go home now." She left her seat and put on her cloak.

Laki rose, too. "I'll go with you."

"You could both stay here tonight," Grandma Nari offered. "Your house will be cold and musty."

"I'll sleep at the house. Laki, you should stay here, considering."

He gave her a nod of understanding. She kissed her grandparents good night and walked out into the twilit village. The stars were coming out, above the tall treetops. Somehow, the trees seemed taller against the stars, though the stars were infinitely farther away. Luskell paused a moment to Listen to their song, though it was too chilly to stand outside for long.

She walked to the other end of the village, to her family's one-room cabin set back in the forest, away from the main road. It was the only house Luskell's family owned, though they used it for only a few weeks here and there throughout the year. When they were away, her father protected the cabin from intruders with a concealing charm that rendered it invisible — and uninteresting — to non-magical eyes. Even neighbors who knew it was there tended to forget about it. Strangers were never even curious. Luskell's power allowed her to see through the spell to the green-painted front door. The magic as she passed through it was gently familiar, like her father's scent.

She opened the door and stepped inside the dark room. She lit the lamp with a thought. The whitewashed log walls glowed softly in its light. The place looked welcoming, but it had been closed up for weeks. Luskell opened the windows to freshen the stale air while she brought in firewood and water, then lit a fire and heated enough water for a sponge bath. She found a pair of shears and trimmed the hair flopping over her eyes. She didn't know or care what it looked like. She tossed the little pile of curls outside, where they might find their way into a nest for birds or squirrels.

When she went to the Mountain, Luskell had left most of her clothing at the cabin. It was a small luxury to change into a fresh nightdress and unpack clean bedding to sleep in. So soft and comfortable, but ... she couldn't sleep.

Her throat ached with homesickness, though the cabin was as much home as anywhere. She had been alone but not lonely most of the time she was on the Mountain, once she got used to it. Knot's Valley was a place where one was meant to be alone. The unoccupied cabin sharpened her longing for family. This was *their* place. She had never been here alone.

At least she could let them know where she was. She made herself comfortable, quieted her mind, and reached out. Her mother would be able to answer; Luskell sought her mind first.

Mamam — I'm in Misty Pass. I'll be home tomorrow afternoon.

Luskell! I wondered if we'd hear from you soon. Are you traveling alone?

Laki has … business in the city, so he's coming with me.

That's good. I won't keep you, then. Good night, Luskell.

Mamam broke the connection before Luskell could explain Laki's business. It was easy to guess what Mamam thought she might be keeping Luskell from. She'd have to straighten out that confusion, but it could wait. She sought her father's mind to let him know she was on her way. He couldn't reply, but he would want to know. Master Bardin was next. She'd completed her quest and earned her staff, later than she'd expected when she began her training, but she'd done it. She had to rely on Mamam or Dadad to tell her brother Crett she was coming home. He was only two — no, two and a half now, but a long way from mind-talking.

Luskell blew out the lamp and settled in to sleep. She considered bending her dreams toward the Other Side and Knot. All she had to do was imagine in detail the person she wanted to encounter on the Other Side, then release herself to sleep and dream her way across the thin boundary between life and death. No. That was a bad habit she needed to break. She should wait for him to come to her. If he ever would again. The last time she'd seen him, he had looked angry, like he didn't want her to visit. Yes, he had often warned her not to, but he had never been angry about it. Was it something she'd done, or had something changed? But the Other Side never changed.

It was so hard, not seeing him and not knowing why he kept away. She accepted that it was strange to have a relationship with her father's father, who had died months before she was born. It didn't keep her from treasuring their time together. Their time in dreams was all they had. Until she'd learned it was unsafe, she had been all too eager to return his visits. Under the right circumstances, she could even make the crossing while awake, but that required someone else dreaming their way over ... or actually dying.

Luskell contented herself with thinking of her family and how good it would be to see them again ... how proud she would be to complete her apprenticeship and receive her wizard's staff ... how comfortable the bed felt ... how sleepy she was ...

Luskell opened heavy eyelids. Soft light filled the cabin, but not lamplight. Someone sat at the table — a tall young man with bright red hair and pale, unfreckled skin. He treated Luskell to a wide grin.

Her brother, Ketwyn. She hadn't gone to him. He had come to her. She flew into his weightless embrace. "Thank you, thank you, thank you! Did you know I was tempted?"

"I guessed. You've resisted a long time."

Luskell looked around the cabin. "This isn't very creative, visiting me where I actually am."

"I like this house. This is where Mama learned to be happy again."

Luskell knew only the bare outline of that time. Ketwyn's death soon after his birth had broken their mother's heart and drained her power. Knot had helped her return to full strength. She had found new purpose in healing and made a home for herself in this cabin. All that was before Luskell's time.

"Do you visit her dreams now?"

He nodded. "It helps for her to see me grown up. Sometimes Grandma Lukett comes with me."

Lukett was their maternal grandmother, Grandpa Eslo's first wife. She had died when Mamam was a child. Luskell carried part of her name.

"How kind! Poor Mamam, she's lost so many people. I forget sometimes."

"But you've been all alone. I would have come sooner, but I thought Knot was still visiting you."

Luskell sat in one of the chairs near him. "Do you know why he stopped? I've missed him."

"He said something about visiting Stell."

"Now I feel guilty. I didn't even think he might be neglecting her." Knot had discovered he could visit his wife, Luskell's other grandmother, though she had no magical power. She was a storyteller, a kind of magic of its own.

"I don't think that's the whole reason," Ketwyn said. "There's something stirring on our side. Something old and powerful, a spirit of legend. He didn't want to draw its attention to you."

"What about you, then?"

"I'm not important. As far as it knows, I'm a baby who never knew anyone or learned anything. I doubt it notices who I visit."

Luskell had never met a "spirit of legend" on the Other Side. "Why would it care about me? Who are you talking about?"

"Old Mother Bones."

Luskell shivered. She knew Old Mother Bones as a character in old stories meant to make children behave. A skeletal hag in tattered clothes who lived in a cave or a hollow tree, depending on who told the story. It was said she could drag a living soul to the Other Side and hold it there until the body died.

"Old Mother Bones is only a story. She's not real ... is she?"

"I haven't met her, but Knot thinks she is. The gossip is she was troubled because someone was crossing over." Ketwyn raised his eyebrows and gazed at Luskell.

"But why would she care? And why does it matter?"

"I'm sorry, I don't know. Knot guesses she's bothered by a living soul trespassing on our side and might try to cause trouble if it doesn't stop. It's probably best you don't cross over until we know more."

"I wouldn't have to if Knot would visit me."

"What if it's dangerous? To you?" Ketwyn looked downcast, which Luskell had never seen before. "Is it all right if I come when I can? Maybe I can find out something useful."

"Of course it's all right, Ketwyn. I want to see you, too." Luskell laid her hand over his. It wasn't warm and solid like Laki's hand, but there was something almost living about it. An energy without substance.

"Good. We'll learn what we can, and I'll let you know. Good night, little sister."

Chapter 4

Luskell woke, refreshed by Ketwyn's visit as much as by the sleep itself. They hadn't forgotten her on the Other Side, but she would have to learn to get along without such frequent visits. Her place was with the living. Even if she was curious about the "spirit of legend." How did a character out of folklore come to dwell among the souls of real people? A mystery.

Luskell longed to wear clean clothes but traveling in a dress held little appeal. She settled for a clean shirt with her grubby trousers and heavy boots. She packed her battered old satchel with the rest of her dirty clothes on the bottom, clean clothes on top, and her fiddle cushioned between them. When she left the house, Luskell stood in the doorway a moment to make sure no one was looking her way. It wouldn't do to appear suddenly out of the concealment.

At the Fogbank, Laki was already eating breakfast. Luskell joined him, and Grandma Nari brought her a plate of sausages, eggs and bread. "If you can't stay, I can at least feed you up. Lunch is in the basket." Grandma studied Luskell more closely. "Did you try to cut your own hair?"

"It was in my eyes and I didn't have a mirror." She stabbed a sausage and took an appreciative bite.

"Curly hair is forgiving, but I could even it up if you like."

"And do the back? I didn't even try, but there's too much of it."

"So you won't be growing it out again?"

"Not right away. Short is less trouble than long, even if I have to keep cutting it."

Grandma went to get her shears. When Luskell had finished breakfast, Grandma trimmed and snipped until she had a substantial pile for her own birds and squirrels.

"I think of your hair as brown," she commented as she went to get the broom and dustpan. "I always forget how much red is in it."

"None compared to Mamam's," Luskell said. "She says it's the same color as Grandma Lukett's, but hers was straight."

"It's too bad she never got to meet you."

"She has, now. I've seen her … over there." There was another person Luskell couldn't visit anymore. The topic reminded her of her third grandmother. "Is there time before the coach comes to write a letter to Deep River? I should let Klamamam know where I am." This was what Aklaka children called their grandmother, the only name Luskell had ever used for Stell, her father's mother and the source of part of her own name.

"If you're quick about it." Grandma Nari provided writing materials before sweeping up the hair.

Dear Klamamam,

*I have finished my time in Knot's Valley.
Aku stayed quiet, so I must have done my
job well enough. It is beautiful there, but I
often wished you were with me to tell
stories after supper. Many nights, Knot
visited my dreams, so I did have some
company. I hope he didn't neglect you too
badly.*

*I'm going back to the city now. Write to me
there. We're still staying with Wyll and
Kiat. It will be crowded but I can hardly
wait to see Crett again. He must be so big!*

Wish me luck as I start my life as a wizard!

*Love,
Luskell*

The westbound coach to the city arrived as Luskell was addressing her letter. She left it with Grandma Nari to put on the eastbound coach. Luskell and Laki bought the cheaper seats on top, it being a sunny morning. Luggage was packed in around them. Only when they were in place did it occur to Luskell that Laki had no bag.

"You're going to the city with no change of clothes?"

"I left my city things in the city."

That meant he'd left them with someone there. "You were staying with her already?"

He didn't bother to shield his emotions. He was offended and indignant, but somehow kept his voice calm. "You should know better than that, Luskell. I left clothing at her place, but I haven't slept there yet."

"I'm sorry," Luskell said, chastened. "I forgot how seriously you take your position." Most Aklaka were free to form many attachments, whether serious or casual, until eventually settling down with a partner for life — often not until they had a child. Laki, as his mother's heir, had to be more careful about casual liaisons. If he fathered a child, he would be married to the child's mother, no matter who she was. If the child were a daughter, she would succeed him as Uklak. Apparently, Luskell was the only one who had received his full attention, and perhaps only because he had believed she planned to stay with him permanently.

"You're forgiven," Laki said with a smile. "With Mamam's blessing, we can now start our life together."

"What about my blessing?" Luskell asked.

"I'd like to have it, but I don't need your permission."

That stung, though he was right. "I hope she deserves you."

"You'll see. You're not jealous?"

"Let's call it ... protective," she said. "I care what happens to you. I'm not changing my mind, in case you were wondering. I have my own path, even if I don't know what it is yet."

"I worry you'll walk it alone."

"If I do, that's my problem, not yours. I might be better off alone. Wizards are difficult to live with." Or so she'd been told, and her own example seemed to bear it out. But sometimes two people with power managed to make a life together. A face rose before her mind's eye: dark blond hair, hazel eyes, a lively smile. Fandek, her mother's apprentice. Luskell liked him more than she had when she first met him; more than she cared to admit. She had resisted getting close to him in the months they were together, in spite of, or perhaps because of, his overwhelming appeal. He had something ... special. She didn't trust it. She forced the image back into darkness.

The road from the pass wound down through mountains and foothills, often with a steep slope above and a deep canyon below. Dense forest hid more distant views. The motion of the coach and the sameness of the scenery lulled Luskell, and Laki wasn't particularly chatty.

"Ketwyn visited me last night," Luskell said, more to break the monotony than anything. She opened Nari's lunch basket and began to nibble on the bread, cheese, and pears she had packed for them.

"What did he have to say?"

Luskell shook her head, trying to remember details. "It didn't all make sense. Do you know anything about 'spirits of legend'?"

"Like Aketnan? Not your mother, though I owe her my life, but the Peacebringer spirit." Laki accepted his share of the food. He laughed as the ripe pear dribbled juice down his chin.

Luskell passed him a cloth to wipe it off. "Mamam doesn't believe Aketnan inhabits her anymore. Where does it go when it has no host? The Other Side?"

Laki frowned in thought. "There's nothing about it in any of the stories. That's a place for the souls of the dead. Aketnan is pure spirit."

"So never human?"

"I don't believe so. Maybe it's merely the name we use when someone rises to the occasion in times of trouble. But I think it's something real."

"Mamam does, too. She — "

Laki held up his hand to silence her. He wore his Listening look, an expression of deep concentration. After a moment, he climbed over the luggage in front of them to speak to the driver. "Get ready to stop."

The driver glanced over his shoulder. "What for?"

"Rockslide."

"Don't joke about a thing like that. I'd have heard—"

A distant rumble and a loud crack interrupted him. He turned his attention back to the road and slowed the horses. When they came around the next bend, a cloud of dust billowed across the road. Rocks filled a deep draw, though only a few smaller stones had rolled into the roadway. But the slide had uprooted a mature fir tree, and the massive trunk blocked traffic in both directions.

"Whoa!" The driver reined up and set the brake. His face was pale as he glanced back at Laki. "Thanks for the warning, young man. Wizard, are you? Didn't know your people had 'em."

"We don't. Not exactly. I'm a Listener. I heard when the slope got ... excited."

The inside passengers leaned out the windows to learn why they'd stopped. When they saw the fallen tree, they all clamored for someone to do something, but Luskell didn't hear any of them give a good suggestion as to what.

The driver scratched his head. "There goes my schedule! Don't usually get downed trees until later in the season." He explained to anyone who would listen that they'd have to sit and wait for a highway guard patrol. If they were lucky, the guards would already know about the tree and bring a saw, but more likely they'd have to go back to their post to get one. "I hope everyone brought lunch, because we could be here a long time."

I could move it, Luskell mind-talked to Laki.

You can levitate something that big?

Size isn't important. That's what Bardin had taught her, and she'd worked hard to master a technique that did not come easily to her.

Luskell climbed down from the coach. As she approached the tree, she lifted the eyepatch and closed her good eye for a moment. The tree still had a strong glow of life in it. She pressed her hand against the deeply grooved bark and Listened. It seemed dimly aware of its changed perspective. At any rate, it was getting bewildering messages from its roots, which weren't used to so much air and so little soil. Luskell reached out to the slide, too, though she usually avoided Listening to rocks. They were ponderous and required more patience than she possessed. These rocks seemed comparatively giddy after their rush down the slope, but once the dust had settled, they slowed down into their new, stable position.

At the sound of hoofbeats, Luskell lowered the eyepatch and peered between branches. She was hoping for a highway guard with a saw, but this had the look of a merchant wagon. The driver reined up close to the fallen tree. Behind it, a smaller cart slowed and stopped, and then the late-morning coach from the city jingled up.

Luskell made her decision. She didn't have any reason to save her power, and what good was power if you didn't use it to help out?

"Listen to me, I have an idea!"

When her shout received no attention, she gripped the branches and pulled herself up onto the trunk, glad she wasn't wearing a dress. She'd been climbing in dresses since she could walk, but there was no reason to make things more difficult than necessary. She stood upright. The drivers and passengers of the various stopped vehicles all discussed what to do at the tops of their voices. It was clear none of them had tools or much of a plan, and tempers were already short.

Luskell magically projected her voice in order to be heard. "Quiet!" Everyone turned and stared. At least they'd stopped yelling. "If we're to move this tree, you can't be so close."

"Move it, how?"

"Wizardry." No sense getting into a long explanation about who the wizard was. That would be obvious soon enough. "Now please make some room."

While those on the downhill side got busy rolling their vehicles back, Luskell climbed down and returned to the coach, considering the problem. The question wasn't whether she could move the tree, but where to put it when she was done. She was tempted to shove it over the side, but that might start another slide or injure some unseen person below. If she could pivot it around, she should be able to lay it down alongside the road.

"Can you back up?" she asked the driver. "I need space so no one gets hurt."

The driver gave her a suspicious look. "Space for what? What's your game, anyway?"

Laki interrupted. "You should do what she says. I'm not a wizard, but she is."

"Ha, that's a good one. Where's your staff then, wizard girl?"

"Waiting for me in the city, so I want to go there. Don't you?"

"So the rumors were true?" The driver scratched the back of his neck. "You're really her?"

"Who else would I be?" Luskell clung to the last shreds of patience.

"But you're so young. You can't be more than twenty."

"I'm almost eighteen. Now, some space?"

"Yes, of course. At once!"

The driver enlisted help from the other passengers to back the horses and coach away from the fallen tree. If nothing else, it provided them something to do besides talk. Laki paced out the approximate length of the tree trunk and kept everyone at a safe distance.

Once she was sure she had enough room to work, Luskell stood in the road facing the fallen tree. She filled her lungs and reached deep for the magic inside her. The heat at her core tingled out through her arms to her fingertips. With steady application of power and controlled breathing, she raised the treetop. She could feel the weight of it, but as if it were something smaller that she could actually lift with her muscles. But still heavy. Very heavy.

Laki? Help.

How? I'm no good with levitation.

Lend ... power.

Luskell hoped he would understand. She couldn't afford to divert power to mind-talking for a long explanation. Luskell held the tree and did her best to control her increasingly labored breathing. Laki gripped her shoulder and the burden lightened as his power poured into her. She breathed deep again, then slowly let out the breath as she pivoted the whole tree on the heavy root mass. She carefully lowered the stout trunk into the shallow ditch along the road. A few branches extended into the roadway, but it was no longer blocked. A crew could come and cut up the tree later, at their convenience.

A few people cheered. The other coach passengers stared from the tree to Luskell, all chatter silenced.

"Please, won't you sit inside?" the driver asked.

Luskell glanced at the fearful passengers. A few backed further away from her. She climbed shakily back to her seat on the roof. She had no desire to make the situation more uncomfortable for herself, let alone for someone who had paid full fare for an inside seat.

Laki took his place beside her. "Showoff," he murmured.

"Just being useful. Dadad would have done the same." Luskell didn't feel like she'd lifted a forest giant, but magical exertion took a physical toll, especially magic that didn't come naturally. "I'm going to rest my eyes a moment. Do you mind?"

She didn't stay awake long enough to hear his answer.

Chapter 5

Luskell woke hungry but comfortable. Her head rested on Laki's shoulder. She jerked upright. That kind of intimacy belonged in the past. At least he hadn't shoved her away, and she hadn't drooled on him. She looked around as the coach rolled into Eukard City. She'd last seen it on a gray winter morning, a lifetime ago. Now the old chestnut trees shaded the broad street with their dense foliage, some of the leaves already yellow. The trees thinned out as they drove into the center of town, where two- and three-story brick buildings crowded together along narrow streets.

She mind-talked to Bardin. *I'm back in the city, Master.*

Meet me at the Wizards' Hall so I can see what you've become.

Luskell wasn't sure what to make of that. What had she

become? Maybe Bardin could tell her.

The coach stopped at the coach office in the heart of Old Town. Luskell stretched and climbed down from the roof. Laki passed her bag down to her, then followed.

A stocky fellow emerged from the stables to unhitch the horses. They nuzzled him and he gently rubbed their noses and offered carrot chunks. Although Luskell had never been introduced to him, there was something in his face she recognized. It came to her in an instant; she knew exactly who he was.

She set the satchel on the ground. "Laki, watch my bag a moment."

The stableman gave her a wide smile when she approached. He was probably near her age, but seemed younger with his open, innocent face — a big boy more than a young man.

"Hello! You're Fandek's brother, aren't you?"

He nodded and smiled more widely. He was shorter than Fandek, who matched Luskell in height. He had hazel eyes like his brother, but greener.

"I'm Luskell. Fandek is ... a friend of mine. He said he found you this job. Do you like it, working with horses?"

The coach driver threw an arm around the boy in a rough hug. "Deklyn doesn't talk, but the horses don't mind."

"You mean he can't talk?"

"I don't know. Can't or doesn't, it amounts to the same thing."

Luskell reached out to Deklyn's mind. Like his face, his thoughts were open and uncomplicated. A part of his mind was dark, a room with the lamp blown out. Something had happened to him, but he didn't remember it now. Probably just as well — it couldn't have been a good thing. He had grown into a good person, anyway, as the horse nuzzling his fingers attested.

Deklyn laid the fingers of his left hand over his left eye, then lifted them away. He repeated the gesture. Luskell turned to the driver, puzzled. "What's he saying?"

"I think he wants you to take off your eyepatch."

"No one wants that."

But Deklyn continued the gesture. She lifted the patch to let him see her scars. He winced but didn't look away. When she looked at him with that eye, he bloomed with life and good health. She was open to his feelings, too. Sympathy and kindness washed over her.

The driver chuckled. "He's full of caring for any hurt thing, see."

So maybe part of him did remember what happened. Luskell replaced the patch. "I'm all right. Maybe better than before." She held out her hand. "I'm glad to meet you, Deklyn."

After a moment's hesitation, he shook hands. He had the same strong, long-fingered hands as his brother. As both his brothers. She turned her shudder into a stronger squeeze. This brother had none of the monster in him.

Laki waited patiently until she returned. "It's hard to tell with the sun in my eyes, but that boy might have a touch of magic about him."

"The horse thinks so."

Laki chuckled in agreement. "I saw you lift the patch. Have you figured out what you see?"

"I think I see ... life. Vigor." She lifted her satchel from the ground. "It's a new power. I haven't done much with it. I might be able to tell by looking if someone is well or ill. Maybe I'll know when they're dying."

"But you don't plan to be a healer."

What have I become? "I don't know what I plan to be."

"It's not so bad to have choices. Do you want to come

with me to Embassy House?"

Luskell's stomach flipped. She had to keep letting him go. "I will if you want me to. Could we stop and see Bardin first? I told him I'd meet him today, and the Wizards' Hall is closer than Embassy House."

It was only a few blocks from the coach office to the Wizards' Hall. Luskell hesitated on the front porch, then opened the door and walked in without knocking. She'd been away a long time but had every right to enter.

"I'll wait outside if you don't mind," Laki said. "Let me know if you need me."

Luskell set her bag down in the entry, under the hooks for cloaks. Opposite was a board with notes pinned to it. Some were addressed by name, while others listed a specific skill. She hadn't paid much attention to it before, but it was a reasonable way for people to ask for magical help, as long as it wasn't an emergency.

The Wizards' Hall had once been the mansion of a wealthy family. Any wizard or apprentice in the city was welcome to eat meals in the large dining room or to relax around the fire in the spacious common room. Those who could afford it paid regular dues to subsidize those who couldn't yet. It wasn't a formal school, but the rooms upstairs were used for teaching and practice.

Luskell stepped into the broad entrance hall and looked around for Bardin. He wasn't in the dining room to her left. A wizard with long white hair and a short, scruffy beard emerged from the common room to her right. He looked Luskell up and down with ice-gray eyes.

"Well, you're a grim-looking fellow, aren't you?"

"Nice to see you, too, Wizard Larem. Is Bardin here?"

"Luskell's back!" A dark-haired boy raced out of the dining room and threw his arms around her.

"Lucky, you're so tall!" Luskell laughed as she hugged

him back. He had barely reached her shoulder before but now came up almost to her chin.

"I shot up over the summer. I'm almost twelve, you know. What happened to your eye?"

"Long story."

Lucky stepped back, grinning. "I've got time." He brushed the front of his shirt. "But why are you sticky?"

Luskell's once-clean shirt was spattered with sap and tree parts. Her hands were grubby, too. "Would you believe I levitated a tree?" She had been working with Lucky when she hit on the technique that allowed her to master levitation, so she knew he would appreciate the accomplishment.

Larem eyed her more closely, frowning as recognition dawned. "Luskell, eh? Crawling back in defeat, I'd wager. If Bardin knows what's good for him, he won't offer a second chance."

Luskell's face grew hot. She counted slowly to herself. Larem had never felt she deserved her first chance. She wouldn't give him the satisfaction of making her lose her temper. "Sorry to disappoint you," she said when she'd regained her calm. "I completed my quest. Bardin asked me to meet him here."

"You beat me," Bardin said from behind her. "Welcome back at last. I was beginning to wonder. Oh ..." He stared when she turned to greet him, then looked away. "Did your quest give you ... trouble?"

Luskell touched her eyepatch. "I gave myself trouble." She looked more closely at the dark circles under his eyes. "Master Bardin, are you unwell?" She resisted the urge to raise the patch and check.

Bardin puffed out a breath and the corners of his mouth lifted in a weary smile. "Strange dreams last night. Couldn't get back to sleep, so I've been up since before dawn."

"I'm sorry to hear that. Nightmares?"

"I'm not sure. They were pleasant at first — my old master Ordahn came for dinner. I told him about you, and he said he was proud of me." Bardin glanced at Larem, who huffed and made a dignified exit into the dining room. "I was about to serve cake when a ... a giant skeleton thrust itself between us, moaning and screaming. Then I woke up."

"Whose skeleton was it?" Luskell asked.

"I don't know. Taller than your friend outside, though. Will you introduce me?"

"Of course." They stepped outside together. "Bardin, this is my friend Nalaklak, who taught me to Listen. Laki, Bardin has tried to make a wizard of me."

Bardin chuckled. "Most of the work was done before I got started. You're good at this Listening, Nalaklak?"

"So they tell me. I use it to assist my father, Ambassador Naliskat."

Luskell elbowed Laki playfully. "You're too modest! He's been Listening since he was three. He has a gift."

Bardin raised an eyebrow and smiled. "In that case, I propose we test Luskell now."

Luskell started. "Now? Wouldn't tomorrow be better, after I've eaten and rested? And maybe washed my hands?"

"A wizard is often called upon to act after a long, tiring day. Or when less than perfectly clean. How you perform under such conditions is, I think, a more accurate test of your ability. When you Listen, what do you Listen to?"

"The Mountain. Trees. Rivers." Luskell ticked off the list on her pitchy fingers. "Rocks, but please, let's not do rocks. We'll be here a month."

Bardin smiled. "Trees, then. What about the maple grove between the library and Balsam's House?"

Without waiting for an answer, Bardin headed across

the square to the grove. Luskell and Laki followed him into the dappled shade. The foliage grew thick and mostly green, though a few of the topmost leaves had started to turn golden.

"Nalaklak, do you speak mind to mind?"

Luskell snorted. "He taught me that, too."

Bardin glanced at her. "All right, here's what we'll do. I will shield Luskell from all mind-talk, thoughts, and emotions. Nalaklak, you'll Listen to this grove and relay to me whatever you pick up. Then you'll be shielded and Luskell can Listen."

"Do you think we'd try to cheat?" Luskell folded her arms and scowled.

Laki squeezed her shoulder. "Your plan sounds fair to me, sir. You don't know me, and Luskell has known me her whole life. We don't have to consciously mind-talk to communicate."

"She'd better turn her back, too."

"Fine." Luskell turned to face the side of Balsam's House, another brick mansion that now served a different purpose, this one as a hospital. The healer Balsam had been born into the family of a wealthy merchant. She never married or had children of her own, so when she inherited the family mansion, she made it over into a house of healing, and made herself a new family of healers and apprentices. She established an endowment to fund the institution and ensure the healers were paid a decent wage; few of them had a family fortune to fall back on. Other wealthy women made donations to keep the place going. Balsam's House would outlive Balsam.

Luskell wasn't looking at Bardin, but she felt his shield drop into place around her. Although it didn't block the sounds of birds, wheels, or voices, another kind of hush fell. Stray thoughts and strong feelings that leaked from

Balsam's House cut off abruptly. It was almost like being back in Knot's Valley. She enjoyed the respite until the shield lifted and the city rushed back in.

"Your turn, Luskell. Listen as long as you need to, then tell me what you heard."

Luskell breathed, relaxed her mind, and reached out to the maple grove. Listening was a similar skill to reading thoughts, only with things that didn't have minds the way people or animals did. From her first experience, Luskell had likened a group of trees to a complex chorus. Each individual tree had multiple voices — roots, trunk, leaves, fruit or cones — working together, and each tree communicated with every other tree in the grove. Groves also passed information to more distant groves of the same kind, as well as to trees of other kinds. They were primarily concerned with water, soil, sun, insects, the seasons; to a lesser extent with the activity of humans and other animals. Luskell Listened to all the voices, and to the individual tree nearest her.

When she'd Listened long enough, she turned to Bardin and Laki. "There's been a drought this summer," she said. "They're eager for the fall rains. Another grove, in the Garden District, is having insect problems, but so far, these trees haven't been affected. They pick up a lot of human emotion from Balsam's House — fear, comfort, compassion. They don't have any use for it, but they kind of hold it. The walls of the house do that, too. I think the trees remember me. I've climbed most of them, one time or another. And this one is recovering from … a wound?" She patted the trunk of the tree nearest her.

Bardin smiled. "I would call it surgery. A branch was scratching on Balsam's window and disturbing her rest, so they pruned it back to the trunk. I have been turning a part of it into your staff, Luskell. I suppose we'd best go finish it.

I had to leave the last step until you got back."

She gasped. "That's it? I passed?"

"You fulfilled your quest. One more step and you're a wizard."

"Yes! Come with me, Laki! You should be there, too."

Laki glanced at the sky. Daylight was fading. "I should go. Someone's waiting, you know."

Luskell lost some of her joy. "Oh. Right." She forced a smile. "I want to meet her before you leave town."

"Come to Embassy House tomorrow."

"Good. Tomorrow." She gripped his hands. "Oh, sorry. I did ask to wash the sap off first."

Laki smiled and raised her sticky fingers to his lips. "We'll see you then, Wizard."

Luskell watched Laki walk away. When he was out of sight, she crossed the square with Bardin and returned to the Wizards' Hall.

Bardin held the door for her. "Who's this 'someone'?"

"The woman he plans to marry." Luskell stepped inside and hung her cloak on one of the hooks above her satchel.

"I don't have your sense for emotion, but I can tell you love that boy. Are you going to let him go without a fight?"

Luskell clenched her teeth, then forced herself to relax. She sighed. "We've been friends forever, and that's what we'll be forever. It's better that way."

"Ah. I know the feeling. But better, how?"

"I'm not suited to be an Uklak's wife."

"And an Uklak is ...?"

"Sorry." Luskell made an effort to speak clearly. "A hereditary leader of an Aklaka band. Laki's trained for the role his whole life."

"And the Aklaka don't marry for love?"

Luskell chose her words with care. "There's great passion in most Aklaka relationships. The Uklak's, too. But the Uklak's spouse is more than a lover. He or she should have gifts that complement the Uklak's. There's not much I can do that Laki can't." She allowed a wry smile. "There's the whole wizard thing, too. Laki's family is accepting, but the rest of the band is wary of ... our kind."

"So it's a wizard thing, not a Luskell thing?"

"Hmph. I wouldn't wish me on anyone."

Bardin's perpetually down-turned mouth bent into a smile. "Well, wizards are famously hard to live with. I can't imagine you're any worse, and you're probably better than many." He gestured up the stairs. "Let's put the final stamp on you."

Bardin led the way up to a workroom. A tapering length of maple lay on the tabletop, about as big around at the thickest as Luskell's wrist and almost as tall as Luskell herself. She reached for it, then stopped herself. "May I touch it?"

"Please, pick it up and hold it. It needs to be tuned to your power."

She grasped it, the grip smooth under her hand. She swung it to test the balance, then struck the thick end against the floor. It made a satisfying thump.

Bardin smiled. "I left it unshod, but you can add a metal cap to the foot if you like."

"I know some good blacksmiths in Deep River. What do we do now?"

"I'll finish the carving while you tell me about your quest."

"But I already showed you — "

"You showed me you accomplished your goal; learned what you hoped to learn. That's only one reason for a quest. It's also important to know you have the resources to get along on your own, to ask your own questions, seek the answers, use your power appropriately. I want to hear the *story*. How did it go?"

Luskell handed over the unfinished staff and settled into a chair. "There's not much to tell. I took the coach to Misty Pass and stayed with my mother for a few days."

"She went to care for your grandfather, didn't she?" Bardin asked.

"He had a bad case of the wobbles and would have died without her." There had been an epidemic of the seasonal illness, more severe than most years and worse in the crowded city than elsewhere. In their first project together, Luskell and Bardin had worked out a technique for protecting people who hadn't been infected yet. Once they had proved it was sound, they shared it with more capable healers. "Mamam was casting protection over all of Misty Pass every time a coach arrived. I'd never seen her so worn out, but no one else got sick."

Bardin nodded thoughtfully. "Are you proud of your mother or of your technique?"

"Both, I guess." Luskell propped her elbows on the table and rested her chin in her hands. Too late she remembered the pitch on her fingers, now on her face, as well. "I was tempted to stay and help her, though I'm still not much of a healer. It was good to see her and my little brother again. I missed them more than I knew." Longing returned, stronger now. She hadn't seen her family in months but now she was walking distance from them. "After a few days, I flew to Knot's Valley so Laki could teach me to Listen." They'd taught each other a great deal more, but Luskell wasn't about to share that part of her quest with Bardin. She hastened to continue her story before she thought about those memories too much. "It was difficult at first. I had to learn to focus, to ignore all kinds of distractions. But he said I had a knack for it."

"I think he was right, based on the sample you gave me.

Did you learn what Listening is for?"

"It's not about trees telling me anything directly, if that's what you mean. Laki said it's about putting your attention outside yourself so you can see what's right in front of you. What you know but don't know you know. I'm still learning that part, but it's been helpful a few times."

"Anything of the kind in the maple grove just now?"

"Maybe something about Balsam's House. It was all mixed up. Or maybe I am."

Bardin smiled. "That's to be expected. So you learned quickly?"

"After a week, I had enough skill to practice on my own. I went down to Deep River to visit my grandmother."

"That's where your friend Jagryn lives, isn't it? Or has wizarding taken him elsewhere?"

"He plans to settle there. He's a good weatherworker — useful in a country wizard. And everyone already knows him. He was having trouble finishing his quest, though. I tried to help him, but I might have made it worse."

"Why do you say that?"

"He wanted to visit the Other Side, the way I do. I told him how I do it in dreams, but it wasn't the same for him. He couldn't sleep when he needed to, so he took drops to help him." Bardin's alarmed expression told her he knew the risk of taking the sedative without supervision. "Jagryn managed to dream himself to the Other Side, but he couldn't get back. I had to go after him, and when he woke up, he was ... confused. We both were. We had a misunderstanding." Luskell didn't want to go into detail about the strange but pleasant dream she and Jagryn had shared. It had damaged their friendship almost beyond repair, mostly because he hadn't told her he was serious about Ruvhonn, and she hadn't guessed until too late. She forced a smile onto her face before Bardin could ask. "But we worked it out and Jagryn eventually did his quest on his own. He's a wizard now. And he got married recently. I hear they're visiting Eukard City right now."

"That's good. You see? Not all wizards are hard to live with. Now, tell me about your eye."

Her hand went by reflex to the patch. "I'd rather not."

"It's important, Luskell."

"The short version is I tried to kill a man, but I missed."

Bardin raised his eyebrows but appeared more interested than shocked. "I'm going to need the long version."

She'd been afraid of that. Did she really want to be a wizard? She sighed. "All right, but you won't like it. You remember the strangler, from last winter?"

"I don't think any of us will forget."

"He left the city the same time I did, and as chance would have it, he ended up in Deep River, too. He was hiding out, in disguise. He attacked a local girl, but I drove him away before he could kill her. I thought he was going to escape, so I called down lightning to stop him. But I missed and hit a stump, instead. It exploded and I got a face full of splinters."

"Oh, dear. You and weatherworking ... I'm sorry you were hurt, but I understand you succeeded in capturing him."

"Fandek did, not me."

"All right, but you saved your friend. You meant well and tried to use your power to help."

Luskell sighed. "It sounds better when you put it that way. My father said something similar, but ... I really wanted to kill him. I have something dark in me."

"We all do. Perhaps you're lucky to learn it so young. You'll need to work on control, but you knew that already."

"That's why I didn't come back right away."

"You stayed in Deep River while your injuries healed?"

"Yes, but it didn't take long. I went back to Knot's Valley."

"Ah — with your friend Laki."

"No. I was alone from Spring Balance until a few days ago." Deep longing for the lonesome high places tugged at Luskell's heart. "I kept Aku, Listened, and worked on myself."

"Time apart can be bracing. Challenging, though, for one who likes company and attention."

For as long as Luskell could remember, she'd always been able to persuade her friends to go along with her schemes and adventures. "The early days were the hardest, getting used to the quiet and solitude. Listening helped, and getting into a routine of hiking, foraging, singing to Aku, maintaining the lodge and my belongings ... And I had visits from the Other Side most nights — my grandfather Knot or my brother Ketwyn."

"And now you're back among living folks."

"Yes. Time to see if I'm a better person than I was. I missed people, but in some ways it was easier." She laughed at a new thought. "I never asked before, but do you live alone?"

"I do and I don't," Bardin replied. "I have two spacious rooms to myself, not far from here, in my eldest sister's home. Our family home, but she inherited it and filled it with children and grandchildren. I have my own private entrance so I can choose whether I encounter them or not."

"So you never had anyone ... special?"

"There was a girl once." Bardin gazed upward, the sweetest smile on his face that Luskell had ever seen there. "I would have married her, but she had other plans for herself. When it seemed those plans were leading her into danger, I told her father. She didn't speak to me for years."

"That's awful! I guess my friends are more forgiving."

Bardin laughed. "Well, we patched it up eventually. Friends forever, as you say. She never married, either. I guess it wasn't anything against me. So, do you still want to be a wizard?"

"I do, if you think I can be."

He held out the staff. "Hold it steady while I do the last of the spell."

Luskell held the staff with both hands. Bardin passed his hands over it without touching the wood while he chanted a brief spell.

From the moment she'd found her power, Luskell had understood the meaning of magical words and phrases. This was different. She didn't know what these words meant, though she sensed a deep magic in them. When he finished, a faintly glowing network sprang out around the staff. She felt it as a thrill and a pang — her power and her home.

"This is mine," she whispered.

"It is. Now you are a wizard. What will you do?"

"I ... don't know." She balanced the staff on both hands. It was part of her, as if she'd grown a third arm. "Will you teach me how to use this?"

"*It* will teach you. You should find difficult magic easier. You won't have to use as much power. You'll feel ... steadier."

"That would be an improvement. I think I'll wait till tomorrow, though. I need food and sleep."

Bardin ushered her out of the workroom. "Meet me tomorrow and we'll put your name in the *Registry of Practitioners*."

"Here or at the library?"

"Here. We need to make the ink first."

"I'll see you then." Luskell started down the stairs.

Bardin followed. "The sun's about down. I could walk with you, see you safe home."

"With an eyepatch and a wizard stick, do you think anyone will bother me?"

"Well, when you put it like that ..." Bardin smiled, but Luskell could sense his lingering concern.

"Don't worry," she assured him. "It'll be as if I'm not even there."

Chapter 6

Despite what she'd told Bardin, Luskell wasn't truly invisible. She had the power and the skill to maintain full concealment, though movement made it harder to sustain. But she was tired and hungry. She didn't want to expend more energy than she had to. She worked the much easier magic of deflecting attention. She would be visible to anyone paying attention, but the spell rendered her so uninteresting, nobody would. She passed unnoticed in the busy streets of Old Town, with only the thought of reaching home.

Home. It had never been a fixed place, but wherever Luskell's family could be found. She drew strength from the prospect of seeing them again soon. She gripped her new staff, itself a source of energy and excitement, and walked as quickly as she could to the rooms above Wyll and Kiat's textile shop. Her parents knew she would arrive today, but not exactly when, and she decided to preserve the surprise. She wanted to make an entrance.

Luskell climbed the outside stairs and stood a moment at the door. She flung it open, thumped her staff on the floor, and cried, "I'm back!"

To an empty room.

She wanted to kick the door shut, then curl up and cry. Why would they leave when they knew she was coming home today? She drew a calming breath and fought off the childish tantrum. She needed to act like the wizard she now was. A quick glance told her they couldn't have been gone long. A fire burned low in the stove, and Crett's toys were scattered across the floor — blocks and a trio of carved bears she recognized as having once been Laki's. She had played with them herself as a child. Luskell closed the door quietly and leaned her staff in the corner behind it, next to her father's. That was another clue. If he meant to be gone long, he'd have taken it with him.

Luskell hung her cloak on one of the hooks by the door. It was good to be back in the familiar place, but had it always been so small? Her half-year alone in a wild place had changed her perspective. She went into her even smaller room to empty her bag and change clothes. And scrub her sticky hands and face, but there wasn't enough water. She found the pail and went outside and down the back stairs. The yard was enclosed on three sides by buildings and on the fourth by a high fence. Delivery wagons used the gate to enter, but most of the time it was kept closed, as it was now. The well and pump in the center were surrounded by their own gated fence. Another woman finished filling her bucket as Luskell approached. She turned from her chore and yelped in fright, dropping her bucket. The water poured onto the ground.

"I'm sorry, I didn't mean to — " In the fading light, Luskell recognized the other woman. "Ruvhonn? What are you ...? I mean, I didn't expect ..." At a loss, she picked up the fallen bucket. "Let me help you with this. Hold it while I work the pump."

"Oh. Thank you." Ruvhonn took it and held it under the stream of water as Luskell pumped. "We're staying with Kiat and Wyll while we visit the city."

"Of course, Jagryn stayed with them when he was here before," Luskell said. "It must be crowded, though."

"Well, not as crowded as it might be. Keela's still in Deep River."

"She must be doing well with Brynnit." Luskell's friend Keela had traveled with her the previous winter, to study with her aunt, Deep River's healer. "Did you know we're right upstairs?"

"Jagryn mentioned it. He didn't think you'd be here, though. Your grandma said you were in the mountains somewhere."

"I was, until yesterday. She gave me his letter last night."

Ruvhonn's bucket was full and Luskell expected her to take it inside, but she reached for Luskell's. "I'll hold yours now. It's only fair."

"You didn't spill it, but all right," Luskell said, and resumed pumping. "Are you enjoying your trip?"

"The city is very ... interesting. Jagryn's time here meant a lot to him." Ruvhonn glanced at Luskell, then quickly away. Even if she didn't know about the secret kisses Jagryn and Luskell had exchanged back in those days, she probably suspected. Knowing honest Jagryn, he'd told her everything.

"Did he tell you about the time we were nearly struck by

lightning?"

Ruvhonn's mouth dropped open. "But he's always so careful!"

"There's a reason Dadad taught him to work weather apart from me."

Ruvhonn nodded. "That makes sense now. Anyway, I'm happy to visit the city with him, but I'm worn out from traveling. I've never been this far from home. And my stomach doesn't like it."

"If you're sick, you should talk to my mother."

"Oh, I'm not sick, I just don't have any appetite at the usual mealtimes. And it's hard to sleep with so many people around."

"I've been completely alone since spring," Luskell said. "It is strange to be back among folks. I hope they don't keep me awake, because I'm worn out, too."

They carried their buckets back to the house, parting at the base of the stairs. It had been an awkward meeting, but not as bad as it might have been. Luskell took her water inside and finally had a chance to wash, change clothes, and unpack. As she returned her fiddle to its shelf in the front room, she heard voices on the stairs.

"Big step! One more! You did it! What a big boy you are!"

"I do every step."

Crett hopped in, then halted and stared at Luskell. In the half year since she'd seen him, his red-gold curls had been trimmed and he'd grown taller. He would always be her baby brother, but he wasn't a baby anymore.

Their father followed Crett inside with a large basket in his arms. "Look who's here, Crett! Who have we been waiting for?"

"'uskell?" His eyes widened and he squealed. "'uskell!" Luskell knelt down and he leaped into her arms.

"I'm not Wuwu anymore?" She'd been looking forward to his name for her, one of his first intelligible words.

Crett scowled. "Dat baby talk, 'uskell." He patted her eyepatch. "Patch off."

"Are you sure? It doesn't look very good under there."

"Patch off."

She lifted the patch so he could see her scars and injured eye. And she could see his life energy. He was bursting with it, strong and healthy. Luskell lowered the patch and hugged him tight. "It's good to see you, Crett."

"I knew you comin'."

"Of course you did — Mamam and Dadad told you, didn't they?" She leaned back to unbutton and remove his coat for him.

"Knew 'fore dat."

"Mm-hm, sure you did." Luskell kissed his cheek and stood up. "So if you knew I was coming, where were you?"

"Gettin' supper." Crett ran with his coat and hung it on a low hook near the door.

Dadad set the basket on the floor and hung his cloak next to Luskell's. "We expected you earlier. When it got late, we decided we'd better get some food so you wouldn't have to go hungry. You still like the chicken pie from the Otter, don't you?"

"Mm, I thought something smelled good. Where's Mamam?"

"They needed her at Balsam's House tonight. She said to go ahead without her. What kept you? Was the coach late?"

"Not as much as it might have been. Let me eat something and I'll tell you all about it."

Luskell removed a book from the table to make room for Dadad to set down the basket and remove the pie. "What's this?" She didn't recognize it and there was no lettering on the dark cover to indicate the subject.

"Something I borrowed from the library. You might find it interesting, too. We can talk about it after Crett goes to bed."

Crett ran to a low shelf near the stove and brought three plates to the table, one at a time, then returned for forks. Luskell smiled and shook her head in disbelief. Such a big boy. Dadad broke through the pie's golden, flaky crust and spooned steaming chicken and gravy onto the plates. Luskell ate half her helping. With the edge off her hunger, she slowed down to relate the story of moving the fallen tree.

"And when we got to town, we went to see Bardin and, well ... now I'm a wizard."

It wasn't the grand entrance she'd planned. In some ways, it was better to see Dadad's startled glance into the corner where her staff leaned next to his, and the delighted smile that followed.

He sat back and gazed at her, grinning. "You are a wonder. Didn't waste a moment, did you?"

"I didn't know Bardin would want to do it today. But I had Laki with me, and he was able to confirm my Listening."

"On top of that business with the tree — a good test, when you'd already been using power. Leave it to Bardin ..."

Luskell finished her supper, basking in her father's pride. After the meal, she played her fiddle and told Crett a story before bed. Once he was tucked in, she and Dadad sat by the stove and talked quietly.

"So, tell me about your book," Luskell said.

He retrieved it from the shelf where she'd moved it. "You know Terulo, don't you? He helped me find it when the librarian couldn't. He has a gift with forgotten things."

"Interesting specialty for a wizard," Luskell said. Terulo

was an apprentice wizard close to her age; a year older at most. He had already been studying with Wizard Larem when she started with Bardin. She liked the apprentice better than the master.

"Yes, unusual but potentially useful. He might make a good librarian someday," Dadad said. "I asked for books on suppression of power."

"Like how you drained Trenn so he wouldn't threaten us?" Luskell shuddered at the memory of that night, not long after she'd discovered her own power.

"Related, but different. It's been on my mind since then, but this is the first chance I've had to look into the subject."

"Why the interest?"

He smiled. "It started with you, actually. Remember you told me you tried to work magic when you were only seven, and when you couldn't, you concluded you never would?"

She laughed. "How wrong could I be?"

"You didn't know, and you didn't think to ask. I suspect you managed to suppress your own power. We expected it to manifest when you were eleven or twelve. Your mother first saw glimmerings around that time."

"It would have saved a lot of trouble if someone had told me!" Luskell said.

"Oh, we tried, but you got so angry, we decided it was safer to let things take their own course. But you held it off until you were almost fifteen."

"Not really that interesting."

"Not on its own. But it nudged me to consider my own experience. The onset of my power happened when I was twelve ... and you know how well that turned out." He waggled his scarred right hand, which he had accidentally set on fire. "I had power I was afraid to use. I studied from books, but I didn't dare try any but the most harmless spells."

"Is that why you're so good at illusions?" Luskell had always admired her father's skill in that area. He could produce a convincing meadow in the middle of a room, complete with babbling brook, fragrant flowers, and visiting wildlife. She had no trouble with illusion magic but had never worked at it. Unlike his, her skunks had no stink.

"It probably is. I wonder, though, if my fear suppressed my power — maybe it wasn't that I *wouldn't* do those other spells, but that I *couldn't*. Until I found a master who could unlock my power in a safe way."

Luskell frowned, trying to understand. "So suppressing your power was a good thing?"

"Possibly. I want to see what else is known about it. It didn't seem to harm either of us, and in fact may have made us stronger than we would have been otherwise. But what would happen if a knowledgeable wizard deliberately suppressed someone else's power. Say a child whose power is manifesting too young to be safe, or a youth who is regarded as a threat. Would the suppression eventually wear off and the power develop normally, or would there be some harm? Draining mature power leaves the person sick and empty, but suppression must feel different."

"I didn't feel anything when it wore off," Luskell said. "You think this book might tell you?"

"I don't know yet, but I hope so." Dadad set the book down and leaned back with a sigh. "It's good to have you back. I wish I could have seen Laki. He didn't want to come home with you?"

"He ... had someone else to see. He's found a wife here, and Kala gave her blessing."

"Oh. I'm sorry."

Luskell nudged his shoulder. "Don't be. That's not how we are."

"If you say so."

"I do. And before you ask, yes, I heard Jagryn got married, too. I met Ruvhonn earlier, downstairs. I'm ... glad they're close by." Luskell was mostly sure this was true.

Whether or not he noticed her discomfort, Dadad changed the subject. "How does it feel to be a wizard at last?"

"I already love having the staff. And I earned the title, so I'll use it. But ..." Luskell searched for the right words. "I'm not sure it's what I *am*. Or all I am. Does that make sense?"

Dadad nodded. "You earned the title of Healer, too, even if it isn't your greatest talent."

"And Listener, and Aku's Keeper," Luskell added.

"Reminds me of someone else," Dadad said. "My father was a wizard of many gifts. Besides his work with Aku, his greatest was probably healing. He was proud of it, but so uncomfortable with people, he rarely used it."

"I've heard that," Luskell said. "But what does it have to do with me? You're right, healing isn't my strongest ability."

"Only that he was more than only one thing. And healing was the last magic he ever did."

"Yes, an injured stranger, wasn't it?" Luskell knew the basics of the story, enough to explain why she'd never met her grandfather in life.

Dadad leaned back and gazed at the ceiling. "Your mother and I had rescued him from Aku. He recovered most of his power, but the ordeal damaged him. He was dying slowly, his life trickling away. Ketty could restore much of what he lost if he didn't overexert himself, especially with magic. But he couldn't keep away from it, even if only little tricks to amuse children. He probably could have gone on for years that way. But then that boy brought his mother to the inn, all battered and bleeding from being trampled and run over."

"Why didn't Mamam take care of her, if Knot wasn't well?" Luskell asked. Mamam had saved Laki when he was badly hurt. She might even have brought him back from death.

"She'd helped deliver a set of twins earlier the same day. She was exhausted, and as we later learned, already expecting you." Dadad turned a warm smile on Luskell. "Knot decided to let her rest, and spent everything he had to restore a mother to her family. He never earned a blue apron at Balsam's House. He never called himself Healer. But at the end, that's who — what — he was."

Luskell pondered this. It didn't answer her questions, but at least she wasn't the only one.

"Does Mamam usually stay at Balsam's House so late?"

Dadad frowned. "No. Balsam can't do as much as she — " He broke off with a faraway look in his eyes. After a moment, he came back to Luskell with a half smile. "Your mother must have known we were talking about her. One of the neighborhood midwives called her out to help with a delivery."

"Lucky family." Luskell had hoped to see her mother before she fell asleep. That didn't seem likely now, but they'd be together in the morning.

After a quiet moment, Dadad spoke again. "Have you seen your grandfather lately?"

The way he said it, she knew he didn't mean Grandpa Eslo in Misty Pass. "Yes, often. He came to me. I didn't go there," she hastened to add before he could ask. "Knot and Ketwyn kept me company almost the whole time. I don't suppose I'll see as much of them now."

"Just as well. Your time and power are better spent among the living."

"Yes, you're probably right."

This seemed the wrong time to mention Old Mother Bones.

Chapter 7

Luskell was on her feet before she knew she was awake. She needed to calm Aku. No, she wasn't there anymore. She was home. She Listened. Nothing.

Listening was more difficult in the city. Every brick and stone had its own slow voice, and every house buzzed with absorbed emotion. She tried to Listen under the noise. It would have been easier were she touching the ground, and not surrounded by walls. She pressed her hands to the wall, which touched the ground, which touched Aku. Luskell reached for the solitude Laki had said she carried inside her. The city's distractions receded, and she felt more connected to the natural world. She didn't detect anything wrong. That didn't mean nothing *was* wrong, but she couldn't sense it. Maybe she'd heard Mamam come home, or Crett had cried out, though it was quiet in the next room now.

Something in a dream must have startled her awake. Had she been dreaming? She couldn't remember anything but an ominous atmosphere. She was used to being on alert for changes in Aku's mood, though. It didn't take much to wake her. She crawled back under the covers. Her bed was still warm, and she was tired enough to slip back into sleep.

Luskell walked in Braffin's Garden at sunset, Ketwyn by her side.

"This is nice." She took in the leafy trees and mellow light. They had the place to themselves. "Did I dream it on my own or did you choose?"

"I might have helped. You're back in the city, but you like to be outside."

"The garden is one of my favorite places in the city."

"I know. When you were small, I used to watch you play here with your big friend."

"Ambug." Luskell smiled. She looked forward to seeing him and her other city friends soon. "He put up with a lot, always giving me horsey rides."

"I was glad you had someone like a brother, but I wished it could have been me."

"You'd be the same age, if you'd ... you know."

"If I'd lived." He grinned, assuring her he wasn't offended.

"I wish you could have been friends with Ambug, too." They circled around the fountain in the middle of the lawn. The grass was greener than it should have been at the end of the dry season. In dreams — good dreams,

anyway — things were nicer than in real life. Any dream with Ketwyn in it was good by definition. "But I'm glad you're here. I woke up earlier and thought Aku was about to blow!"

"She's not your responsibility now. She has a new Keeper, right?"

"Yes, but I worry he won't give her enough attention." They passed the statue of King Braffin. It looked more like Dadad and wasn't in its usual place. Dreams ... and an idea. "Could you maybe ask Knot to visit his dreams and make sure he's doing his job?"

"Did Knot pester you about such things while you were there?"

"No, because I didn't need pestering."

"And you have no reason to think the new Keeper needs it, either. You woke up worried, but nothing actually happened."

"Well, no, but ..."

"You have to adjust to your new life. Let the old one go. Knot would say it isn't good for Aku to be too attached to you. It probably isn't good for you to be too attached to her, either."

"I guess. It's hard, though."

Ketwyn's mouth moved but he spoke with Mamam's voice. "Luskell? Do you hear me?"

Luskell woke to her mother's voice in her mind. After the night she'd had, she assumed it was another dream.

I need your help. Can you come?

Not a dream, then. Luskell sat up and tried to focus her

bleary thoughts. *What do you need me for?*

There's a birth going wrong. I'll explain when you get here. Mamam gave the address of a house on the edge of Old Town. *Don't come to the street door. Use the alley behind the house. Knock at the back door and I'll let you in.* She ended the connection.

Luskell dropped back for a moment, then got up and dressed in her dirty travel clothes again. She preferred them when hard work or danger were likely. She put on her eye patch and tiptoed out. In the front room, she almost tripped over Crett's trundle bed, where he slept with his thumb in his mouth. Dadad had fallen asleep sitting up by the stove.

Luskell shook him awake. "You should go to bed," she whispered.

"I'm fine. I'll wait up for your mother."

"I just heard from her — she won't be home anytime soon. In fact, she asked me to help her. Get some sleep. We'll be home in the morning."

Luskell threw on her warm cloak against the autumn chill, picked up her staff and went out. It was dark, and late enough that the streets weren't crowded, but early enough that the taverns were emptying out. Luskell wasn't in the mood to deal with strolling drunks. And Mamam's call had sounded urgent. Even if Luskell deflected attention so she wasn't bothered, walking was the slow way to get there. It was time to try something she'd wanted to test since the moment she first gripped her staff.

Luskell stood at the top of the stairs and tucked her eyepatch into her pocket. She focused her mind and became an owl. She flapped on silent wings out over the streets and houses of Old Town. Her talons grasped a twig — her staff, transformed along with her. Any ordinary object she might have held would have been left behind. So it was true. The staff was part of her and transformed when she did.

To her owl eyes, the night was bright, though clouds covered the moon and stars. Luskell ignored the city's rodents and arrived at the house in less than half the time it would have taken to walk. She resumed her own form and was about to knock at the street door when she remembered Mamam's instructions. Going around to the alley door seemed beneath the dignity of a wizard, but that's where Mamam expected her.

She walked back to the cross street and down to the alley's mouth, impenetrably dark after owl vision. Before she put the patch back on, she looked down the alley to see what her wizard eye might catch. A small bright form scurried away — a rat, full of life — but nothing more threatening presented itself. She put the patch on and made her way to the back door of the house. When she knocked, Mamam let her in.

"Thanks for coming so quickly."

A man stood with his back to the room, staring out the small window at nothing. He turned and Mamam gave him an encouraging nod before she led Luskell into the other room. The laboring mother lay on a bed. The young woman attending her looked up and Luskell recognized Cedar, an old friend. Though only a year or so older than Luskell, Cedar was already a skilled midwife.

Cedar frowned. "A wizard? This is no place for a man."

Luskell removed her cloak and leaned the staff in the corner. "Cedar, it's me."

"Luskell? What happened to your eye?"

"Later." Luskell lifted the eyepatch for a moment. Mamam and Cedar shone steady, but the mother-to-be flickered like a candle drowning in its own wax. This birth was going wrong, but what was Luskell supposed to do about it? "Mamam, why do you need my help? This is your area."

"Babe's in a bad position. Between us, Cedar and I should be able to move him around to come out, but poor Nalya's bleeding more than she should, and she's about spent. I can deal with the bleeding, but I need you to ... stay with her. Keep her ... awake."

Luskell bowed her head to hide her indignation. What kind of work was that for a wizard? The laboring mother cried out as another pain took her. When it passed, she dropped back, weak and sobbing. Luskell knelt by the bed and gripped her hand. "Hold on, Nalya. I'm Luskell. I'm here to help you."

Mamam and Cedar spoke quietly, but Luskell focused her attention on Nalya. If this was her job, she would do it well. They gazed at each other and Nalya gripped Luskell's hand and squeezed hard through the pains. Luskell followed the thoughts in Nalya's mind. She wanted her mother ... She feared it would go on forever ... The pains would never stop ... So tired ...

After one particularly wracking episode, her eyes drooped shut and her fingers went limp. Luskell patted Nalya's cheek. "Nalya? Wake up. Come on, wake up now." When she got no response, she closed her own eye and followed the fading thoughts. When Luskell opened her eyes, she stood with Nalya behind the house ... but not in the dark alley. They stood at the bottom of a grassy hillside, bright but with no sun in view. Distant figures climbed the hill and disappeared over the top.

Luskell squeezed Nalya's shoulder gently. "Come back inside."

"But it's so peaceful here. So restful. Can't I stay?" She took a step forward, then another.

Luskell grabbed Nalya's hand and drew her back.

Although Luskell had been here many times, this was a new perspective. She'd never stood all the way at the bottom of the hill. But she knew the temptation to stay. She looked at Nalya, a young woman not many years older than she was — maybe twenty at the oldest. A new wife, having her first child. But in this world, her belly wasn't big, and she didn't hold a baby.

"Your little one lives, Nalya. Without you, maybe not for long. Come back now."

With effort, Nalya turned her head from the pleasant hillside and looked at Luskell. "Where's your eyepatch?"

"I don't need it here."

"Where is 'here'?"

"The Other Side." Luskell pointed up the hill. "Those are the souls of the newly dead. It isn't your time to join them."

Nalya stared. "Who are you?"

"I'm Luskell. I'm here to help you. My mother's doing everything she can, and she's the best there is, but your baby needs you most of all. Let's go in." She gave a gentle tug on Nalya's hand.

Nalya cast one longing glance up the hill, but nodded and turned away. "All right. Don't leave me."

Luskell jerked and opened her eye. They were back in the room with Mamam and Cedar. Nalya groaned low and pushed.

"That's the way," Mamam said.

Nalya was back, but for how long? Luskell doubted a stranger with an eyepatch would be a strong enough anchor. She would do all she could, but Nalya needed someone she knew. Luskell caught Cedar's eye. "Get her husband in here."

"This is no place for a —"

"Get him. Now."

Cedar looked like she might argue but didn't. Moments

later, she led the terrified young man in from the other room.

Luskell tried to smile. "Hold her other hand and talk to her."

"What ... what should I say?"

"I don't know! Sweet talk, like when you were courting. Give her something else to pay attention to. I'll help."

Luskell laid her free hand on Nalya's head. She pushed healing, life-giving power into Nalya as Nalya pushed her child into the world. When at last the baby shouted, both parents wept and laughed. Luskell had only enough energy for an exhausted smile.

Mamam left the new family in Cedar's able care and drew Luskell into the other room. "Good idea, bringing the husband in. She tried to leave, didn't she?"

"Yes. How long were we gone?"

"Not ... long. I was about to worry, but you brought her back. Thank you. Are you all right?"

"Mm. Tired."

"More than tired, I think. I'm sorry, my wizard girl, I hoped it wouldn't come to that. But no one else does what you do. I won't ask again."

"No, it's all right. No ... harm ... done." Luskell moved heavily, weighed down by exhaustion and a lingering sadness. Whether from visiting the Other Side or from having to leave, she couldn't say.

"Come with me." Mamam took Luskell's arm.

Luskell stumbled outside, leaning on her staff and her mother, though Mamam was much smaller than Luskell. It was still dark out, but when they left the alley for the open street, the first pale light of dawn showed in the east. She didn't pay attention to where they were going. They were going home, of course. But when she looked up, they were outside a grand brick mansion.

"Balsam's House? Mamam, you're not going back to work now?"

"No, there's someone here you need to see. Come on, step up."

Luskell climbed the steps onto the porch and plodded inside. But she wasn't sick. Why would Mamam bring her here?

"Luskell! When did you get back?"

The familiar voice made her look up. Her mother's apprentice, Fandek, came to meet them in the wide hallway. He wore a delighted smile. It warmed Luskell but she wasn't ready to see him. She tried to turn around, but Mamam held her firm.

"Luskell could use some of your sunshine."

"Yes, ma'am. Right away." Fandek placed both hands on Luskell's head. She was no less tired, but the ache of exhaustion melted away. Her low spirits lifted, to the point where she wasn't sure her feet touched the floor.

Mamam chuckled. "That's probably enough."

Fandek lifted his hands from Luskell's head and placed them on her shoulders. "Good to see you."

She leaned against him and held him in a one-armed hug. "Oh, Fandek ..."

"Maybe more than enough."

At Mamam's comment, Fandek gently pushed Luskell away and held her out at arm's length. "So, a staff. You're a wizard now?"

"Just since today. And you're a healer."

"An apprentice." He flicked his brown apron. "But healing suits me."

"Thank you, Fandek. I can't tell you how much that helped."

"I'm glad. But we have so much to talk about!"

Maman drew Luskell back. "She needs to sleep now, but

I thank you, too."

"Tomorrow, then?"

Luskell smiled up at his eager, handsome face. "I'd like that."

Luskell and her mother left Balsam's House and walked home as the black sky lightened to gray. The long night dragged at Luskell, but she felt better, no doubt due to whatever Fandek had done. She glanced sidelong at Mamam.

"His *sunshine*?"

"Sh! Some people are sleeping," Mamam whispered. "That's just what I call it. Fandek's gift has been a real blessing at Balsam's House."

Luskell had experienced Fandek's talent before, though she hadn't tried to name it. Even before he knew he had an aptitude for healing, he'd been able to lift Luskell's spirits simply by being there. When he learned to work a pain charm, his natural talent leaked out as a touch of euphoria that was more than mere absence of pain. That alone was reason to distrust her affection for him. What if she liked only how he made her feel? There was also the matter of his older brother, the reason for her ruined eye.

She couldn't blame Fandek for his brother's deeds. He was right. They did have a lot to talk about.

Chapter 8

Luskell climbed the steps to their rooms, grateful to be almost back in bed. "So are you on staff at Balsam's House now, or only working with Fandek?"

"I'm Director. *Acting* Director," Mamam corrected. "Balsam isn't well, so she asked me to help."

Luskell and her mother stopped talking as they tiptoed into the darkened room. Snores met them from the big bed in the corner. Dadad must have taken Luskell's advice. Crett giggled in his sleep but didn't wake.

"Thank you again, Luskell," Mamam whispered. "I'm sure you didn't expect to be working your first night back."

"I'm glad I could be useful."

"You can sleep late tomorrow."

"Count on it. No, wait — I'm meeting Bardin to put my

name in the Registry. I shouldn't be late."

"See you in the morning, then. Sleep well."

Although no longer low-spirited, Luskell felt the fatigue of the long day and use of power. If anyone visited her dreams, she didn't remember in the morning.

A morning that came too soon. She was excited enough about this last step in her wizard's training that she didn't mind too much. She was less pleased about the prospect of meeting Laki's intended. She wanted him to be happy. She didn't believe he might choose someone unworthy. But she had gotten used to him loving *her*. Was she that easy to get over?

Wizard business came first. Luskell tried to quell her excitement enough to eat some breakfast with Mamam and Crett. Dadad had already gone out, so any advice or encouragement from him would have to wait until the deed was done. She put on the same gray dress she had worn the day she went looking for a master to make her his apprentice. It wasn't her favorite, but seemed sober and grown-up, maybe even wizardly.

Bardin waited for her by the fire at the Wizards' Hall. "The staff suits you. Shall we finish the job?"

They returned to the upstairs workroom, where Bardin had laid out the materials needed to make the ink.

"How is this different from the ink for writing spells?" Luskell asked.

"It will have *you* in it. We begin the same way, though." He placed a dish of wood shavings in front of her. "These are from your staff. You should have no problem burning them to ash." Bardin allowed a smile to lift the corners of his mouth.

Overexcited at her first lesson, Luskell had consumed an entire candle with her fire spell. She had gained control since then. She set the shavings alight without speaking the words. They burned fast and hot, and were soon reduced to a small pile of ash. When the ashes were cool, she stirred in pure water until the mixture was soupy and black, then added a drop of distilled spirit to preserve the ink.

"Now it needs a drop of your blood." Bardin held out a small, sharp blade.

"I thought the wood from my staff was how it had me in it." Luskell took the blade and cleaned it with a bit of the spirit. She drew it across the tip of the middle finger of her left hand and squeezed a drop of blood into the dish of ink. "How does any boy get through this step?" She cleaned the cut and healed it.

"They're not *all* squeamish. Now, repeat after me." Bardin said a brief incantation over the ink. Luskell repeated it while stirring. The words sounded more like Aklaka than Eukardian but didn't have an obvious meaning in either language; similar to the ritual with the staff. Bardin poured the finished ink into a tiny pot and corked it. "Let's go put your name in the book."

They crossed the square to the library. Morning light shone down on the main reading room through the great glass dome and tall windows. Bardin and Luskell climbed the spiral staircase to the mezzanine that overlooked the reading room. This level held spell books and volumes of magical history, as well as folk tales and mythology. Near the books was a display of historical artifacts in three small alcoves: on the left, the Agate Staff of Azzar, a stone carving that looked like wood, with a painting of people in fancy clothes and crowns doing something in a tent in the desert; on the right, a faded document, the Treaty of the Waters;

and in the middle, *The Registry of Practitioners.*

A black-haired young man sat at a table near the windows, several books open in front of him. "Ah!" A soft cry escaped him, and he scribbled something on a blank sheet to the side of the books.

"Terulo!" Luskell called, also softly; they were in a library, after all. "What are you doing?"

He turned, mouth open in surprise. "You came back! And you have a staff? Wonderful!"

"I can't imagine your master agrees." Terulo had been a quiet supporter of Luskell's wizardly ambition, while most of the other masters and apprentices had been dismissive; his master Larem most of all. His hair was longer but more neatly combed than the last time she had seen him. A dark reddish beard surrounded his mouth, sparse but neatly trimmed. "But what's all this?" Luskell waved at the books and papers in front of him.

"My quest."

"You're doing your quest in the library?"

"Why not? There are piles of books and old documents here that no one's really gone through. My power isn't enough to be much use on its own, but I might discover something unknown or forgotten. I've always had a knack for it."

"So my father told me. You helped him find a book."

"That's right, it wasn't in the librarian's records, but I found it in a box in the storage closet. This kind of work suits me, and I can afford to do it rather than find something else."

Terulo came from a wealthy family — Luskell remembered him telling her they owned an island — so he did have the leisure to be a scholar on his own.

"So what's your quest?" she asked.

"I started out researching enchanted objects. These

days, spell ink and the wizard's staff are the only ones in common use, but long ago there were others. Is there a reason, or is it 'just not done' anymore?"

Luskell had never given much thought to enchanted objects, though she'd had a close encounter with a cursed knife once. Crude magic, easily countered by skilled practitioners. As she had seen the previous day, a wizard's staff resulted from a more intricate process. If it was older than the other spells she knew, that might explain why she didn't understand the language.

Bardin nodded appreciatively. "A worthwhile project, indeed. There's so much we don't understand or have forgotten. Even the ritual for crafting the staff is not well understood. We do it because it works, but I'm not sure anyone knows *why* it works."

Terulo grinned. "If I find out, I'll let you know. But I've stumbled onto something else I want to finish first — a forgotten spell."

"Ooh! That sounds more exciting," Luskell said.

"And a more defined goal for a quest," Bardin said. "Where did you discover it?"

"I've been finding torn fragments of pages tucked into several different books. I have enough of them now to see they're all from the same page. It's a spell I've never heard about, but I believe it opens a doorway between where you are and another location you know or can see."

"I've never heard of that, either, but it sounds useful." Luskell imagined stepping in an instant from one neighborhood to another, or from Eukard City to Deep River. From the living world to the Other Side, even.

"I'm glad you think so. I'll need you to help me test it if it gets that far," Terulo said. "I have enough magic to read from spellbooks and understand how a spell works. Not enough to perform the magic myself. But you should have no trouble."

"You can count on me."

"Come, Luskell," Bardin said. "It's time to put your name in the book."

"Leave room for mine!" Terulo said. "I'll be eighteen next month."

The *Registry of Practitioners* was an oversized tome that had its own curtained alcove. It listed the names and specialties of every adult magic wielder in the city since its founding hundreds of years before. Though a few months shy of her eighteenth birthday, Luskell got to add her name now because she had earned her wizard's staff already. She would have had to wait until she was of age to add her name as a healer, though she had achieved that rank more than a year before. Whoever made the rules must have regarded a wizard's staff as more important than a healer's apron.

Bardin drew back the curtain and waved her forward. She noticed Jagryn's entry several lines above where she would sign. He had come of age before he earned his staff. The entry said *apprentice*, so he hadn't stopped by to update it yet. Fandek had signed, too, as an apprentice healer. Luskell hoped he would get to update his entry soon, too.

She uncorked her pot of ink and dipped in a pen. In the best handwriting she could manage, she wrote her name with a symbol indicating she was a woman. For her attainment, she wrote *wizard* with perhaps more boldness than necessary, but it felt good. Then she had to choose up to four specialties.

"I'll put Transformation, for sure," she said. "And Mind-Talking."

"You did Listening for your quest."

"I know, but no one else knows what it is. And I'm only

a beginner. I'll put Concealment, though."

"What about Crossing Over?" Bardin asked. "If anything is your specialty, that is."

"Only one other person put it, long ago. Maybe other people could do it but never wrote it down. I wasn't sure it was useful until last night."

"What happened last night?"

"I ... brought someone back. It wasn't her time." Luskell shook her head. "I've been trying not to cross over, though. It feels wrong to write it if I'm not doing it."

"Leave it off. You can always add it later if you change your mind."

Luskell dipped her pen again to write her three specialties.

When the ink was dry, Bardin opened the book to a random page in the middle. "Show me Luskell." The pages rustled and turned by themselves to the page she had just signed. "Show me Transformation." The rustling grew louder and seemed to come from all around them. Glittering ribbons of light emerged from many pages, from deep in the past to the immediate present.

"So that's it?" Luskell asked.

"Everything is complete." Bardin held out his hand for her to shake. "Welcome, Wizard Luskell."

Chapter 9

Luskell left the library dazed and giddy. *Wizard* Luskell. She had her staff in hand and her name in the book. It changed nothing, and everything. What would she do now?

Eat lunch seemed a good place to start. It was early, but she hadn't had much appetite for breakfast.

"Luskell? I didn't know you were back."

She looked around at the familiar voice and lost her appetite again. Jagryn, arm-in-arm with Ruvhonn, who apparently had not mentioned their chance meeting the night before. She'd wanted to see him, of course, but not without any preparation or enough sleep. But she was a wizard now, supposedly wise and mature. She could do this.

"I got in late yesterday." Luskell gripped her staff and

made herself smile. "It's … good to see you."

Jagryn looked older than his nineteen years, maybe because of the staff in his hand and the short, full beard he now wore. And the sprinkle of gray in his wavy brown hair. His quest to the Other Side had cost him. His youth was more apparent when he lost the worried look and let a wide grin light his face. A gold ring glinted from his left earlobe, a match for the two Ruvhonn wore, and in accordance with an old Deep River custom. Ruvhonn had already worn the right one when Luskell saw her the previous winter. The left ones were the outward sign of the agreement they'd come to after Luskell left Deep River, fulfilled with their marriage on Long Day.

Ruvhonn pressed against Jagryn. They were the same age, born within days of each other. She had not lost all her girlishness, though she'd been through a harrowing time, too. Now her pink cheeks positively glowed and sunlight gleamed off her golden hair, the braids neatly coiled around her head.

"We got here day before yesterday," Jagryn said. "Did you see my letter?"

"Yes, Grandma gave it to me the same day you wrote it." Luskell wanted to thank him for preparing her, but that implied there might have been a problem. "I'm so happy for you." She wrapped Jagryn in a one-armed hug. She hadn't bothered to shield herself and now it was too late. A complicated wave of emotion washed over her and swirled with her own mess of feelings. The old attraction sparked to life, muddled with regret and hurt. Jagryn's part of the mix included an overriding affection for his wife.

Reminded of her presence, Luskell reached out with her staff arm to include Ruvhonn in the embrace. Ruvhonn stiffened, almost as startled as she had been at the pump. Something Luskell wouldn't have detected from a distance made itself plain when they touched. No wonder Ruvhonn glowed.

"Oh! Congratulations!" Luskell stepped back, her smile unforced.

Ruvhonn blushed deeper and giggled. "You make it sound like the wedding just happened, but we've been married three months."

"It's not such a long time. And it did just happen for me." Luskell hoped that was enough to cover her enthusiasm. They didn't know yet and it wasn't her place to reveal it, but if all went well, they'd be parents before their first anniversary.

"I'm on my way to update my entry in the Registry," Jagryn said. "Then I'm going to show Ruvhonn my favorite places from when I was here before."

"I filled in my entry this morning," Luskell said. "Oh, do you remember Terulo? He's up there doing research on a forgotten spell and asked me to help with testing. I'm excited just thinking about it. It reminds me of when you and I used to work together. Wouldn't it be fun to do something together while you're here?"

Jagryn frowned. "It's probably not a good idea for us to do magic together." His expression softened. "But maybe we could all have supper later?"

Luskell hid her disappointment. He was right, she needed to learn to work alone. "I'd like that. No, I can't — I promised Laki I'd meet him. Guess who else is getting married?"

"You and Laki?" Jagryn asked, full of hope and a speck of jealousy. "Your grandma said you went to Knot's Valley."

"I was there *alone*. And Laki is marrying someone he met here. He says he doesn't need my blessing, but he'd like to have it."

"Oh, Luskell ..."

"I don't need your pity. I made my choice and I'm fine with it. You're not the only one who completed a quest and earned a staff."

"And your eye? Any better?"

She touched the patch. "Different. Maybe better. I can see the life in you." She lifted it quickly, relieved to see they both had a healthy glow. Ruvhonn's light had something extra in it, confirming what Luskell had already sensed. "Sorry, it'll never be a pretty sight. You're both better than fine. Now, if you'll excuse me, I had a late night. I hope I can get some rest before I meet Laki."

"All right. It was good seeing you, Luskell. Till later." Jagryn lifted his hand, and Ruvhonn waved, too.

Luskell headed for home, relieved to have the dreaded first meeting out of the way. It could have gone worse, and maybe future encounters would be warmer. When she got there, she was surprised and pleased to find the whole family gathered — the first time she'd seen all three of them together since spring.

Crett ran to her and tugged her by the hand to the table. "You left me!"

Mamam laughed. "She's only been gone a few hours, Crett."

Luskell helped herself to a bowl of soup and took a seat. "Well, I'm a real wizard now. I've got my staff and my name's in the book."

"What did you list as specialties?" Dadad asked.

"Transformation, Mind-Talking, and Concealment."

"But not Crossing Over. I'm glad you're keeping your promise."

"It didn't seem right to advertise something I'm not likely to do. But if there's a need, like last night, I won't let my gift go to waste."

Mamam nodded. "She saved a life. Saved a family,

maybe."

Luskell sighed. "I don't know yet what I'll be doing on a daily basis."

"Whatever you call yourself, your skills are welcome at Balsam's House anytime," Mamam said.

"Maybe as a temporary thing, till I know what I want to do. But how do I know?"

"I find the needs call out to me without too much looking," Dadad said. "You can check the board at the Wizards' Hall. Or come out with me if you want to. The first time, at least."

"That sounds good to me."

"You don't need to get serious yet," Mamam added. "I ordered you a new good dress. You should go to Tulia's tomorrow for a fitting."

"I don't need a new dress. I doubt I'll be going to dances much." But Luskell thought longingly of her beautiful green silk dress, worn only three times before she outgrew it.

"You should have something nice, even if not a party dress. You're young to be doing what you're doing. A respectable dress will go a long way. And Tulia said she could re-make your green dress."

"That would be all right, I guess. And I'd like to see Daisy, too." Tulia's daughter Daisy was a childhood friend, but Luskell hadn't seen her much since they left the neighborhood free school when they were thirteen.

"And then in the afternoon you could watch Crett and his little friends," Mamam said as she cleared soup bowls from the table. "Several of us take turns, but it will help to have one more."

"Play now!" Crett shouted.

Dadad scooped him up. "Come on, big fellow, nap time first."

"No nap!" Crett squirmed, but Dadad tucked him under one arm and pulled out the trundle bed with the other hand.

"Wasn't Fandek going to stop by today?" Mamam asked.

Luskell felt like she was falling. "Oh. That was real?"

"You seemed happy to see him last night."

"No, I was, it's just … last night is kind of fuzzy. I thought that part might have been a dream." Luskell spooned up the last of her soup and passed the bowl to Mamam. "I told Laki I'd visit him today. I'll see Fandek another time. But first I need to close my eyes for a while."

"No nap!" Crett repeated.

"Are you sure?" Luskell left her chair and curled up on the little bed next to him. "A nap sounds so good to me right now." She rubbed his back and quietly sang "Aku's Lullaby."

Crett's eyes drooped closed. Luskell shut her own eyes, grateful for a moment's peace. She'd been on the go almost constantly since her return to the city, with only one night of broken sleep. A nap was all she needed to —

Luskell! Can you hear me?

The mind voice was weak and broken up, but clear enough to recognize.

Luskell groaned and rolled onto her back, her eyes still closed. *Yes, Fandek, I hear you. Where are you?* Maybe he had to work today and needed to delay their meeting.

Um. On the stairs. I can't talk over distance the way you do.

When someone knocked on the door, Luskell pushed herself up and went to get it. "Here's Fandek now."

Dadad laughed. "There's how to act like a real wizard."

She opened the door and pasted on a smile that turned real the moment she looked into Fandek's eyes. She wanted to be angry — how could he make her happy just by being there? She couldn't sustain the irritation. "Good afternoon!

Your mind-talking has improved a lot."

"No, it hasn't, but thanks. You must feel better than you did last night."

"I ... took a little nap." *And got a dose of your sunshine.* To be polite, she invited him in.

Fandek nodded toward Luskell's parents where they sat at the table. "Good afternoon, ma'am, sir."

Crett jumped out of bed and ran over with his cheeks puffed out. Fandek dropped to his level and made fish lips. The grotesque face contest continued until Crett got hiccups from laughing. Luskell guessed this was part of an ongoing game between them. Crett's regard spoke well of Fandek, but there wasn't much chance for a real conversation with everybody around.

"There's something I have to do today," Luskell said. "You can come along if you want to."

Fandek stood up from the floor and brushed off his knees. "Sure! Yeah! Whatever you want." Crett hugged Fandek's leg.

Luskell picked up her staff. Holding it steadied her, as Bardin had promised.

"No cloak?" Mamam asked.

"It's much too warm out," Luskell objected.

"It will cool off when the sun goes down."

"I don't plan to be out that late." Laki was her oldest friend and she would always be happy to see him, but this promised to be an uncomfortable meeting. No need to draw it out. "See you later."

She stepped outside and reached for Laki's mind. She knew roughly where he was and found him without much trouble. *Laki? Is this a good time?*

Yes, if you're ready. Come to the back and knock on the kitchen door.

Fandek extracted himself from Crett and they

descended to the street in silence. Luskell didn't want to start the conversation, but Fandek didn't seem any more willing. "You're ... a lot more polite than you used to be," she said.

"I hope so! I can't imagine being rude to Mistress Ketty."

Luskell snorted, at the formal title and the very idea. "I know what you mean." She wasn't sure what it was, but her mother inspired good behavior, at least in people other than her own children.

"Crane's a good example, too. He set me straight, back when he was filling in for my master." Fandek looked around as they reached the square at the heart of Old Town, a large space fronted by the library, Balsam's House, and the Wizards' Hall. "So where are we going?"

"Government District, to see my friend Laki."

"Oh? Oh." Fandek's inexpertly shielded feelings allowed his disappointment to leak through. She'd sung Laki's praises often enough.

"He traveled with me from the Mountain, but now he's going to join his people. I promised to see him before he leaves." Luskell almost laughed at the obvious way Fandek's spirits rose at that news.

It had been sunny, but now the clouds thickened, promising rain later. That was typical for the time of year and didn't deter the crowds coming and going on business. Luskell didn't bother to deflect attention as they walked. In daylight, the eyepatch and staff were likely enough to put off anyone who might accost her. She didn't like to admit Fandek's presence probably did as much.

"How was the Mountain?"

Luskell welcomed the easy question. He'd last seen her before she went there, so it was a logical opening. "Good. She kept me busy and out of trouble. We understand each other."

"I thought you might stay there."

"It doesn't work that way. Aku gets a new keeper every half year, so she doesn't get too attached."

"But you want to go back?"

She glanced at him sidelong. It was an astute comment, considering this was their first chance to talk about it. "I miss her, but I need to learn to stay out of trouble on my own. What about you? I see you're working at Balsam's House. Do you live there, too?"

"They said it wouldn't be right, with all the other healers being women." Fandek gestured with his thumb over his shoulder, back the way they'd come. "I stayed with your folks most of the summer."

Luskell stopped, horrified. "They gave you my room?"

Fandek laughed. "No, they knew you would hate that. I shared Wyllik's room downstairs."

"Must have been crowded."

"I don't know. I'd never had much room to myself. I was fine with it." He frowned. "Wyllik never said anything, but he was obviously uncomfortable. Not so much with me, but like he was working something out. But I had meals upstairs or at Balsam's House, so ..."

"So you've probably had enough of the little one," Luskell said to fill the pause. She found it interesting how attuned Fandek was to people's feelings, but didn't want to point it out. She walked on, more relaxed.

"It was good to spend time with Crett. He's funny." Fandek glanced at Luskell. "Being around him made me think I might want to be a father someday, if I could be a good one like yours."

And not a horror like yours, she thought. He didn't need her to say it aloud, nor was this the time to encourage his goal of fatherhood. He might assume she was ready to help. "I missed Crett so much!" she blurted.

"He missed you, too. But since I've been working at Balsam's House and earning a wage, I have my own room around the corner." He pointed as they crossed the square, to a venerable stone building with two floors above the ground level cheeseshop. "Do you want to see?"

"Another time. Laki's waiting, and ... Oh!" Luskell halted, rubbing her forehead in frustration. "I can't believe I forgot! I shouldn't arrive empty handed."

"Will cheese do?"

"It'll have to." Luskell drew her moneybag from her pocket and weighed it in her hand. Not full, but a few coins jingled.

They entered the pungent smelling shop. Wheels and wedges of different kinds of cheese filled the shelves. To save time, Luskell asked for a small wedge of a favorite variety, mild and nutty ... and not too smelly. She paid and slipped the wrapped parcel into her pocket. They stepped back into the street.

"Now that I won't embarrass myself, we can go see Laki," she said.

"All right. So, this way?" Fandek pointed.

A major street led off the square, out of the densely built Old Town into the more gracious Government District, where the large houses had gardens, and tall trees lined the street. It wasn't the Mountain, but Luskell found relief in the space and green.

"Does Laki know about Jagryn?" Fandek asked.

The question startled Luskell back to the moment. "Not sure what you mean."

"When we were in Deep River, it seemed like you and Jagryn were ... close. And you still wear his eyepatch."

"He did a good job on it. And as it happens, he's in town now, too. With his *wife*. Do you remember Ruvhonn?"

"He really did it, huh? Well, good for him. For them."

"Anyway, Laki and Jagryn are both my friends, and they're friends with each other. We started out learning magic together, meeting in secret and each of us sharing whatever we knew." Luskell laughed, recalling how little she knew at the time. "That's when I learned I had power of my own. I was so thrilled, I turned around and kissed Jagryn. Didn't know until after that he was sweet on me. And I didn't understand why Laki was upset."

"But you're supposed to be sensitive to people's feelings," Fandek said.

"That ability hadn't developed yet. I barely knew what *I* was feeling. I had only recently started to like boys. I thought I could be sweet on Jagryn, too, but it turned out I was more sweet on him being sweet on me. And Laki thought we were destined for each other, when he was really foreseeing Crett."

Fandek nodded slowly. "So you're all still friends and no hard feelings?"

"I hope so," Luskell said. "They both know how much they meant to me and still do, and they've moved ahead with their lives."

But she hadn't told either of them how she felt about Fandek. How could she, when she wasn't sure what to call it herself?

Chapter 10

Luskell cast around for a topic not related to Laki or Jagryn or parenthood or her feelings. "I saw your little brother at the coach office. He seems to love his work in the stables."

"Deklyn always liked animals better than people. They don't expect him to talk."

Luskell chuckled in agreement. "I know someone like that. Remember Jagryn's uncle in Deep River? He talks to animals and they listen."

"I remember, the fellow who used to be sweet on your mother."

"That's right," Luskell said. "He's no wizard, but he has a touch of magic."

"Magic. You don't suppose Deklyn ...?" Fandek looked at Luskell with eyes full of hope.

"Laki thought he saw something. He couldn't say for sure, but it does tend to run in families. Be sure you don't speak spells aloud where he can hear."

"I'll keep him safe. Magic or not, I'm glad Deklyn's happy."

"Thanks to you," Luskell said. "Did he ... ever talk?"

"Baby babble — mama, dada. He called me Fafa. But after the accident ..." Fandek shuddered at a memory Luskell didn't have the heart to read. She remembered that room with the light out.

"Mamam would be able to tell for sure, about the magic. How's it working out with her?"

"She's a good teacher, but sometimes I wonder why I bother. Is there anything she can't do? But I want to please her, so I go ahead and try. She says I'm making progress." Fandek sighed. "She's amazing."

Luskell snorted. "Don't you fall in love with her, whatever you do."

"I'd be too afraid!"

"She can be scary, all right."

"Well, yes, but I meant of Crane."

"What? Why?"

"He's not just *a* wizard. He's *the* wizard."

Luskell had been away long enough to almost forget her father's reputation. "But he's also the sweetest man in the world."

"Said the sweet man's daughter. But he always knows what I'm thinking."

"So shield your thoughts when you don't want him to know."

"Um ... then he knows I'm thinking of you."

Luskell couldn't help the squawk of laughter that escaped her. "So shield them all the time!" She thought about that for a few steps. "Maybe I'm the one you should be afraid of."

"I was. I probably will be again. Now, I'm just glad you're back."

Luskell was glad to be back, too. She'd thought about Fandek sometimes while she was on the Mountain. The real thing was even nicer looking than her memory of him. He'd let his dark blond hair grow almost to his shoulders. He was probably emulating Dadad, who had always worn his hair long. Fandek didn't seem to be trying for a beard, though. She imagined him with one. He looked good either way. Something about being with him made Luskell … happy. But she couldn't tell him or trust the feeling until she was away from him.

They walked on, talking of trivial things. Fandek's fingers brushed Luskell's and a thrill like lightning ran up her arm. She thought he was about to hold her hand. She wanted him to, but didn't trust that, either. She casually lifted her hand and conjured a sprig of lupine. The purple flowerets became butterflies that changed to blue, then green, before bursting into fireworks.

Fandek laughed. "Showoff."

She grinned and took a bow. "I haven't done that trick in months. No fun without an audience."

"I could never manage illusions without saying the words," Fandek said. "Kind of defeats the purpose."

And he wasn't good at hiding his thoughts and feelings. Was Fandek exactly what he seemed? Luskell shook the idea away. "The first time I tried it, I nearly set the house on fire. With practice I got better, but I know people who are much better at illusions than I am. And you have your own special talents."

They reached Embassy House soon after. The large, elegant structure had been divided into spacious apartments for the various diplomatic parties that spent part of the year in the city.

"I've never been up here before." Fandek gazed at the mansion with obvious awe. "You say you lived here?"

"Not year-round, and only on part of one floor. And it's been a long time. Come on, this way."

She led him around to the back. She hadn't expected that as a wizard she would be sent to so many back doors like a servant or deliveryman. Why did Laki want to meet there? Maybe the rest of the house was already closed up for the season. She swallowed her pride and knocked. Muffled laughter drifted through the heavy door. It opened and Laki greeted her. His welcoming smile faltered slightly when Fandek stepped into view. He shielded his feelings expertly, but Luskell read the flicker of something like jealousy in his expression. No, not jealousy. Protectiveness. They had that in common.

"Welcome, Luskell and ...?"

"Laki, this is Fandek, Mamam's apprentice. Fandek, meet Nalaklak. He Listens and translates for his father, the Aklaka ambassador."

To Luskell's surprise, Fandek held his hands out palm up for the traditional Aklaka greeting. "We met briefly, earlier in the summer."

Laki nodded. "Of course, the day I gave my toy bears to Crett. You and Aketnan — Ketty — were on your way to Balsam's House, so we didn't have a chance to talk." He glanced at Luskell. *Is he the one you choose?*

I don't know yet.

"I know those bears well. Crett loves them," Fandek said. "But maybe I misunderstood. I thought you were heir to something bigger than translating."

"My mother is Uklak — the head — of our band. I will succeed her someday. But not too soon, I hope. Please, come in."

They followed him through an enclosed porch where dish towels hung on a drying rack. A dwindling stack of firewood sat outside an inner door. They passed through into the large kitchen, illuminated at this hour by daylight shining through high windows. As a child, Luskell had loved to visit this kitchen, which was equipped to prepare everything from a light meal for one to a banquet for twenty. She would sit on a stool in the corner and watch the head cook and her assistants work their magic. As long as she stayed out of the way and didn't ask too many questions, they'd tell her all about the dishes they were preparing and let her taste.

On this day, the kitchen was quiet. Most of the utensils and cookware were stacked or hung in their places, but one large pot was in use. A tall young woman stood at the big iron cookstove and stirred something that filled the room with a savory aroma. She wore a big apron over a simple dress of reddish brown, sleeves rolled to the elbow. She turned toward them with a smile on her angular face, her dark gaze full of watchful intelligence.

Luskell didn't know her name, but she was sure she'd seen her before. At Embassy House, but not working in the kitchen. The memory refused to open but carried a vague sense of unease.

"Luskell, Fandek, I'd like you to meet Tatakla, who has consented to stay with me." As Laki spoke the name, a sunbeam of warm affection filled the room.

Luskell looked around for anyone else. The cook left the stove to join them.

Really, Laki? A kitchen maid?

Nothing in his expression showed he'd heard her mind talk, but he replied the same way. *Cook's assistant. And much more.*

Tatakla stood a little taller than Luskell, with darker

skin and straight brown hair pulled back in a long braid. She held out her hands for the Aklaka greeting, then shook hands Eukardian style. "It is good to meet you both. I've heard so much about Luskell." Tatakla spoke Eukardian with a slight accent, similar to Laki's but subtly different.

Her smile was genuine, but Luskell picked up a touch of jealousy, too. Unless it was her own, or Fandek's. What a terrible idea this was!

"I'm glad to meet you, too." Luskell gave a weak smile. "Laki didn't tell me you were Aklaka." It was a guess, but Tatakla's height, her features, her accent, all pointed that way.

"My mother was Foryani, my father was Aklaka — Latu band. And you?"

Luskell blinked. "Um ... I have some Aklaka on my father's side, too. I don't know which band. Or ... did you say Latu?"

Tatakla nodded. "A mountain in Foryin — one of Aku's little brothers. How can you not know your band?"

"I wasn't raised Aklaka," Luskell explained. "I don't actually have much Aklaka blood, but it came through stronger than the Eukardian."

Laki took Tatakla's hand. "In more ways than appearance. Luskell shows promise as a Listener. She has just completed a half year as Aku's Keeper."

"Does Latu have a Keeper, also?" Luskell asked, trying to be polite. Tatakla's lips tightened and a flood of grief and anger washed over Luskell before she shielded herself. She took a step back and looked to Laki for help. "Have I said something wrong?"

"You didn't know. Latu took Tatakla's father."

"Oh, I ... I'm so sorry!"

"He shouldn't have been there if he couldn't do the job!" Tatakla turned away from them, her hands over her face.

Luskell regretted the whole visit. There was something about Tatakla she didn't trust, but that didn't excuse opening this wound. Laki had sent the conversation in that direction, though. It wasn't entirely her fault. They all stood around awkwardly while the pot on the stove quietly bubbled.

"What are you cooking?" Fandek asked. "It smells delicious."

Tatakla turned to him with a grateful smile and wiped her eyes. "It's time to close up the kitchen for the season, so it's a soup with a bit of everything — late vegetables, leftover scraps of meat, stock from the bones. There's too much for Laki and me. You'll have to stay for supper."

"Oh, I don't know." Luskell looked to Fandek for rescue. "You probably have to get back to Balsam's House, don't you?"

"No, I'm off today. I can stay if you can. And you can add the you-know-what." Fandek winked.

"I almost forgot! Here. It's cheese." Luskell took it from her pocket, unsure who to hand it to.

Laki and Tatakla both reached for it, laughing as they bumped hands. Laki withdrew and let Tatakla take it.

She sniffed the package appreciatively. "Mmm, this will go well with our supper. Thank you."

Fandek turned to Tatakla and Laki with a smile. "You both speak Eukardian so well."

Laki draped an arm around Luskell's shoulders. "I learned from Luskell as a child — only fair, since I taught her to speak Aklaka when she was learning to talk."

Tatakla took his other hand. "I knew a little when I first came here, but I wasn't fluent until I'd been in this job awhile. Laki helped me, though. Now I often dream in it, but I swear in Foryani!"

"Why did you come here if you couldn't speak the

language?" Fandek asked.

She looked at him and didn't answer right away. She sighed and said, "I come from two peoples, but I never felt quite at home in either of them. I thought a third place might be better."

"And was it?"

She leaned against Laki. "In some ways."

The conversation continued over the meal of Tatakla's hearty soup and a loaf of freshly baked bread, enhanced with Luskell's cheese — just enough for four. For Fandek's sake, they kept to Eukardian, though Aklaka words sometimes popped up, along with one or two unrecognizable expressions that must have been Foryani swears.

Luskell found herself liking Tatakla, though the distrust lingered. "I spent part of every summer at Embassy House until I was fourteen, a lot of it down here. Could we have met before?"

"I've been here in the kitchen only three years, but before that I was an aide to the Foryani delegation."

"Yes, of course! I saw you at a banquet my parents hosted, probably four or five years ago. You had on a beautiful gown that night, but I remember your face."

"I'm sorry, I don't remember you."

"I wasn't supposed to be there, but what twelve-year-old wants to be sent to bed right after supper?"

Tatakla laughed. "So you spied. Good for you. I also remember that banquet. There was a man, not Aklaka but with Aklaka features —"

"My father." The memory came flooding back, all the dressed-up adults around the table, and Tatakla openly flirting with Dadad. Mamam had caught Luskell spying and sent her to bed, so that was all Luskell remembered of the evening. No wonder she distrusted Tatakla.

"Was that who it was? I enjoyed his company very much. You are a lucky girl."

"Well, he is the sweetest man in the world." Fandek smiled and squeezed Luskell's hand under the table. He must have given her a dose of his sunshine because her anger settled before it got messy.

Tatakla went on to tell how she'd come to her present position. She had spent her youth with her father's band and felt Aklaka at heart. Then he was killed when Latu erupted on his watch. Her mother couldn't bear to stay and took Tatakla back to her hometown in Foryin. Tatakla knew the language because her mother never quite mastered Aklaka. Her mother wasted away and died not long after — of a broken heart, they said. Tatakla moved to the capital for a new start, where she met someone from Eukard and began to learn the language.

"My facility with languages came to the attention of the ambassador and I was hired as an assistant and translator."

"Why are you working in the kitchen?" Luskell asked.

"There's nothing for me in Foryin. I like it here. Rather than go back with my delegation, I took this job, assisting the head cook during the summer and the caretaker the rest of the year. Then Laki appeared." Tatakla put an arm around Laki and leaned her head on his shoulder. "When was that, two years ago?"

"No, three, when I first started assisting my father," Laki said. "But we didn't get well acquainted until the next summer."

Three summers ago, Luskell had traveled to the city with Laki and Jagryn because the dead had warned her in a dream of danger to her parents. After their rescue mission, Laki had stayed to help his father while Luskell and Jagryn returned with her parents to Deep River, where Crett was born. Two summers ago, Luskell had been with her family in Deep River, then in Misty Pass. She had returned to the city in the fall to train and work at Balsam's House but had seen Laki only rarely. He had never let on he might be seeing someone. Not even when Luskell visited him in Knot's Valley.

The shock must have shown on her face because Laki gave her a puzzled look. *What's wrong?*

How could you? You were already seeing her when we were together last winter!

We were friends. I was interested, but I didn't make her any promises. I was waiting for your decision.

Luskell gave him a slight nod to show she understood. It was obvious how much he loved Tatakla, a love that had been growing for longer than a few months. But he had loved Luskell enough — or believed enough in his vision of the two of them with a child — to hold back until he knew her decision. Not for the first time, she thought how much easier it was to deal with a mountain.

Chapter II

When Laki lit the lamp in the middle of the table, Luskell jumped up from her seat. How had it gotten so late? "We need to get back to Old Town. Thank you for supper."

Laki rose, too. "I hope we see you again before we leave."

She gave him a mischievous smile. "But I haven't given my blessing yet."

"Your approval would be welcome, but I don't need your permission, Luskell."

Luskell embraced him and allowed herself a pang and a sigh over what might have been. She let him go, yet again, and grasped Tatakla's hand. "Take good care of each other."

Laki gripped Fandek's hand. "You take care of Luskell."

"How?" Fandek wore a panicked look.

"That's the secret you'll have to work out."

Luskell and Fandek walked out into the deepening twilight. The clouds made it darker than it should have been. And colder. Luskell could almost hear Mamam's *I told you so* about the cloak she hadn't worn.

"You didn't tell me Laki was getting married," Fandek said.

"I didn't know you'd care."

"But ... you know how I feel about you."

"It wasn't about you." Partly true. "It was about ... her. Tatakla. I hadn't met her before, and I didn't want to talk about her or think about her or believe it was real."

"Wait — you thought you could win him back or something?"

"No!"

"So you didn't want him, but you didn't want anyone else to have him, either."

It was uncomfortable, how any man could be so astute. Luskell breathed deeply and made herself speak calmly. "It's not that I don't — didn't — want him. It's that I know I shouldn't have him. And I didn't know if she was good enough for him."

"Is she?"

Luskell sighed. "Maybe. The meeting went better than it might have." Due at least in part to Fandek's sunshine, she was sure. He'd had at least brief contact with everyone there. She should have been grateful for anything that eased the awkwardness. It didn't help her trust him or her own feelings.

Fat raindrops splatted on Luskell's head. She quickened her pace. "I suppose it was too much to hope we could walk home without getting wet."

Fandek laughed. "Your mother said to take your cloak.

But it's not that far back to Old Town. We're already across Fortress Street."

"I thought you hadn't been to the Government District before."

"I didn't say that. I never had a reason to go as far as Embassy House. It's not on the way to Old Gray."

Old Gray was the nickname of the fortress that housed the prison. "Oh. He's still there?"

"You think they'd let him out?"

"No, I just thought ..."

"... he'd be dead by now. Me, too. But he started confessing to old killings no one had connected to him, so they kept him around."

"What good does it do now?" Luskell asked. "It doesn't bring anyone back."

"No. I guess it's a comfort to families whose daughters went off to the city and never came home. They know what happened. And it keeps my brother around a little longer."

"Weren't you afraid of him?"

"I used to be. Not so much now."

"But he's a monster!"

"He is and he isn't." Fandek sighed and rested his hands on his head for a moment. "He says he didn't want to do those things. He talks about it like there's someone else who puts on his skin. I guess that's the monster. It'll all be over soon, anyway. They're going to hang him at the end of the month."

A fitting end for a man who strangled his victims, but Luskell didn't say so aloud. She didn't feel sorry for the murderer, but she did have some pity for Fandek. "Will you keep visiting him until then?"

Fandek nodded. "He's in a dark place."

Luskell pictured a lightless dungeon. "The prison is dark?"

"It's grim, but not that kind of dark. He's scared and hopeless." He paused. "I wonder, could you come with me sometime? You could tell him about the Other Side."

"Why would I want to help a monster?"

"Because he wasn't always? I don't know. I bring him a little sunshine. It's all I have."

"You have a gift," Luskell admitted. "Do you use it much at Balsam's House?"

"It's a real help with small children. They're sick and scared and surrounded by strangers ... Has Crett ever been sick?"

"Only mild things. Mamam keeps off all the serious illnesses. But he caught a cold when he was two months old and we were all miserable."

"Yeah. I like how I can put little ones at ease."

A feeble voice cried out. Luskell halted at the mouth of an alley, almost dark in the rainy twilight.

"Did you hear that?" Without waiting for an answer, Luskell entered the alley. Halfway to the next street, two shadowy lumps struggled. Luskell lifted her eyepatch as she jogged toward them. The two forms glimmered, one bright, one weak. As her good eye adjusted, Luskell saw the stronger figure raise a knife.

Luskell gripped her staff in both hands and swung as hard as she could. The solid maple thumped the assailant's forearm. He yelped as the knife skittered away, then swung around to face her. Luskell remembered magic and hit him with a repelling charm that knocked him off his feet. He scrambled up again and ran away, Fandek in pursuit.

As soon as Luskell got a good look at the victim, she recognized him, a beggar in the neighborhood. "Ettam, are you hurt? Did he take anything?"

Ettam groaned and lifted one arm. "Stabbed me. Not enough ... coins."

A few scattered copper dulleens gleamed in the fading light. Luskell called up an illusion of fire over her staff. It had no heat but gave off a steady glow to see by. As Luskell looked Ettam over more closely, she wished she'd given chase and Fandek had stayed. She was a fast runner, even in a dress, and the poor soul needed a healer. He bled from at least two stab wounds, but there was more wrong than that. "You're sick."

"Pretty sick," he agreed.

She pressed her fingers to the wounds and called on her power to stop the bleeding. It started as warmth in her chest and flowed tingling down her arms to her hands. "Where do you live? You shouldn't be out in the rain."

"No ... home."

"Balsam's House, then. Do you think you can walk?"

He shook his head. Luskell looked up and down the alley. Fandek wasn't back yet, and she didn't want to wait. She stood back and levitated the sick beggar. It should have been easy. He was much smaller than the giant fallen tree. Lifting something flexible and living and in pain turned out to be much more difficult, and that was before she tried to move him. She managed to shift him a few steps before she had to set him down, harder than she intended. He groaned.

"I'm sorry! I thought I could move you, but this won't work."

"There's no need to move me. I ... won't be here long."

The rain fell faster. Luskell cast a spell tent over them to keep it off. She let the illusion fire go but gathered pieces of a broken crate as fuel for a small real fire. She was good with fire magic and had enough mastery of healing to ease some of Ettam's pain. Whatever she could do was too little, though. He was dying. They both knew it. She resisted following his thoughts. She wasn't supposed to go there.

Ettam shivered. "So cold."

Luskell built up the fire, though the spell tent was already too warm. "Soon you'll be someplace comfortable. People you've loved will be there to meet you."

"Easy to say. What if there's nothing? Or worse than here?"

"You'll see. I can help you sleep, if you like."

"Afraid to sleep ..."

Luskell was sure it would help, but she couldn't force it on him. She continued to use the pain charm, though there was a pocket of suffering just out of her reach. He moaned and shivered and twitched. He lost consciousness but still lived and suffered. Luskell had to leave the spell tent. She couldn't watch him, and she couldn't do anything for him. She leaned on her staff in the rain, feeling useless and miserable. She changed her mind and dived back into the spell tent. She reached for his thoughts or dreams, but there was nothing. The flicker of life was out. Ettam had gone alone.

Fandek ran back into the alley, puffing with effort. Another man followed him, wearing the tall hat of a Guard.

"I caught the robber! Lucky a Guard patrol was passing. How's this one?"

Luskell bowed her head in sorrow. "Dead. I think he was already dying before he was attacked." She extinguished the fire and let the spell tent go.

The Guard stepped up. "We'll have the body taken to Balsam's House to be prepared for burial."

Luskell acknowledged the offer silently. She had no voice to reply. She turned and ran out of the alley, tears streaming down her face. Fandek caught up with her. "Hey! Hey, what is it?"

"I ... I could've helped him, and I didn't!"

"Luskell, if he was as sick as you say, even Ketty couldn't have healed him. I'm sure you did what you could."

"That's the problem — I *didn't* do what I could. He was afraid, and I let him go alone. I should have gone with him!"

"But you're not supposed to —"

"I don't care! I could have, and I didn't!"

Fandek tried to take her in his arms. She shoved him away.

"Fine. Do you want some sunshine?"

"No!" she sobbed.

"Do you want to go home?"

She shook her head. Anything but that, where everybody was full of wisdom and advice and understanding. But they didn't understand this.

"Come back with me. You're getting soaked out here."

Luskell let Fandek guide her the short distance to his room, around the corner from Balsam's House. It was almost too much to walk, but she didn't want to be carried.

He opened the street door. "Sorry about the smell."

"The world needs cheese more than it needs magic." Luskell dragged herself up the stairs behind him.

He unlocked a door and held it open for her. She stumbled against a table in the dark.

"Sorry. Here." At a word from Fandek, a lamp flared and settled down to a warm glow.

Luskell drew breath to speak, but all that came out was a sob. She collapsed against him and wept. After a startled moment, he put his arms around her. She let him hold her. She didn't have the strength left to push away. Didn't want to. The tears kept coming. Fandek stroked her hair and her face. He kissed her eye, kissed her eyepatch, kissed her cheeks. Desires she'd put aside these last months flickered to life. Her mouth sought his. As they kissed, desire roared, threatening to burn away her melancholy. She pulled back. "Stop."

"Are you sure? Sunshine's not the only way to feel better."

"I don't want to!"

"I'll bet you'd want to if Laki were here, or Jagryn."

"How dare you!" Luskell scowled and raised her hand to threaten a slap, though she lacked the strength to deliver it.

Fandek rubbed his forehead. "Sorry, I didn't mean it. Sometimes I still say the first rude thing that pops into my head." He gave her a lopsided smile. "This isn't how I pictured our reunion."

Luskell had tried not to picture it. She sank onto his one chair. "I spoil everything. You don't want that, and I don't want to feel better. Not yet. I don't deserve it." But now she had a glimmer of an idea. "I only need to sleep."

"Alone, I take it."

"Yes. Do you want me to leave?" She started to get up.

Fandek waved her back into her seat. "It's fine, you can stay. I promised Laki I'd take care of you, didn't I? Will you be all right if I run over to Balsam's House? I want to make sure about Ettam's body."

"Go. I'm just going to sleep."

"You won't ... hurt yourself or anything?"

"No, I promise."

"All right. If you change your mind about the sunshine, I'll be here when you wake up."

Chapter 12

Fandek left and locked the door behind him. Luskell took in the tiny room, not much bigger than hers and furnished with a narrow bed, a small table, one chair, and a couple of crates set up as shelves to hold his few possessions. A chimney from below was the only source of heat. The place smelled strongly of cheese.

The room's one adornment was a small medallion, about the size of a ten-dul piece but with a scalloped edge and dark with age. It hung on a cord from a nail in the wall. When Luskell held it to get a closer look, she felt ... something. Not exactly magical, but like a weak dose of sunshine through a veil of cloud. It was probably only that she felt better because she had a plan.

Luskell removed her eyepatch and stripped off her

damp dress and stockings, hanging them over the chairback to dry. Her shift hadn't gotten wet in the rain. She climbed under the covers and gripped her staff as she lay down. It took real effort to let it go, especially anywhere away from home. Sleeping in a strange place, it couldn't hurt to have a weapon at hand.

She took a moment before she slept to remember Ettam — how he looked, the sound of his voice, everything she knew about him. He had a thin scar across his throat, from an attack with a cursed blade, the same one Luskell had later encountered herself. The attacker had meant to cause chaos and distract Luskell's father from a more sophisticated plot. Ettam, a convenient victim selected at random, had survived the attack thanks to quick work by Luskell's parents and Balsam, but she wondered if that's when his troubles had started. Was he a beggar before the attack?

When the picture was as complete as she could make it, she let go and slid into sleep.

She opened her eyes again in the grassy meadow at the top of that long slope under a bright, sunless sky. She looked around for Ettam, but she was alone. She shivered, though the air was warm; she'd never been alone on the Other Side before. Then again, she'd never sought a spirit newly departed. She had either arrived with them, or they had been dead for some time. Perhaps Ettam didn't know how to answer her call the way the more experienced dead did.

Luskell got to her feet and sniffed. A faint odor of cheese had followed her, a tie to the living world. That gave her confidence to explore.

Above the level meadow, the hillside continued in a gentle slope. Luskell had sometimes seen spirits coming to meet her from that direction, so she set off. She didn't know what was beyond this hill. Did the landscape continue grassy and bright, or was there something else? The walk was long, though not strenuous; but neither did the scene change. It was as dull as if time had stopped.

At last Luskell reached the top. Below her, a broad valley spread, gleaming with a vast city. She tingled at this sight. Had any living soul seen it before? The graceful, translucent structures seemed more grown than built, with barely a straight line anywhere, and countless balconies unsupported by anything Luskell could see. Before she'd had a chance to fully take it in, the figure of a man appeared before her; Aklaka by the looks of him though short by their standards, barely taller than Luskell herself. He was no one she remembered meeting, though his dark eyes and angular features held something familiar. He spoke rapidly in a dialect different from the one she knew. She caught the words "daughter" and "Listener."

"More slowly, please," she said, and spoke slowly herself.

"You are the Listener who crosses over. I didn't know how to find you, but you came to me! I felt you arrive!" He smiled, revealing a wide gap between his front teeth.

"I have my own reason to be here. Why did you want to find me?"

"My daughter is ashamed of me. You can tell Tatakla it wasn't my fault!"

Tatakla's father? Yes, there was a resemblance. "If I see her, I will." No guarantee she would, but it didn't hurt to hear his story, as long as he kept it brief. "What happened?"

"It was my turn to stay with Latu. Anyone with Listening ability takes a season. I could sense an eruption building as well as anyone. I knew the song. But no one can predict a steam explosion."

"Is that what it was? I'm sorry that happened to you, and to your family."

"There wasn't much left of me after."

Before Luskell could ask any more questions, two figures hurried toward her. Ettam, looking bewildered, and a younger man — someone else from her past.

"Go back! You shouldn't be here, Luskell!"

"Trenn? Why —?"

"I owed Ettam an apology."

Of course. Luskell knew that. Trenn had been the villain with the cursed knife, though he had changed in death, impossible as that seemed. "So do I. Please give me a moment. Ettam, I'm sorry."

"What do you mean? I should thank you. You kept the rain off and soothed my pain."

"But I could have come with you here. I could have … eased your crossing. I'm sorry I made you go alone."

"Everyone goes alone."

"Almost everyone."

"This is not your world, Luskell." Trenn stepped up to her and turned her around to face back down the hill.

"But what if it is? I have a power — I should be using it!"

"Knot won't like it."

"Then he should tell me himself."

A smile softened Trenn's stern expression. "I'm sure he will. You'd better go now. We all feel it when you cross over, and not everyone here is your friend."

Luskell lifted her hands in resignation. "Fine, I'm going. But don't think I won't be back." She strode off down the hill. *Knot wouldn't like it? Well, Knot wasn't her boss. He didn't get to say.*

Luskell had climbed a lot of hills in her life. This was

the only one to feel longer going down than it had coming up. Time ran differently here, or not at all. And that city drew her. Her pride saved her from turning back. She wouldn't give Trenn the satisfaction of seeing her waver. She could come here, and she could go home.

About halfway down, Luskell paused. In her fury, she'd been driving her staff deep into the turf. But what staff? Her hand grasped something, though, invisible but solid. She stared until she saw it — all sparkle and no stick. The ghost of her staff. It was part of her. It wasn't only the cheese smell that anchored her to the living world.

As she continued, her feet dragged, and she drove her staff into the turf not in fury but to hold herself up and keep moving. Had she made any progress at all? She turned to look back the way she'd come. A faint trail of sparkles extended behind her, like the magical markers in the Registry; like the ghostly glitter around her staff. She had made progress but not as much as she'd hoped.

A figure watched her from the top of the hill. Not Trenn. A towering skeleton dressed in tattered clothes, half again as tall as Luskell herself, and staring at her with blazing eyes.

Old Mother Bones.

Luskell drew up her remaining strength and tried to run. Ketwyn had warned her. Knot had tried to protect her. She'd brought this on herself.

"Skell! Skell!" A long-tailed black-and-white bird soared overhead.

Footfalls thudded behind Luskell, gaining fast. She didn't dare pause to look, but it sounded four-footed, not two. A horse galloping over grass. A soft whicker confirmed the guess. First a magpie, then a horse? Were there animals on the Other Side? She'd never seen any before, but she'd also never come this far.

A big chestnut horse passed Luskell and cut across her path, halting its gallop suddenly. She put out her hands to stop herself. The horse was warm and almost solid, its coat smooth under her fingers. It had none of the sharp horse-sweat smell of a living animal. It seemed familiar, though Luskell had never owned a horse.

Luskell glanced behind her. Old Mother Bones loomed in the distance. Was she closer than she had been? The horse nudged her until she looked around. It glanced over its back.

"I think you want to help." Luskell scrambled up and grasped the mane. "Let's get out of here."

The horse galloped down the hill and across the level meadow, not stopping until they'd reached the brink of the steep downhill slope. Luskell assumed she'd be safe if she could get that far. She'd never seen a spirit cross that boundary, but did the restriction hold for a legend?

She slid off the horse's back. "Thanks."

It twitched its ears at Luskell and was out of sight faster than a living horse could run. Luskell turned toward the slope. Far away at the bottom, she could see herself sleeping, and Fandek watching over her. Her heart twanged. Cheese and her staff and something more ...

She plunged down ...

... and woke. Daylight shone through a small window into the little cheese-scented room. Just as she'd seen from the Other Side, Fandek sat near the bed watching her. Relief to match her own washed off him when he saw her awake. She looked at him with her wizard eye, which revealed a blaze of health and youth.

"Has your eye improved?"

"Some," she said. "It's different, anyway."

He glanced at the shift she'd slept in, then turned away. "So, um, there's warm water if you want to wash. I'll step out."

"Thank you." When he'd left, she got up to wash and dress. When she had her clothes on and her eyepatch in place, she called him back by mindtalk.

"Sit down, Luskell," Fandek said. "We need to talk."

"I know. I'm sorry I've been so awful to you. You've never been anything but a friend to me. Well, after a bumpy start, I mean."

"I'm glad you feel that way, but that's not what I mean. I want to talk to you about your health."

"Why?"

"Because I'm an apprentice healer and this is what I'm supposed to learn to do. Now please, sit."

Luskell perched on the edge of the bed with her staff next to her. "I'll play along, but there's nothing wrong with me. I just needed to sleep."

Fandek sat in the chair and faced her. He snorted a laugh. "You're exactly like your mother."

She looked up. She was nothing like her powerful mother, who could save anyone.

"I'm not."

"You both throw around heavy power till you've got nothing left, then end up spent and in a dark mood."

Luskell had seen her mother like this; not often, true, but enough to recognize what he was talking about. And she'd heard stories from before she was born, about the time after Ketwyn died, and that other time when Laki was badly hurt and her mother brought him back from the Other Side. She'd never put the magic and the mood together. "It's not the same. Anyway, I'm fine now."

"You use your power for different things, but it looks the same. I'll admit, you both have far more power than I ever will, but it's not infinite." His expression softened. "I'm afraid you'll hurt yourself."

Her heart twanged again. "It's kind of you to care, Fandek, but you don't know what you're talking about. I was upset about Ettam, that's all."

"Two nights in a row, I've seen you exhausted and in low spirits."

"Coincidence."

"So it's not going to be a daily thing? That's a relief. I still want to ask you a few questions."

"Go ahead." Luskell had heard healers, including her mother, interview patients. She'd done it herself. It cost her nothing to give Fandek some experience.

"So we'd typically talk about meals and work habits. You being a wizard, we'll have to include magic, which I guess is work habits. Let's go back to the day before yesterday. How much magic did you do?"

"Really, not much. I was on the coach with Laki most of the day." She considered. "Well, there was the fallen tree."

"Fallen tree?"

"Huge fir, blocking the road. I moved it."

"You moved it. By yourself?"

"Mostly. Laki helped some."

"Luskell, remember — we learned levitation together. It was as hard for you as for me."

"I got better at it."

"But it's still difficult? Especially to move something that big. I'd call that throwing around heavy power."

"I rested on the coach." More than rested. She had slept like the dead all the way to the city.

"What did you do when you got to town, go straight home?"

"No, we went to see Bardin. He wanted to test me while Laki was there, so we went to the maple grove and I Listened. Then we finished my staff."

"And all this on an empty stomach, no doubt."

"I ate when I got home. Dadad and Crett brought home a pie from the Otter."

Fandek grinned. "My favorite! And then what?"

"I sang Crett to sleep and went to bed early."

"So how come I saw you later that night?" Fandek looked straight at her, as if he'd won a point.

Luskell huffed impatiently. "Mamam called me out to help her on a birth. She needed someone to sort of anchor the mother while she focused on the child, so I flew there as fast as I could." There was no point in hiding the transformation. Better to confess it before he asked.

"Anchor the mother?"

"She was weak from labor and bleeding. I ... kept her in this world."

"Did you, by chance, have to go and bring her back?"

"Not ... exactly. She nearly slipped away, but we didn't lose her."

"How much power did that take?"

"A lot," Luskell admitted. "I wasn't sure I could bring her back twice. I had to keep her here. That's why you saw me in such a state. Healing takes more out of me than a lot of other magic. I probably would have been fine with a good night's sleep, but the sunshine was a help."

"It's popular around Balsam's House, with patients and healers alike."

"Do you give it to Mamam?"

"Sometimes. She's prone to melancholy when she's worn down."

"I know. I didn't think I was like her, but I guess I am." Luskell held her hands out, palms up. "In my defense, I didn't do any magic yesterday, other than mixing ink and the illusion you saw, until we found Ettam. I should have let you take care of him while I beat up the robber."

"Next time." Fandek flashed a quick grin, then turned

back to business. "How much time do you spend on the Other Side?"

"I didn't go there the whole time I was with Aku. I was there with Nalya only a short time. And I let Ettam go alone." She held her dream of the Other Side and Old Mother Bones inside her. She had gotten away, thanks to that horse. If it was real and not a dream. She'd have to ask Ketwyn if there were animals on the Other Side. But Fandek didn't need to know.

"All right, I guess you're taking care of yourself, as long as you remember to eat and sleep." He reached for her staff. "This is supposed to help conserve your power, right?" As his fingers closed around the wood, his eyes widened and he let it go just as Luskell grabbed it back. "What was that? It made me dizzy."

"Sorry, I should have warned you. It's tuned to my power. Another magic user won't be able to hold it comfortably unless I give permission."

"But will it help?"

"I'm still learning to use it, but yes, it should." She pushed it against the floor and stood. "I forgot — I didn't have it yet when I levitated the tree. And I didn't think to use it with Nalya or Ettam." She thought again of the sparkling ghost staff she held on the Other Side. Could she have gone so far without it, and could she have returned? But she didn't say it aloud. "I should go home. They must be wondering where I am. And I'm supposed to see someone about a dress." She made a wry face.

"Actually, I saw Ketty at Balsam's House last night. I told her you were safe." Fandek stood. "Come on, I'll walk you home before I go to work. Unless you want breakfast at Balsam's House."

"Good idea. I think I know how I can be useful."

Chapter 13

"So you don't always work nights?" Luskell asked Fandek as they walked from the cheese shop to Balsam's House.

"I usually work when your mother asks me to. The other night, though, I swapped shifts with someone."

Luskell smiled. "Hanny?"

"How'd you know?"

"Lucky guess. Does she still use that story about her brother being in town?"

"No, her husband. He just got back from some kind of wizarding trip. You remember Virosh, don't you?"

"We've met. Weatherworker, isn't he?" Virosh had been one of many men who didn't believe Luskell could or should be a wizard. "So she married him?"

"Not long after you went on your quest."

Luskell had to work to picture the flirtatious Hanny settled down as someone's wife. Being attacked by the strangler last winter had sobered both Hanny and her lover, a young wizard who had studied with Bardin before Luskell did. Maybe it wasn't so surprising they decided to make it official.

They arrived at the hospital. Anyone in Eukard City too ill or injured to be cared for at home — or who had no home — came to Balsam's House. Anyone with a talent for healing was wise to go to Balsam's House, too. A healer trained there had the skill and experience to serve anywhere. Even Luskell had completed the training, though she lacked natural ability in that area. She left Balsam's House on her seventeenth birthday and vowed to herself not to return, determined to become a wizard instead. She had to swallow a big bite of pride to break her vow.

Luskell and Fandek crossed the porch. Fandek opened the door and stood back to allow a group of people to exit. An old woman shuffled out, supported by two men who looked to be her son and grandson. The woman appeared so frail, Luskell lifted her eyepatch. Her wizard eye confirmed her suspicions.

"They're going the wrong way," she murmured to Fandek.

He held out his hand to the woman. "Are you leaving us already, Denna?"

She took his hand. "I'd rather die at home."

"Will you take some sunshine before you go?"

"Gladly, dear boy, if you can spare it."

Fandek smiled. "It's yours."

She sighed and stood straighter. "Thank you. If I don't see you again ..."

"Send for me if you need a lift." He squeezed her hand

gently and let her go.

"But ... but ..." Luskell protested as the three climbed into a waiting buggy. "How can you — how can Mamam let her leave when she's so ill?"

"We've done all we can. She chose to go home. We can't *make* people stay, especially if we can't help them."

They entered the wide hall. Patients waiting to be seen sat on benches along the walls. Healers moved among them, speaking quietly. The sound of distant crying carried from another room, but the noise level didn't rise much above a gentle hum. The atmosphere teemed with fear and worry, though an overriding sense of trust contained these strong emotions. When she'd been working here, Luskell had remained open, but now she shielded herself. It was too much after meeting Denna. There would be plenty of time for other people's feelings.

To the left, doors opened to small rooms that offered privacy for examination and treatment. Farther along were wards for the chronic or contagious patients who needed to stay for more care. At the end of the hall, the healers' dormitory was located near the wards. On the right, double doors opened into the healers' dining room. A broad stairway led up to the director's office and Balsam's private apartment.

A blue-aproned healer emerged from a treatment room with a woman and a child whose arm hung in a sling. She spoke to them, all competence and calm, and ushered her patient and his mother out. When she turned, her gaze passed over Luskell, then snapped back. Her mouth opened in surprise. "It's ... Luskell, isn't it? I thought you went off to be a wizard."

Luskell recognized Shura, a girl close to her own age who had started her training after Luskell left. When Luskell had first met her, she wore the brown apprentice's apron. They had met only once, but the occasion was memorable — the morning after Hanny was attacked.

"I did. I mean, I am. A wizard, that is." Luskell offered her staff as proof.

"So what are you doing back here?" Shura glanced at the eyepatch and away, like she didn't want to be caught looking at it.

"I have ... a new skill." Luskell tapped the patch. "This is part of it. I think it might be useful. Is my ... is the director here?" They weren't well acquainted; Shura probably didn't know who Luskell's mother was. That could wait until later, too.

Shura nodded up the stairs. "In her office. Be sure to knock so she can put her hair on." She covered her mouth and her cheeks reddened. "I didn't mean to say that out loud!"

Luskell flipped her hand through her own short curls. "I've seen it. She won't mind." Mamam had worn her hair short for years, displaying an illusion of whatever hairstyle was appropriate. Luskell hadn't bothered, but it might be a useful trick to learn now that she was back in the city.

Fandek took her arm and steered her toward the dining room. "Breakfast first." It wasn't a question.

Luskell didn't argue. She had plenty of appetite. She took a seat at the table. In spite of, or perhaps because of having the scent of cheese in her nostrils all night, she filled a plate with cheese, then added a roll and two juicy plums.

"So this new skill — " Fandek began.

Luskell put up a hand. "Are we eating or talking?" She smiled. "I'll tell you all about it after I've had a chance to see Mamam. She'll know whether it's useful or not."

After breakfast, Fandek went about his duties, and Luskell climbed the stairs. She knocked as she'd been instructed, but also mind-talked *It's Luskell* so Mamam wouldn't bother with an illusion.

"Come in!"

Luskell entered the office and closed the door behind her. Mamam sat at a desk with her back to a window that looked out into the maple grove. She frowned at the books and loose papers in front of her. The healers of Balsam's House kept notes on every patient treated, which were entered in logs. Luskell understood the need for records of what worked and what didn't, but hadn't enjoyed the paperwork. Mamam gave her a tired smile that hinted it wasn't her favorite part of the job, either.

Luskell sat across from her. Mamam's short coppery hair was sprinkled with silver, and new lines had appeared between her eyebrows and at the corners of her mouth. "Do you ever go home? Fandek said you were here last night."

"I didn't stay long, but I'm glad I was here when they brought Ettam's body." She shook her head. "Poor man. Of all things, a knife attack again! It must have been terrible for him."

"But that's not what killed him, is it?"

"No, he's been failing for a while. There wasn't anything more we could do for him. At least someone was with him at the end." Mamam gave Luskell a proud, fond smile. Then she frowned. "Something's different. Like there's ... less of you?"

Luskell was glad her emotions were carefully shielded. She wasn't ready to share her shame over leaving Ettam, or her secret visit to the Other Side. But less of her? That sounded ominous. She lost something each time she visited the Other Side, but not always enough for Mamam to notice. She'd have to be careful. "Are you officially the director here, or is this temporary?"

Mamam glanced to the side, as if looking through the wall into Balsam's apartment. "Not temporary, I'm afraid."

"Can I see her? Or is she too ...?"

"I'm sure Balsam would welcome a visit from you. She was sleeping when I checked on her, but maybe later."

"I can wait. What's wrong with her? She wasn't ill when I left."

"She probably was, but she didn't know it yet." Mamam sighed and ran her fingers through her hair. "You were working here during the epidemic last winter; you know how busy it was. She thought she was suffering from overwork, but even after things quieted down, she didn't get any better. By the time I came back, it was too late to do much for her except take over most of her work."

"Oh no, really? Maybe I should be helping, too."

"I'd be happy to have you. Not today, though. You should take a day, see about your dress, play with Crett."

Luskell smiled. "If it means that much to you ..."

"You deserve some time off. Anyway, I thought you didn't want to be a healer."

"I have ... a new power that might be useful."

Mamam lost her distracted air. "Maybe that's what's different. Tell me about it."

Luskell tapped her eyepatch. "I have a wizard eye. It shows me how much life is in someone."

"So you know when people will die?"

"Sort of. Not like telling the future. I know if someone is dying right now. Like the woman who just left. Denna?"

Mamam sighed. "We can't cure everything."

"Is that why you left Grandpa when he's still not well?" Luskell asked.

Mamam leaned her elbows on the desk and rested her head in her hands. "He's as well as I could make him. I can treat symptoms and even clear infections, but that kind of damage … well, it's like your eye. I could spend all my power — maybe risk my life — repairing his lungs or your eye, and it might make things worse."

"Sometimes I forget you have limits. I'm sorry."

Mamam waved off the apology. "This wizard eye of yours could be useful when we have to decide who to treat first, or if someone is getting sicker but it's not obvious. How would you feel about visiting Balsam's House once a day to scan the patients? You could choose to stay and work or go out into the city and find people who need help."

"Like Dadad does! Yes, I'll do that." It sounded more wizardly than working inside all day.

Mamam laid a blank page on the desk and began to write out Luskell's contract. "I can see how you might not want to be under my eye all the time." Mamam's green eyes twinkled with amusement. "Although you might want to work closer to Fandek."

"Why would I?" Luskell's emotions were shielded, but she feared she had given too much away by her quick, defensive reply.

"Luskell, you don't have to pretend. He told me you were with him last night. Which surprised me. I always thought you and Laki would work something out, and I wasn't sure you'd get over him so quickly."

"What? No, Fandek and I … we're not … I mean, I like him better than I used to, but …" Luskell remembered kissing Fandek. Her cheeks burned, defeating the purpose of the shield. "Well, it's not appropriate as long as he's your apprentice, is it?"

"He won't be my apprentice much longer. So you weren't with him last night?"

"Only to sleep. I was upset about Ettam, and it was late. I didn't want to wake Crett." Luskell made herself breathe slowly to keep from babbling. "I don't want to rush anything."

"That didn't stop you last winter with Laki. And Jagryn?"

Luskell didn't remember telling Mamam anything about what may or may not have happened with Jagryn, but that didn't mean she didn't know. "Then you know why I need to slow down."

"I'm not rushing you; you're not even eighteen. I want you to be happy, maybe have a family when you're ready. A wizard's life doesn't have to be lonely."

"It won't be if I crowd in with you and Dadad and Crett!"

"We've been talking about finding someplace bigger, if we ever have a moment to think about it. Not like Embassy House, but ..."

Luskell welcomed this opening. Mamam might have the answer to her question. "Speaking of Embassy House, do you remember a dinner in our apartment for all the delegations, five or six years ago?"

"That must have been the year we ended up hosting when Naliskat wasn't feeling well. Five years ago sounds right. Why do you ask?"

"There was a girl with the Foryin party, who was flirting with Dadad! And now she's going to marry Laki. I don't know what to think."

Mamam threw back her head and laughed. "Oh, Luskell, you're jealous! I thought you didn't want to be with him."

"That's not the point! It was a shock to see her again."

"She wasn't flirting with your father."

"How do you know?" Luskell slumped back in her chair. "Maybe it doesn't matter. Should I go back and give my blessing?"

"They don't need it, but I'm sure Laki would appreciate

it." Mamam studied Luskell in a way she recognized. Mamam had a kind of wizard eye, too. It showed her who had power and how much. She blinked and her gaze returned to normal. "Are you using your power for something?"

"You mean right now? Nothing except shielding the way I always do. Why?"

"It looks like you're … well, I'd call it bleeding power. Not a lot, but constantly."

"Will it hurt me?" She remembered what Dadad had said about Knot before he died, his life trickling away. This was her power, not her life, but one fed the other.

"Probably not, at least in the short run. I can't imagine it's doing you any good, though. This might explain why you've been so worn down since you got back."

Fandek had noticed the same thing, but maybe it wasn't something she was doing to herself, as he had accused. Now that Mamam had pointed it out, she could feel the trickle of power that rose within her as a tingling warmth and flowed away. But where? She wasn't directing it or using it, at least not consciously. Yet it seemed to have a direction.

"I'll work on it. I'm glad you saw it. I might never have figured it out on my own."

Their business concluded, Mamam went to the inner door that separated the office from Balsam's apartment. "Wait here. I'll see if she's awake."

Luskell listened to the murmur of voices in the next room — Mamam's familiar voice, clear and strong, and another voice she almost didn't recognize. How could those feeble tones belong to Balsam, a healer of commanding presence?

Mamam returned. "Go on in. She's excited to see you, but please don't tire her."

Luskell entered the sitting room and closed the door behind her. Sturdy, upholstered chairs and a settee faced the hearth, where a low fire crackled invitingly, but that room was unoccupied. In the corner room beyond, Balsam lay in bed, propped up on pillows. Daylight streamed through large windows. In the strong light, Balsam's iron gray hair looked faded to ash and her cheeks, washed out and pale.

She beamed when she saw Luskell, looking more like her old self. "Luskell! How good to see you! Come closer, where it's light."

Luskell approached. Outside the window, yellowing maple leaves fluttered, and in the distance, Aku gleamed white. "Look, the Mountain's out." As she gazed at it, she felt a tug at her heart like homesickness.

Balsam stretched up to see, then slumped back. "You wish you were still up there?"

"No, but I haven't seen her since I left."

"And you've been back how long?"

"Since ... day before yesterday? Seems longer. It's been a busy couple of days."

"But the Mountain draws you."

"Yes." Was that where her power was flowing? She'd grown used to constantly sensing for Aku's moods. But it wasn't her job now. Luskell forced herself to look away from Aku. She pictured the solitude she now held inside her, a compact bundle with a thread of power connecting it to the Mountain. She tied a knot in the thread and cut it off. An inner silence descended. A loss. But the solitude remained, and as long as her feet touched the ground, she would still be touching Aku. "But I can't go back. Not as Keeper, anyway. That was a special circumstance I doubt will be repeated. I need to get on with things. I didn't know I'd miss her this much. It's so much ... simpler, up there."

"Oh, yes. Soothing a volcano certainly sounds like a simple life." Balsam grinned.

Luskell laughed. "When you put it that way ... I mean it, though. I could believe I was the only person in the world. I was responsible for myself and Aku and nothing else."

"I suppose the city might be overwhelming after such a solitary experience."

"It is, a little. I'm getting used to it. It's good to see my family again. Crett has gotten so big!" Luskell gazed out the window again. "I'm glad you have a good view from your room."

"This was my nanny's room, when I was a child," Balsam replied. "The sitting room was where I played and had lessons, and I slept in what's now my office. Or rather, your mother's office." Balsam frowned, and Luskell sensed her loss. She wasn't the only one missing an old life. "Less of a view there, that's for sure."

"It's hard to imagine this place as one family's home." Luskell pictured her family's rooms, and the house in Misty Pass. "Even at Embassy House, we had only part of one floor."

Balsam nodded. "There are a few more rooms off my sitting room, too. They're closed up for now, but I think I've made better use of this big house than my parents did." She grinned, suddenly mischievous. "I didn't always appreciate it. When I was around your age, I used to climb out the window and go looking for trouble."

"I can't believe you got into much trouble."

"Not for want of trying." Balsam cackled and her eyes brightened. "As soon as I found my bit of magic, I fell in with a lowlife crowd of fortune-tellers and fake magicians who didn't all have my best interests at heart. My father was all for locking me up. Lucky for me, my grandfather had a younger half-sister who could train my talent and get me out of the city at the same time. My Aunt Elika."

Luskell laughed. "Does anyone get trained before they get into trouble? Besides Jagryn, I mean."

"I know, trouble is often the first sign of power." Balsam eyed Luskell's staff. "So you're a wizard now, staff and everything."

"It came from the tree outside your window." Luskell held it out for Balsam to see.

"Trust Bardin to find a good use for that pesky branch." Balsam closed her eyes and released a long sigh. She was quiet so long, Luskell thought she'd fallen asleep. Eyes closed, Balsam spoke again. "Do you know Elika?"

"I know who she was," Luskell answered carefully. "The healer in Deep River, years ago. She died when my father was a boy."

"I know that! But you've met her, yes?"

"Oh. Well, yes." No point in pretending when Balsam already knew of Luskell's odd ability. "She gave me a message for someone once. And I saw her a few other times." Luskell left out the detail that on one occasion, she had purposely visited the Other Side in order to rebuke the deceased Elika for endangering Jagryn. That was too strange. "She … seemed very sure of herself."

"Oh, she was!" Balsam laughed until the laughter turned into a choking cough. Luskell poured her a cup of water. Balsam sipped it. "You'd think she was always right. Well, she usually was. When I found my little bit of power, I wanted to make a great show of it. Elika taught me the show has its place. She let people believe her house was haunted, and she let me tell my scary stories." She paused, a frown creasing her forehead. "Do they still believe the house is haunted?"

"I don't think so. Jagryn fixed it up so he could live in it. Do you remember him — Dadad's apprentice? Elika's great-grandson."

"Oh, yes, I liked him. Are you two ...?"

"Not even close. He's a wizard now, and recently married to a girl from Deep River."

"Ah, he'll be sharing the house. I always thought it was perfect for one, cozy for two, crowded for three, which will happen soon enough, I'm sure. But we managed, Elika, Sudi, and I."

Luskell smiled over the secret she knew. "Jagryn and his wife are visiting the city if you want to see them."

"Oh? Yes, maybe. Great-grandson, though — imagine that. And a wizard. I hope Elika's pleased. Where was I going with that? Yes, the show is all well and good, but doing something for folks was the real point. Is it the same for wizards?"

"It must be, or why would we bother with illusions? It looks like I'll be working here again, at least for a while."

"But you'd rather not."

"It's all right. I won't always be working in the house." Luskell pulled a chair close to the bedside and sat down. "I have a new ability I can use here and out in the neighborhoods."

"I know you don't like to be cooped up. So what's this ability?"

"This eye lets me see who's dying." Luskell lifted her eyepatch. There was life in the old woman yet. Not much. It burned low like the fire in the next room.

"That's not always something a healer can fix." To her credit, Balsam didn't flinch at the sight of Luskell's scars.

"I know. Do you remember the night before I left here, when I sat up with Mirion and went with her to the Other Side?"

"I was sorry to put you through that, but you behaved admirably."

"But do you remember what you told me afterward?"

"No, but I'm sure it was something very wise." Balsam cackled at her own joke. "I've never known anyone who could do what you do. I wouldn't mind having an experienced guide, when my time comes."

"I'm sure that won't be for a long time."

Balsam looked straight at Luskell. "We both know that's not true. I'll plan to send for you. Like the midwife, but at the other end."

"That's what you told me before!" Luskell hadn't spoken openly of this to anyone else, but she'd been thinking about it. "People keep telling me I shouldn't visit the Other Side at all."

"But it's not only the Mountain that draws you?"

Luskell gasped. She remembered how hard it was to turn away from the vast city she'd glimpsed, and the trail of sparkles behind her. "Maybe. I don't know. I was with a dying man last night. I didn't go with him, and I've felt ever since I should have. Maybe that should be my specialty."

Balsam smiled. "There's a place for some show, if that's not all there is to it. Is it safe?"

"Not completely, but if I'm careful, I — "

The door from the office swung open and Mamam put her head into the sitting room. "Luskell? You should let Balsam rest now."

"I'll be right out." Luskell turned back to Balsam. "Please don't tell her what I said. She has enough to worry about, running this place and training an apprentice, on top of keeping up with a toddler."

"Apprentice — Fandek, isn't it? With the sunshine?"

"You call it that, too?"

"What else?" Balsam nodded thoughtfully. "It's a natural gift with him, and useful in a place like this. I wasn't sure at first about training him here, but now I hope he'll stay after his apprenticeship is complete. He didn't have an easy start in life, you know."

"I've heard some of it."

"I cared for his mother a few times when she'd been knocked around worse than usual. She always said she'd fallen, but nobody's that clumsy. Then when she brought the baby in — "

"Deklyn?"

"You know him?"

"He works at the coach office, with the horses."

"I know. I keep my horse there. When he was about a year old, Fanlyn brought him in with a dent in his skull and a story about a tumble. I didn't believe that one, either. I hated to send them home, but what could I do? Couldn't have been more than a year later, she died."

"Fandek thinks she was murdered."

"Yes, so he told me. Somehow, all that didn't twist him. He kept Deklyn safe, and now he's a healer."

"He has a gift for it."

"More than that. He has real compassion. He's a good man."

Luskell tried to hide the flush that rose in her cheeks.

"I see you agree." Balsam did nothing to hide her amusement. "Seems it's more than the Mountain and the Other Side that draw you."

Chapter 14

Luskell left her mother's office and headed down the stairs, her mind on Balsam, and Aku, and the Other Side. Not on Fandek. Not at all. She nearly collided with a healer at the bottom of the steps.

"Oops, sorry, Hanny!"

"Luskell!" Far from being angry, the other woman wrapped her in a hug. "It's about time you stopped by."

"It's good to see you!" Luskell held her friend out to look at her. Hanny's pink cheeks and bright smile spoke of good health, though her curvy figure was thinner than Luskell remembered and she had circles under her eyes like Luskell had seen on Bardin.

"May I have a look under the patch?" Hanny asked. "Professional curiosity."

Luskell lifted it, relieved Hanny had a strong glow of health about her.

Hanny examined Luskell's scars without flinching. "More scars than I'd expect with Ketty providing treatment."

"She didn't get there until the next day, so another healer removed the splinters and cleaned the wounds. I was secretly happy to finally have something to show, though not about the eye."

"Can you see anything with it?"

"Not regular things," Luskell said. "It shows me something that should be useful around here, though."

"Ha, so you're a healer after all." Hanny grinned as Luskell lowered the patch.

"I don't know for sure what I am." Luskell frowned. She had assumed earning her staff would answer that question once and for all, not raise more questions. "Fandek says you married Virosh. He must be in town if you're working during the day."

Hanny blushed pinker. "I'm switching to days, anyway. But I wish he didn't have to go out on ships. I sleep better when he's here. Well, everything's better, but ..." She sighed. "When I can't sleep, he makes it rain on our roof. It's so soothing. I was lucky he was home last night."

"It rained everywhere last night," Luskell said. "I was out in it."

"I needed more comfort than the sound of raindrops."

"Why, what happened?" Luskell asked.

"Nightmares. About ... you know." Hanny pressed her lips together and touched her throat.

Luskell nodded. The strangler. Hanny had been the last woman attacked before the strangler left the city, and one of the lucky few to survive.

Hanny glanced at Luskell's eyepatch. "I'm sorry you

were hurt, but thank you for helping capture him. He can't hang soon enough for me."

Luskell squeezed Hanny's shoulder. "Sleep better tonight."

"If I see Fandek before I go home, I'll ask for a dose of sunshine."

Luskell left Balsam's House, absorbed in thoughts of her new role. She was sure her wizard eye would be helpful, even in cases where she didn't go to the Other Side. But if she crossed over, it would be for others, not herself.

She tried to shake off lingering unease. Had she really seen Old Mother Bones on the Other Side? Had the soul of a horse rescued her? No, her visit must have become an ordinary dream shading into nightmare. She'd never seen an animal on the Other Side, or a soul in rags, let alone one that was nothing but bones. Her imagination had gotten the better of her. That was why she preferred to cross over awake. Dreams couldn't be trusted.

She slid her hand into her pocket and touched the little pot of ink, left there from the day before. It seemed much longer since she'd signed the *Registry*, but it was already time to update her entry.

She crossed to the library, which was just opening for the day. She climbed the stairs to the mezzanine and paused before the curtained alcove, then parted the curtains and approached the *Registry of Practitioners*. Jagryn had updated his entry with the attainment of Wizard. His specialties were Weatherworking, Transformation, and Illusions. Luskell took out her ink and added Crossing Over to her own entry. If the dead wanted her to stay away, they would have to give her a good reason.

When she came out, Terulo was taking his seat under the windows.

He glanced around at her. "Back so soon?"

"I decided to add another specialty. Any progress here?"

"I'm still looking for a big chunk of that forgotten spell, but I've found some interesting references to enchanted buildings."

"Enchanted, how? Like how we cast invisibility over our house in Misty Pass? Or like the protective spells they use on the doorways at Balsam's House?"

"I think this is different. The protection wears off and has to be renewed every day, doesn't it?"

"Yes. The invisibility lasts longer because no one disturbs it, but it has to be renewed every now and then, too. So how is this different?"

"The magic is worked right into the building stones. I don't know how yet, but it seems similar to the wizard's staff. When done right, it's permanent, as much a part of the building as the stones."

"Any examples that are still around?"

"At least one — Fortress Prison. It's supposed to have suppression spells worked into it, to prevent magic being used to trick guards or break prisoners out. I read something about the Governor's Mansion, too, but it's not clear if it's the same thing or more like what they use at Balsam's House."

"The old governor had someone working for him to shield his thoughts from people like my parents," Luskell said. "Either he didn't know about the enchantment or didn't trust it."

"Or it wore off and no one remembers how to restore it," Terulo observed. "See what I mean about how much we don't know?"

Luskell laughed, drawing a stern look from the librarian below. "Say, you might know. I once overheard someone talking about how the library is haunted."

Terulo stifled a laugh. "My cousin believes that. He had a scare here, something about footsteps and flying cloak."

"That wasn't a haunt, that was me!" Luskell said. "But a few of those fellows believed it before that. I don't see how it could be, though. The Other Side is vast but closed, from what I can tell. Spirits of the dead can enter dreams but not the living world." But a legend had made its way to the Other Side ...

"The library is the oldest intact building in the city, and it's built on the remains of something even older," Terulo said. "I suppose that's why it ended up with the little museum exhibit." He gestured toward the alcoves on either side of the Registry. "That kind of place gets a reputation, especially when it's full of magic books."

"It's not like they do anything," Luskell objected.

"Most don't, but the *Registries* — "

"There's more than one?"

"Oh yeah, this one only goes back about three hundred years. The earlier volumes are stored in the archives. But they rustle at times. That could start a ghost story."

Luskell considered all those signatures in ink with magical blood in it, pages responding to names or specialties. "So that's why we whisper," she murmured as softly as she could.

Luskell left the library to see about her other errand. She avoided puddles from the previous night's rain and reached the far side of the square. She turned away from home, toward the dressmaker Tulia's shop. She still wasn't sure she needed a new dress, but if Mamam thought so, maybe she did.

A bell jingled as she entered the shop. "Hello?" she called.

Shelves held neatly folded cloth and spools of thread. A length of fabric lay on the big cutting table, paper patterns pinned in place. A small, plump woman stood up from behind the table, scissors in hand, hair pulled back in a knot at her nape. Luskell remembered Tulia as having black hair streaked with white, but the white hairs now outnumbered the black.

"Who's there?"

"It's Luskell." She supposed she had changed even more than Tulia, what with cutting her hair and losing an eye. "My mother says you have a dress for me to try on."

"Well, of course it's you!" Tulia clucked softly. "You shouldn't wear gray; makes you invisible."

Luskell laughed. "You don't think it's wizardly? Anyway, I don't need a dress to make me invisible." She concealed herself.

Tulia gasped, then laughed. "Good one! Yes, a new dress is what you need. I'm pleased with how it turned out. It's the latest style — all the fine women are wearing it. There's a sketch on the wall. Take a look while I get your dress."

At first glance, the sketch showed a Guard's uniform. Not quite, though. The woman in the picture (apparently at least Luskell's height) wore a fitted skirt to her ankles, topped with a belted tunic of the same fabric. It fastened with decorative buttons down the left-hand side and had wide sleeves to the elbow, over a blouse in a contrasting color. It looked very elegant. Luskell couldn't imagine running or climbing in it.

"Here we are!" Tulia announced. She carried a paper-wrapped parcel. "Ketty brought in your old dress and asked me to remake it somehow."

"I wish it still fit. I never had anything so beautiful."

"Some of my best work. But it was a girl's dress and you're a woman now, or near enough. I can't imagine you wore it more than twice."

"Three times."

"All right, but not enough to come close to wearing it out. I took off the bodice and the hem flounce. I can add a new skirt to those, and with the jacket, it'll make over into a new dress for another girl. The skirt had more than enough fabric for a blouse."

Luskell gestured toward the sketch. "How does anyone walk in such a narrow skirt?"

"That's the clever part. If you're standing, the skirt falls straight — very elegant. But it has pleats all around, from just above the knee. They're lined to match the blouse, so when you walk, you get this flash of color. Here, you should see it."

Tulia unwrapped the paper to reveal the familiar green silk Luskell associated with dancing and working delicate magic. The dressmaker lifted the blouse aside to reveal the rest of the outfit. Mamam had chosen a blue woolen fabric close to the color of Luskell's cloak, but with narrow green stripes that matched the silk.

"Ketty has a good eye for color," Tulia said.

Perhaps dressmakers could read minds as well as wizards. "I wasn't sure I needed a new dress, but now I think I do."

"Go in the back and put it on. We'll see how well your mother guessed your measurements."

Luskell stepped into the curtained room to change. The silk was smooth and much lighter in weight as a simple blouse than it had felt as a whole dress. The full sleeves gathered to deep cuffs, so they wouldn't drag in food or ink. The skirt was narrower than any Luskell had worn but not tight.

"The skirt has a pocket!" she squealed. It was hidden at the side where the waistband closed.

Tulia laughed. "Not everyone wants them, but your mother said you would. The tunic has them, too."

It took Luskell a few tries to button the tunic; she was used to side ties. Belted, it fell between her hips and her knees. What she thought at first were decorative features turned out to be actual pockets, as promised, like a real Guard's uniform. And when she walked out of the room, the pleats opened up with a glimpse of green.

"Look at you! You could be on the Governor's staff!"

"I like it, and it fits well enough."

"Let me check." Tulia fussed with seams and bands. "I thought Ketty was exaggerating when she said how long to make the skirt, but she was right. It's a bit loose in the waist and hips."

"I lost what girth I had in the mountains, but it's sure to come back now."

The door jingled open to admit a black-haired young woman, barely taller than Tulia and almost as plump.

"Daisy!" Luskell cried. Cedar wasn't her only friend named for a plant. Tree and flower names had once been the fashion only of wealthy families in the city, but had gained popularity among working people, which meant the fine folk had mostly stopped using them.

Daisy stared. "Luskell? What happened to your ... hair?"

"And my eye? It's all right, Daisy. I cut my hair off to make life easier and I hurt my eye by trying to be a wizard before I was ready."

Tulia stared at Luskell's face for the first time. "I never even noticed. Not sure eyepatches will ever be in fashion for women, but it works for you."

"Then it's true?" Daisy asked. "You're going to be a wizard?"

"Am one." Luskell gestured toward her staff where it leaned against the wall.

Tulia stepped back and admired her work. "Now you tell your news, Daisy. The reason I need a new assistant."

Daisy blushed and looked at her feet. "I'm engaged to Ambug."

After a moment of shock, Luskell burst out laughing. "Sorry, but that's five of my friends who have announced engagements or marriage in the last two days."

"You must have done a spell," Daisy giggled.

"Well, I did introduce you two. At least I don't have to worry about Cedar."

"Maybe not officially. She's fond enough of Shura that they got a place together near Balsam's House. Do you know her? Maybe you worked together there."

"We never worked together, but I met Shura right before I left town last winter. I thought I sensed something between them. I'm glad they're still together."

Daisy smiled. "She brings out the soft in Cedar. I never knew anyone but babies to do that."

"We should do something together now that I'm back," Luskell said.

"Yes! A picnic at Braffin's Garden while the weather's good. I'll plan it and let you know."

"Just the three of us, like old times." Luskell smiled, remembering childhood days with her friends. "No, four; I wouldn't want to leave Ambug out of it."

"We should include Shura, too. And your special someone, if you have one?"

Luskell hesitated long enough to pique Daisy's curiosity. "Let me think about it. I might come alone," she said before her friend could pry.

"Luskell, can you stay to lunch with us?" Tulia asked.

"I wish I could. I promised to watch Crett this

afternoon, so I'd better go."

"All right. I'll finish this hem and have your dress sent over."

"How much do I owe you?"

Tulia shook her head. "Ketty already paid. I always give her a good deal." She glanced at her daughter. When Daisy was fourteen, she'd contracted an infection that would have killed her if not for Mamam's care. Tulia paid her with Luskell's green silk dress, and good deals in perpetuity.

Chapter 15

When Luskell got home, Dadad and Crett were about to dig into a lunch of bread, cheese, and apples. In spite of its similarity to her breakfast, the simple meal appealed to her.

"There you are!" Dadad closed his library book and set it aside. "We were starting to worry when you didn't come home for supper last night."

"Laki invited us to eat with them — him and Tatakla."

"His bride-to-be? Her name sounds familiar; I wonder if we've met." Dadad stroked his beard.

"Probably at Embassy House." Luskell didn't care to linger on the subject. "We didn't stay all that late, but things got messy on the way home."

"Your mother told me some of it when she came back

from Balsam's House." Dadad grabbed an apple from Crett before the boy could fling it across the room. He cut up the apple and gave a slice to Crett. "Terrible about Ettam. At least he had someone familiar with him at the end. As long as you didn't — "

"I didn't," Luskell interrupted. "But I added Crossing Over to the registry. If I'm going to work at Balsam's House even part of the time, I'll encounter people dying. I'm not going to hide my ability." Luskell crunched into her own apple and met Dadad's worried gaze, daring him to challenge her.

He blinked. "I know you won't use it frivolously. Crett, not such a big bite." He helped Crett break his bread into smaller pieces so he wouldn't choke. "If you can handle the small one on your own, I'd like to make the rounds. There's never not a need."

"So I've seen. Maybe tomorrow I'll go out with you."

Dadad beamed at her. "I'd like that."

"Anything I should know?"

"He needs a nap, and then he gets to play outside with his little friends. None of them are older than five, so they take some watching."

"Is magic allowed?" Luskell winked at Crett.

Crett clapped his hands. "Yes! Yes! Yes!"

"Only as a last resort." Dadad struggled to keep a straight face. "I'm sure you'll be fine. They're a good bunch. I'll see you around suppertime." He cleared his plate, took up his staff, and left.

Luskell removed her brother's shoes. "Who are your friends, Crett?"

"Dalym's my bes' fren'. An' dere's Jumi, an' Frizza. An' Vell. She's big."

Luskell guessed Vell must be the five-year-old. "Such a big group! Anyone else I should know about?"

"Oh! Grammy Bo come when I sleepin'!"

"That's nice. We probably won't see her today." Luskell didn't know all the neighbors but imagined a kindly old woman who might sometimes sit with Crett while he napped or when her parents had to go out in the evening. "Today Luskell's here while you sleep. Is that all right?"

"No nap!" Crett rubbed his eyes.

Luskell picked him up. He felt different than he used to. "No diaper?"

"Big boy now."

She set him down so he could show her how he used the pot. She pulled out the trundle bed. Had it always taken up so much room? "You don't have to nap. Just close your eyes and I'll play my fiddle for you."

He flopped onto the bed and closed his eyes, giggling. "Not sleepin'!"

Luskell tuned her fiddle and played a quick dance tune. Crett banged his feet against the bed. She played the same tune at half tempo, followed by a new one she'd made up for Aku. She gradually transitioned to "Aku's Lullaby" and sang along. Crett visibly relaxed, stuck his thumb into his mouth, and settled down to rest. When she was sure the nap was really happening, Luskell put the fiddle away. She heated water and washed the lunch dishes, then swept the room. It wasn't how she'd pictured her life as a wizard, doing housework and childcare. But she was a member of this household and that's how it had always been: everyone pitched in. She couldn't expect much sympathy if she complained.

When the chores were done, she stretched out on her parents' bed and closed her eyes. She'd had nothing but uneasy or interrupted sleep for days. In spite of Crett's resistance, a nap seemed like a great idea. She dozed off in no time.

A face loomed over her, waxy skin taut over sharp bones. The eyes blazed with rage. As the mouth opened to speak, Crett yelped in his sleep. Luskell jerked awake, heart thumping. Crett murmured, "Go 'way," and rolled over, sucking his thumb and content once more. Luskell thought about reading his dream, but there was no real need. It couldn't have been worse than hers, already fading. An angry face, about to speak ...

Crett woke and stretched. "You napped me!" he accused.

"You must have needed it. Come on, let's get your shoes on." Luskell lifted him from the bed onto a chair.

"No!" His favorite word these days.

"Oh, but it's time to meet your friends. I want to watch you play."

"No! Moo come!" Crett's lip trembled and his eyes filled with tears.

"What's 'moo'?" Luskell supposed it must mean *cow*. Where had Crett seen a cow? Maybe in Deep River, but they'd left there months ago. There was a cattle market several blocks away. The streets nearby were too narrow to drive the herds, though, so they wouldn't have come close.

"Moo come!" Crett repeated.

"Then we'll have to protect each other." Luskell stuffed Crett's feet into shoes, got his coat on, and carried him outside to the back stairs. She had no hand free for her staff. She left it safe in the room.

Down in the yard, four children were already hard at play, digging, building, making mud.

"See? You're missing out. Which one is Dalym?"

Crett shook his head and buried his face in her shoulder.

Kiat from downstairs hung laundry on lines while she watched the children. As Luskell and Crett reached the top of the steps, a comparatively big girl suddenly jumped up and charged at the others. Shrieking and giggling, they ran, and she chased. Crett reached his hands toward them.

"See? You don't want to miss out."

"Moo come!"

Luskell looked where he pointed. The gate stood open. A bellow resounded from the lane beyond. A brown-furred beast galloped into the yard, tossing horns.

Kiat dropped her laundry basket. "Up! Up!" She scooped up the smallest children and ran for the stairs. The others followed. None of them, including Luskell, had ever seen a large animal loose in the yard.

"Crett, stay here." Luskell set him on his feet and wrapped his fingers around the railing.

Kiat was halfway up the stairs with the two toddlers. One of the older children followed her, but the girl who had been chasing them tripped and sprawled on the ground.

Luskell climbed up and crouched on the railing, drew a breath, and silently transformed to a swallow. She swooped toward the rampaging animal. She lighted on its back and took her own form again. A wild grab, another, and she held a horn in each hand. It was a young bull, not full grown. It didn't think or feel as a human would, but she sensed its fear and anger. It had escaped some threat, but it didn't want to be where it was. It twisted and bucked. Luskell clung on as it tried to throw her off.

She wrenched the bull's head to the side, turning it away from the child on the ground. With a dry mouth, she sang "Aku's Lullaby" and poured calming magic through the beast's horns. It slowed its mad gallop and stopped twisting as the drovers came through the gate. Luskell slid from its back but kept her grip on the horns

"There's something you don't see every day." One of the men winked at Luskell. "A one-eyed girl riding a bull in a dress. People would pay to watch that act in a traveling show."

The other man slipped a lead rope over the bull's head. "Aw, look, gentle as a new calf."

"I'm not going to put a dress on him, though." Luskell let go and backed away, glad her long skirt hid her shaking knees.

"What? No, I meant *you* were ..."

She ignored the drover and helped the frightened girl to her feet. "Are you Vell? It's all right now. You're safe." They climbed the stairs to join the others. Crett clung to the railing where Luskell had left him, silent tears rolling down his cheeks.

Luskell picked him up and held him tight. "It's all right, Crett. I'm here."

"Moo come!"

"Yes, you were right. Moo come." She patted him and wondered, *But how did you know?*

None of the children wanted to play anymore. Luskell took Crett back inside and sat on the floor with him to build a house of blocks for his toy bears.

"When you were napping, you told someone to go away." She tried to speak casually, as if they hadn't both been frightened. "Were you talking to the bull that came into the yard?"

Crett nodded and clutched the biggest bear close. "Moo come." He stared up at Luskell. "You rided it!"

"I didn't plan to, but I guess it worked. I sang to the bull like I sing to you and he calmed down."

Crett giggled. "Sing to the moo-cow! Silly."

"Did you ... dream I was coming home, before anyone told you?"

"You sittin' on top of the coach. With Laki?"

"Yes! You saw that? You're even younger than he was when ..."

Luskell didn't finish the thought. She picked up one of

the smaller bears. They had been Laki's when he was a child, carved for him by his grandfather. Laki's full name, Nalaklak, meant "Great Bear." She supposed his nickname meant "Little Bear." Laki had begun having visions before he was four years old, so it wasn't impossible Crett had started to dream of the future.

When Dadad came home, he had Mamam with him, and they brought supper from the tavern again.

"Did the small folk give you trouble?" Dadad joked. "Any excitement this afternoon?"

"Moo come!" Crett shouted.

They both looked to Luskell for an explanation. "There was a little excitement." She told them about the open gate, the escaped bull, her transformation and ride, but saved the most troubling detail for last.

"Crett knew before it happened. He tried to warn me. And he knew I was coming home before you told him."

"He knew? Or he guessed?" Mamam asked.

"He dreamed I was riding on top of the coach with Laki," Luskell said. "During his nap today, he dreamed about loose cattle in the yard. So you tell me."

Dadad picked up Crett and settled him at the table. He stole a glance at the book of suppression spells. "He's too young."

"It's unusual, but can happen," Mamam said. "I discovered my power when I was only nine."

"Nine isn't two," Dadad said.

"Agreed," Mamam said. "But what do we do about it? Do you know enough to suppress his power?"

Dadad sighed. "Not yet."

"At the very least, we should all remember to work spells without speaking," Mamam said. "Luskell, aren't you glad Bardin had you master that skill?"

Luskell shuddered at the idea of an angry toddler

shouting the fire spell. "I thought maybe Laki could help," she said. "Chamokat must have done more for him than teach him to Listen."

"He didn't leave town yet?"

"They're here for a few more days."

"Ask him," Dadad said. "This is beyond any of our expertise."

Luskell settled herself and reached for Laki's mind. She was glad he was near enough to answer.

Laki, I … we … no, Crett needs your help. He's having visions of the future.

Younger than I was! When did this start?

Not sure. He saw us on the coach, but there might have been something earlier he doesn't remember.

Yes, I'll help. He's too young to deal with it alone.

That's what I thought, and you've been through it.

We'll stop by in the morning.

Thank you.

Luskell broke the connection, relieved to know Laki would help. Was this what his vision, the two of them with a child, had really been about? She almost didn't care that he'd said *We*. She could deal with seeing Tatakla one more time.

Chapter 16

Morning came, the day Luskell would finally go out and start her life as a wizard. After Mamam left for Balsam's house, Crett clung to Luskell.

"Don't go! You stay wif me!"

She picked him up and swung him around. "Silly, didn't I stay with you yesterday? And I'll be back later. But now I have to go be a wizard."

"Be wizard wif me!"

Laughing, she turned to her father. "How do I argue with that?"

"We can go out together later, after Laki is finished here," Dadad assured her. "Or I can meet you, if you want to go to Balsam's House first."

Luskell accepted that as a good compromise. She would

slip out while Crett was busy with Laki.

When Tatakla walked in with Laki, Dadad's eyes went as wide as his smile. "How long has it been?"

"Four years since I was with the Foryin delegation. After that I was in the kitchen, but our paths did not cross."

He poured cups of tea for everyone. "Please, sit, and we can catch up. Your Eukardian is much improved."

"Thank you. I get a lot of practice living here year-round."

"But now you're returning to the Aklaka life?"

"It will still be new, going to a different band. I'm looking forward to it. It's time for a change."

Laki got down on the floor with Crett and the toy bears to ask about his dreams. There wasn't much for Luskell to do. She went outside and shut the door, but she couldn't bring herself to leave. She leaned on the railing and gazed out at the city. The breeze carried the odor of the cattle market, though she couldn't see or hear it. Was that why Crett had dreamed of the bull, or did he really see the future? She tried Listening. It was frustrating with all the dead wood and stone. They gave off the absorbed feelings from the building's inhabitants, drowning out the voices of nature, but had no story of their own. Luskell was about to give up and go to Balsam's House when the door opened behind her.

Tatakla joined her at the railing. "Your brother is very sweet."

The shared affection for Crett softened Luskell's distrust. "We're so far apart in age," she said. "He's my brother, but it's like he's my baby, too. He means everything to me."

"You were wise to call Laki to help."

"I hope so. I'd hate for Crett to be scared by his visions, or think he's doing something wrong."

"Could he hurt himself?" Tatakla asked. "I know so little of your magic."

"Maybe. Dadad and I both started with fire ..." Luskell had scorched a book, but Dadad had injured himself badly, and he'd been twelve, not two. "We have to keep him safe. There was another brother ..." How to explain about Ketwyn? "Mamam would be devastated if anything bad happened to Crett. I know she felt lucky to have me, but with Crett, she was tempting fate."

"I think I met her at least once," Tatakla said. "A small woman with red hair?"

"She's bigger on the inside. They call her Aketnan." Luskell glanced up at Tatakla. "Do you have the same legend?"

"The Peacebringer. Yes. So it chose her?"

"That's what they say. I'm not sure it's still around."

They stood in silence, watching the city and smelling cow-scented air.

Tatakla gripped the railing. "I think ... you do not like me."

Luskell turned to look at Tatakla, who continued to gaze out over the street. "Do you read thoughts, too?"

"I have no such gift. It is easy to guess."

"I want to like you, for Laki's sake. I want to believe he would choose someone worthy. But ..."

"But you want him for yourself?"

"No!" Luskell took several deliberate breaths to calm herself. "No. I let him go. I told him to find someone else. He found you. But ... I can't forget."

"Forget what?"

"I saw you ... flirting with my father." It sounded childish, but the scene played out again before Luskell's mind's eye, fresh as if it were happening in front of her. At twelve, Luskell had already been as tall as most of the adults in the room, but skinny and undeveloped. She watched as a confident young woman in a beautiful evening dress leaned toward Dadad, who was seated across from her. She smiled and laughed, and he responded with smiles of his own.

Tatakla turned to face Luskell, leaning an elbow on the railing. "Is that what you thought? Let me tell how it really was. Imagine me, nineteen years old, a newcomer in a strange city in a foreign land. I had an important job with the Foryin delegation. I was supposed to be good with languages, but I was discovering my Eukardian was not as good as I'd believed. Yet I did not feel exactly Foryani, and I had mixed feelings about my Aklaka heritage." She sighed and gazed beyond Luskell. "I was ashamed of how my father died, but I was homesick, too. Looking forward to meeting the Aklaka ambassador. But he was ill. I felt ... unsure that night."

"You didn't look unsure."

"All because of the dress. But I was seated across from a man who I thought had some Aklaka features. Perhaps he was mixed like me? Then he told a funny Aklaka story with a terrible accent, but without any self-consciousness. When I laughed before he translated it, he gave me a smile that completely put me at ease. After that I felt better about my Aklaka side, and about learning my new job. That's what you saw."

Luskell re-imagined the scene. It was exactly the same as before, but now she could picture the young woman as anxious and then reassured rather than confident and seductive. "He is good at putting people at ease," she allowed. "He knows what it's like to not fit in."

"You are lucky to have him for your father." Tatakla bowed her head and squeezed her eyes shut.

Luskell remembered her dream in Fandek's room. "I'm

sorry about your father. I can see why Aku's keeper is always single."

"I wish our Uklak had been so sensible. But every Listener has to take at least one turn."

"They serve for a season, right?" Luskell asked. "I'm sure some of Aku's keepers would appreciate the shorter term, though they might have to serve more often if there aren't enough Listeners."

"I'm glad Laki won't have to serve again," Tatakla said. "He's skilled enough, though, he wouldn't let anything happen to him. Not like my dadad."

When she used that tender word, Luskell opened herself to Tatakla's feelings. Before when she spoke of her father, she'd been filled with more rage than sorrow. Now grief drowned most of the anger. Luskell laid her hand on Tatakla's.

"It wasn't his fault."

Tatakla scowled but didn't pull her hand away. "Of course it was his fault. He took on a job he couldn't handle, and it got him killed."

"Do you really believe your Uklak would allow an unqualified person to act as keeper?" Luskell asked the question of herself, too. "It was a steam explosion, not an eruption. No warning. It would have taken the best Listener by surprise." *Even Laki,* Luskell thought with a shudder. *Even me.*

"How would you know such a thing?"

Luskell drew a deep calming breath. "Has Laki told you about my... talent? I can ... climb up from the valley." That was the Aklaka term. "I can cross over. After our supper the other night, I dreamed of the Other Side. I met your father there."

"What do you mean you met him?"

"He introduced himself. He gave me a message for you:

He's so sorry to have left you."

"If you really wanted to like me, you wouldn't mock me about this, of all things."

"If I really didn't like you, I wouldn't care how you felt about your dadad," Luskell countered. "All I know is, I dreamed of an Aklaka man in his middle years, shorter than most, with dark eyes like yours and a gap between his front teeth."

Tatakla's frown turned into an astonished gape. "His teeth ..." She squeezed her eyes shut. "You saw him?"

"I did, and his only thought was that you not be ashamed of him."

"Thank you. I will try." Tatakla wiped her eyes and managed a half smile. "I think Laki will be a good father, now that I've seen him with your brother."

Luskell welcomed the change of subject. "I think so, too. He has more patience than I do."

"And am I good enough for him?"

"He doesn't need my blessing, but I will give it if he asks. Promise to take care of him."

Luskell left for Balsam's House in better spirits. She didn't plan to work a shift, but she was eager to try out the idea of scanning patients. She donned the blue apron of a healer and considered where to begin.

"Luskell? I thought you weren't going to work here." Shura blocked her path, frowning. "Are you a wizard or a healer? Choose a side."

"Can't I choose both?" Luskell had only encountered Shura's gentle side before. She admired the forcefulness but didn't care to be its target. "My father's a wizard and he sometimes helps out here. Why can't I?"

"You don't have the right to that apron, though."

"I completed the training, same as anyone." Luskell almost laughed as she remembered her first day at Balsam's House. She had grabbed a blue apron because that's what she'd seen her mother wear. Balsam had to gently explain how she would need to wear an apprentice's brown apron at first, though she'd had some private training already. "And I thought it might make the eyepatch less upsetting."

"I can't argue with you there," Shura said.

"If it helps, Director Ketty knows I'm here. I won't get in anyone's way."

Luskell didn't want to frighten anyone with her scars, so she discreetly lifted her patch to look around from the doorway of the chronic ward. The people there were all stable. One older man was sicker than the others, but not declining at the moment. The patients in the contagious ward were farther from the door. She cast protection over herself and slipped through the spell in the doorway that prevented contagion from escaping. It had been recently refreshed; Luskell thought she detected Hanny's touch. Anyone inside, whether healer or patient, needed individual shielding. While she scanned the patients, Luskell refreshed the protection on each of them. There were only three in this ward, two on the mend, the other miserable with a fever, rash, and sore throat but not getting worse. It was such a contrast to last winter's epidemic.

Dadad, I'm ready. Meet me at Balsam's House.

Have lunch there and I'll meet you afterward. See you soon, Wizard Luskell. He put proud emphasis on *Wizard*.

She was on her way to the front door after lunch when a woman rushed in, carrying a child no older than Crett, hair and clothes dripping. "My baby! Help my baby!"

Shura came out of the nearest examination room. "Bring her here. What happened?"

"She fell into the pond! I only turned my back for a moment!"

Luskell lifted her patch. The child's light barely flickered.

Mamam! Downstairs! Drowning victim!

It couldn't be too late. Luskell knelt beside the bed as Shura felt for a pulse. She followed the fading spark and crossed without hesitation to the Other Side. The little girl already climbed the hill, but slowly, as if reluctant to go. A ribbon of sparkles fluttered from Luskell past the child and over the top of the hill.

"Stop." Luskell climbed after her and caught up. "Come back."

The child paused. Luskell chanced a look back. Mamam was in the room now. Together, they could do this.

"Your mama is waiting for you, see?"

"Mama cryin'?"

"She doesn't want you to go so far from her. Let's go back." Luskell held out her hand and the girl grasped it. They walked together down the slope. It wasn't as hard a trek as in Luskell's last dream of the place, but so slow. "Can you run? You look like a fast runner."

"I fast runner!" The child broke into a short-legged trot. It wasn't much faster than walking, but the energy helped.

Luskell opened her eyes. The girl coughed and spewed

pond water all over the bed, and Shura, and Mamam. They helped her sit up to make sure she got it all out.

Mamam met Luskell's gaze over the child's shoulder. "Not bad for your first day. Do you feel all right?"

"I didn't have to go far. You might have managed without me."

"It was easier with you. Thanks."

Mamam wrapped the child in a blanket and took her and the mother to find dry clothes and something to eat.

"I don't know what you did, but it was ... effective." Shura stripped off the soaked bedding and changed her wet apron for a dry one. "I'm sorry I gave you a hard time earlier. Bad sleep last night."

"Nightmares?"

"I ... don't remember. Maybe. I think I dreamed about something ... big. Ominous."

"I've had a few of those myself lately." A towering figure in rags, looming bony faces. And so had Bardin, Luskell recalled. A giant skeleton. If that wasn't big and ominous, what was? "Something like that can throw off your whole day." She didn't want to frighten Shura, but something mysterious was going on.

Shura nodded. "Cedar always sings your praises. Were you and she ever ..."

"We were good friends back when we went to the free school together," Luskell hastened to assure her. "We'd try to outrun the boys in footraces and see who could climb highest in trees. But I always seemed to like boys. Well, men now."

"I liked some boys, but with Cedar, it's different. More real."

"Our friend Daisy says you bring out the soft in her."

Shura blushed. "Does anyone bring out the soft in you?"

"My baby brother, Crett." Luskell was relieved to have

such an easy answer at the ready.

"I know Crett! So your mother is ..." Shura glanced out the way Mamam had gone. "She's a lot to live up to."

"You don't have to tell me."

"Tell you what?" Mamam entered the room with Fandek behind her. "Luskell, I want to test a theory. May Fandek give you a little sunshine?"

"I don't need it, but all right."

He touched her head and her spirits lifted, though they hadn't been low. She held herself back from leaning into his touch as she had that first night. Mamam watched carefully and nodded.

"Thank you, Fandek. You may go."

He smiled and lifted his hands from Luskell's head, reluctant to leave but obedient to his mentor. With a little wave, he turned and left the room.

"So what were we testing?" Luskell asked, sorry to see him go.

"When you cross over, you leave some of yourself on the Other Side, right? I think that's what I sensed when there seemed to be less of you."

"I admit it, I tried to go after Ettam."

"I understand. And I believe Fandek's sunshine restores most of what you lose. This isn't license to stay longer than might be safe, but if you're going to use this ability, you should keep it in mind."

"That's ... interesting. I will." *Most* wasn't *all*, but better than nothing. As long as she stayed close to Fandek. She could live with that. She wished she didn't like the idea so much. She wouldn't cross over for frivolous reasons, but she wouldn't hold herself back if there was a need. If she could help someone else.

"And you should work on the issue of bleeding power."

"I thought I fixed it!"

"Oh? What did you do?"

"I was ... connected to Aku." Luskell searched for the pocket of solitude. Still there, but no longer tied to the Mountain. "I ... let her go"

"It's better, down to a trickle. I'll keep an eye on it, and you'll make sure it isn't directed elsewhere."

Elsewhere. Balsam had said the Other Side drew Luskell. She imagined that strange translucent city and the faint sparkling trail behind her on the hillside. When she concentrated, she could detect the trickle of power, barely anything. She tried to pinch it off or hold it back. It kept dribbling out. It wouldn't hurt her as long as she stayed healthy and strong, but she didn't want to waste it for nothing. If the energy of a living soul was like a drug to the dead, what was magic power? Luskell couldn't work any magic on the Other Side — beyond the act of being there — so her power must have been different there. But when she crossed over, the souls of the dead felt it. If her power crossed over, even if it couldn't do anything, they would know.

More troubling still: What if it had awakened Old Mother Bones?

Chapter 17

"Who's watching Crett?" Luskell asked Dadad when he met her at Balsam's House.

"Laki and Tatakla. They're both smitten with the little fellow." His warm smile was full of affection for all concerned. "They'll want one of their own before long."

"Better them than me, I guess. So, where to first?"

Dadad gestured toward the Wizards' Hall and led the way to the entry, where he examined the array of requests pinned to the board. He plucked off two addressed specifically to him, plus another general request. Luskell didn't see anything that suited her skills. It was too early to expect anything addressed to her by name.

"I've helped these people before." He displayed the first two. "This other one seems like my kind of thing. The first one is near here."

They walked together to an area of Old Town past the coach office. Luskell hadn't spent much time there but knew the main streets and crossings. Dadad consulted one of the notes, nodded, and walked up to a door. He knocked and waited long enough that Luskell was ready to move on. The door opened and a woman peered out. Her graying hair looked hastily pinned up and she had dark circles under her eyes.

"Oh, Wizard Crane, you're here! Sorry to bother you again, but ... Well, you know. Please, come in." The woman stood back and held the door for them. Someone was crying and shouting from the back of the house.

"My daughter is with me today," Dadad said. "She's newly a wizard and learning the ropes."

"The wizard girl? All right, bring her along." The woman was too distracted to even notice Luskell's eyepatch.

They followed to the back bedroom. An older woman shuffled up and down the length of the room. She wept and shouted, "I've lost it! I can't find it!" Her long white hair had once been neatly braided but had mostly come loose as she rubbed and tugged at it. A quick look with the wizard eye showed Luskell she was in good physical health for her age, but clearly not well.

Luskell opened herself to the woman's agitation and loss, and almost wished she hadn't. What object could be so important that losing it caused this much fuss?

"I'll help you." Dadad held out his left hand, the one without scars. "We found it last time, remember?"

The old woman gripped his hand and looked into his eyes. "I think ... I remember ... you."

He led her to a chair. She sat and he pulled another chair around to face her. "I'm going to put my hands on your head. Is that all right?"

She nodded, and he laid both hands gently on top of her head. He closed his eyes, his lips moving silently.

The woman visibly calmed; she even smiled. "You'll find it. I know you will."

"It wasn't really lost. Your name is …"

"My name is Haleen. Do you know my daughter Leenya?" Luskell detected not even a hint of distress now.

"It is very nice to meet you both. I am Crane, and this my daughter, Luskell."

Luskell waited to ask until Leenya had pressed a coin into Dadad's hand and they were well away from the house. "What did you do?

Dadad sighed. "Haleen is losing her memory. Sometimes she can't remember her own name, and it doesn't do any good for her daughter to tell her. It's lost; she doesn't know who she is. I'm sure you can see how that would be upsetting."

Luskell considered. Would she know who she was if she didn't know what she was called? She thought she would, but there was no good way to test it and she didn't care to try. It was tricky enough to know whether she was a wizard, a healer … or something else. "I think I see. But if it doesn't do any good to tell her, what did you do?"

"I tidied up her thoughts so she could find what she needed. She'll feel better until they get out of order again. There may come a time when I can't help her, but until then …" He glanced back toward the house.

"Will we do the other notes now?"

"Let's walk the neighborhood first," he said. "Walk and pay attention. Look and listen. Not necessarily in the

Aklaka way, though it could be helpful. Reach out for thoughts and feelings. Let people talk. They often come to a solution on their own."

"Not so different from Balsam's House."

Luskell looked around the quiet street. It didn't seem like a neighborhood with a lot of needs, but one never knew.

Someone bumped into Dadad from behind. "Careful there!" He turned and put out a hand to steady the youngster, a boy of five or six who had been walking backward. Tears streamed down his face. "It's all right. Tell me the problem."

"My kitty ran off! I chased after her but now she's lost and so is my house!"

"I'm good with lost things." Dadad rested a hand on the child's head and shared with Luskell the images he found there: a black-and-brown cat, a house with sunflowers out front, the sign on a shoemaker's shop. "Your house is not very lost. It's just the streets don't run straight and it's easy to get mixed up. We'll walk you home, all right?"

"But what about Rags?"

"Is that your kitty's name?" Dadad smiled and ruffled the child's hair. "Knowing cats, she might be home ahead of you."

They followed a cross street into the neighborhood and soon found the shoemaker's and then the boy's house. As Dadad had predicted, the cat was having a bath on the porch as if she had been there all day.

"Rags isn't lost! How did you know?"

"Cats usually know their way around and they rarely go far," Dadad said. "It's better to wait for them than try to follow."

The boy scooped up the cat, which rubbed her face against his. "Come on, Rags, let's go inside."

"I see what you mean," Luskell said when she and Dadad were alone. "The needs find you."

"Most of the time." Dadad turned to go.

Luskell lingered under the sunflowers. "We should get a cat. I mean, if Mamam is director at Balsam's House, we're here permanently, right?"

"Well, some of us are. You're old enough to make your own choice."

"Not yet, though. I haven't even been back a week!"

"It's good to have you back." Dadad tousled her hair. "I'm not sure it's a good idea to crowd another creature in with us."

"Mamam said something about finding a bigger place," Luskell said.

"Yes, we're thinking about it." He smiled. "I never lived with a cat, but I was friends with a few in Deep River."

"Me, too," Luskell said. "Maybe if we're settled, we can get one."

"Or let one find us, the way the needs do. You can take the next one."

Luskell wasn't sure she was ready. How would she know what some random person needed? And then a woman wailed. The grief behind it struck Luskell at her core. She automatically shielded herself. But no, she needed her ability to feel what they felt.

"Should I come along?" Dadad asked.

"This feels like one for me to handle alone." She couldn't have said what about it felt that way, but she'd been learning to trust her instincts. "I'll be all right. See you later."

He went on his way and she followed the sound and the feeling to a house across the street. The door stood open. Luskell walked up to it but knocked rather than enter unannounced.

"Hello? Do you need help?"

A woman lay on the floor, weeping. She lifted her head and screamed. She stifled the cry with a hand over her mouth.

"Sorry," Luskell said. "I didn't mean to startle you. It's the eyepatch, isn't it?"

"No, it's ... your stick. Thought you were a wizard."

And two wizards would have been at least one too many, even if Dadad was the sweetest man in the world. "I am a wizard," Luskell said in the gentlest voice she could manage. "But I mean you no harm. I'll help if I can."

"The girl wizard? I heard the rumors, but ... Never mind. It's too late. Come in if you want."

Luskell stepped into the pleasant front room and saw the cause of the woman's grief. The girl had been cleaned up and lovingly laid out, but even before a glimpse with the wizard eye, it was clear no spark of life remained. The bruising and misshapen head ... There was no following this one to bring her back.

Luskell knelt by the woman. "I'm so sorry. What happened?"

"She was coming back from a friend's house last night about suppertime. Neighbors said a cart horse bolted and she was ... she was trampled and run over." The woman got up on her knees. "Folks brought her home, but she was already ..." The woman wept silently now, gazing at her dead daughter. "The worst part of it is, I scolded her before she went out. The last thing she heard from me ... She'd lost my silver bracelet, a family heirloom her father gave me when we were married. It seems silly now. But I'd planned to give it to her on her own wedding day. Now she'll never ... Only thirteen!"

Luskell didn't see anything she could do to help. She wished she'd let Dadad come with her. But he'd said let them talk.

"I'm Luskell, by the way." She held out her hand.

"Palu."

Luskell took Palu's hand and squeezed it gently. "Do you have anyone to stay with you, Palu? Do you need food or ...?"

"The neighbors helped clean her up and lay her out. They'll be back tomorrow for the burial, with plenty of food. For now, I sent them all away."

"What about her father?"

"Drowning his sorrows at the tavern, I expect." Palu spoke without anger, but Luskell detected a touch of resentment. He had left her alone when she needed him most.

"Tell me about your daughter," Luskell said, an idea taking shape. "What was she like?"

"Hard to see it now, but my Luma was a pretty child. And happy. She had a big laugh, loud and free. Always singing while she worked or played."

"She had a nice voice?"

"No! A terrible voice, off-pitch and shrieky. But she didn't care. It made her happy, so it made me happy. Now I'll never hear it anymore." Tears flowed down Palu's face.

"She had 'Lu' in her name like I do," Luskell said. "Mine is from my grandma. Luma got hers from your name, didn't she?"

"I'd planned to give her one of those flower names, but Marik wanted to be traditional. When he put it together, Lu and Ma, it was so simple and pretty, I couldn't argue."

"I wish I'd known her." Luskell didn't see much else she could do there. Her idea would have to wait. "How would it be if I sent her father home? You shouldn't be alone and I'm not much help."

"He's at the Otter. Do you know it?"

"Yes. May I stop back tomorrow and see how you're doing?"

"If you want to. We'll go to the graveyard early, back here by noon at the latest."

Luskell strode into the tavern. "Which one of you is Marik? Luma's father?"

A man raised his head from the table. He looked more mournful than drunk. "Me. Why?"

"Your wife needs you. Go home. Please."

Whether it was the staff or the eye patch or her plea, he stood. She watched him walk away until she was sure he wasn't coming back.

Chapter 18

Luskell wandered back toward Balsam's House. It was still early in the afternoon. She had planned to keep walking the neighborhood, scanning for needs, but what if she encountered someone else dead or dying? Twice in one day already seemed like a lot. She lingered near Balsam's House, undecided whether to work more there or go home. Before she'd made up her mind, Fandek came out.

"You're off early." She hoped her face didn't show how much her spirits lifted at the sight of him. She was ready to be friends, but her desires wanted to skip that step, exactly the kind of rashness that always led her into trouble.

"I'm going to visit my brother," he said. "You could come along."

"I don't know. Is it allowed?" Visiting a murderer in

prison? Helping a dying person suddenly didn't seem so bad.

"I never thought about it, but it won't hurt to ask." Fandek set off toward the prison and Luskell fell in beside him. "Are you settling in all right?"

"I'm happy to be back, but it's an adjustment." She considered how she'd spent the first half of the day. "This was the first day I tried using my wizard eye. I helped bring a child back, so that's promising. But there was another I was too late to save."

"Sorry. That's always hard," Fandek said, and she could tell he meant it. They walked a few steps in companionable silence before he spoke up again. "Are you going to Daisy's picnic tomorrow?"

Luskell stopped in her tracks. "How do you know about it?"

Fandek turned to face her. "Shura mentioned it. She seemed surprised you hadn't invited me yet."

"I told Daisy ..." Luskell stopped her sputtering and took a calming breath. Not his fault. "It started out as something for Daisy, Cedar, and me, but she didn't want to leave Ambug and Shura out."

"Oh, it would be fun to see Bug again!"

"You know Ambug?"

"I grew up in the Garden District, remember? Sometimes when Pop was in a mood, Mom would gather up me and Kerf and take us over to the Osprey to wait it out." He started walking again. "Later, I took Deklyn. Ellys offered to take us in permanently. It wasn't unusual, orphans finding a new family in the neighborhood, but Pop wouldn't hear of it. We were *his*." Fandek scowled at the memory. "It helped to have a temporary refuge, though. Bug kept us entertained and his mother always had something good for us to eat."

Luskell smiled. "I spent a lot of time with them, too. I wonder if you and I ever met as children."

"No. I would remember you."

His certainty silenced her for a time. She found her voice enough to change the subject. "But you know what else? Crett's been having visions."

"Yeah, he's told me things that could only be dreams, but they seemed more ... solid. Like they actually made sense, as much as anything someone his age tells you can make sense."

"Really? So this has been going on for ... how long?"

"I don't know. A few weeks, maybe? Could be longer. He said somebody told him my brother was going to die. He wanted to know what that meant. I don't think any of us had mentioned it, or even that I had brothers."

"Laki's trying to help him. He had a similar experience around the same age."

The conversation cut off when they arrived at the prison and approached the guard at the gate.

"Fandek, here to see Kerf."

The guard checked a list. "All right. Welcome back."

"May my friend visit, too?"

"Not unless she's on the list."

Fandek turned to Luskell with an apologetic shrug. "Thanks for coming with me."

"Anytime." *Pretend to escort me.*

Fandek twitched but didn't do anything to reveal their secret communication. "I'll ... walk you." He turned the guard. "I'll be back. This will only take a moment."

Luskell took his arm and they walked back the way they'd come, then turned the corner, out of sight. "Go on back. I'll be right behind you." She put on full concealment and followed him to the prison gate.

When the guard opened the gate for Fandek, Luskell

slipped through behind him. Too late to turn back, she remembered what Terulo had said about suppression spells worked into the stones of the walls. She half-expected a ward against invisible wizards to reveal her, or sound an alarm, or block her entry. But nothing of the kind occurred, not even the gentle touch of her father's concealment spell. She continued, unseen, on her way to visit a murderer whom she had helped capture.

The guard led them down a stone-walled hallway lit at intervals by fat candles in sconces. They passed several ordinary-looking doors, then reached an unusually stout door banded with iron. The guard looked through a small, barred opening. He unlocked the door with a big black key and waved Fandek through. Luskell followed, keeping as quiet as she could.

They descended a short flight of steps to another corridor lined with what Luskell assumed to be prison cells. They had the same kind of heavy door with a barred opening and a slot for a food tray. It was too quiet for them all to be full.

The guard stopped outside a door about halfway down and peered through the barred opening. "Hey, Kerf, you've got a visitor."

From within, a voice growled, "Who?"

"Same as always, your brother. Stand back, now."

From inside echoed a sound of metal on stone. The guard unlocked the cell door. "You've got an hour. I'll pass by on my rounds before then. Shout if you need anything." He opened the door and Fandek entered with Luskell right behind him. They were locked in with the strangler.

Kerf sat in a pile of bedding in the corner farthest from the door. The last time Luskell had seen him, he'd shaved both his face and his head, and sometimes wore a black false beard as a disguise. All these months later, his own hair and beard had grown out in shaggy dark-gold profusion. When he stood, he was of similar height to Fandek, but skinnier. He moved awkwardly in leg irons, the chain only long enough to reach the food tray when it was slid through.

"Well, brother, what have you brought me today?"

"Salve, sunshine ... and another visitor."

Luskell dropped concealment. Kerf started back, his chain grating against the floor.

"What do you know, the ugly witch who called me a monster."

"I'm not a witch."

"She's not ugly," Fandek said at the same time.

"If you say so. I can't believe you're with her."

"He's not," Luskell snapped.

"I'm not, but I would be."

That silenced both Luskell and Kerf. To cover her embarrassment, she lifted the patch. Kerf burned with steady light but lower and paler than a person in perfect health. "You'll live long enough to be executed."

Kerf sank back down to his bed. "Could have told you that. It's not long now."

Fandek knelt in front of him, closer to those hands than Luskell would have liked. He applied salve to sores on Kerf's ankles where the iron rubbed. It struck Luskell that a person of power and ill intent could easily unlock the irons, open the door, and spirit the prisoner away. This prison was not as well-guarded as it appeared.

Fandek spoke healing words that must have included sunshine because Kerf's spirits lifted.

"You must be Fandek's wizard-girl friend. What's your name again?"

"Luskell. I know your name already. I'm not sure why I'm here."

Fandek took up a position near the door so he could listen for the guard. "I hoped you'd tell him about the Other Side. Since he's going there soon."

"What do you want to know?"

"First off, why you're the expert." Kerf squinted at her in the dim light. "You've been there, have you?" His face sneered but his thoughts and feelings lifted with a hope he didn't dare cling to.

"I've ... visited. Crossing over is one of my abilities."

"Is it terrible there? Will I be punished for my crimes?"

"Not exactly. It's peaceful. And boring. You'll probably meet your victims, without any power over them. That could be ... uncomfortable. It could lead to some measure of redemption, though."

"Will I see my mother again?"

"Probably. Maybe your father, too."

"Not my first wish. Mom, though ... I'd like to tell her sorry."

"It wasn't your fault she died," Fandek said. "You were only a boy."

"What happened?" Luskell asked. "Were you there when she ...?"

"... was murdered?" Kerf looked straight at her and spoke in a matter-of-fact tone, but his hands trembled. "Yeah, I stood there and watched. Pop used to knock both of us around, but when he really wanted to keep Mom in line, he'd choke her till she passed out. Sometimes it didn't even leave a mark. When she came to, she'd be quiet and ... tame, the way he liked her. When I was small, I'd run and hide, but later, I'd spy on him and watch. It made me feel ... strange. My fingers itched to be that powerful. But the last time, she didn't wake up. I had to get out of there." He sagged and Fandek returned to give him more sunshine. "You called me a monster. I'm not but ... I have a monster in me. If I have to die to kill it, then it's worth it."

Luskell moved closer. "May I read your thoughts?"

"What good would that do?"

"Maybe none, I don't know." She remembered Dadad saying something terrible had happened that twisted Kerf beyond fixing. "It might tell us something useful."

She rested her hands on his tangled, dirty hair. She'd tried reading his thoughts once before, when she didn't yet know he was the strangler. She hadn't been touching him and had not managed to make any sense of his mind. When she reached for his thoughts now, she found a jumble: normal fear and despair, twisted desires, fractured memories of his father beating and killing his mother; of small Fandek shutting his eyes and protecting even smaller Deklyn. And caged within, the monster: the compulsion to kill with his bare hands, locked down through force of will. It stirred, all its attention on Luskell. Kerf trembled with the effort to hold it in. She jumped back as his hands rose toward her throat.

"Don't touch me!" she spat.

"Sorry," Kerf said. "See what I mean? It's not me. I try to control it but ... I'm too weak."

"Good thing you'll be dead soon," she said.

Kerf nodded. "I wish you'd kill me now and get it over with. You wanted to before, with the lightning."

Too shocked to answer, Luskell wondered. He was right, she had wanted to, but could she? Would she?

"Guard's coming," Fandek whispered.

Luskell concealed herself again. Fandek let the guard know they were ready to leave, though the full hour wasn't up. She followed Fandek out and dropped concealment when they were a block away from the prison.

Fandek turned to her with a sad smile. "Thank you for coming with me. He's been worried."

"I don't know if I helped. I woke up the monster."

"I can't imagine it sleeps much."

Luskell considered that as she walked. She was glad for Fandek's company during the visit and afterward. How had he endured these visits alone? "You ... can come with me to the picnic. If you want."

"Really? I'd like to. Does that mean we're courting now?" He reached for her hand.

"No." Luskell drew her hand back before he could clasp it. Their fingertips brushed and she half-regretted her move. There was something more than sunshine in his touch. "I mean, I don't know. This picnic is for friends. We'll start there, all right?"

Fandek sighed. "Not so long ago, you didn't like me at all. I should be happier you consider me a friend."

"It's all I trust myself to give right now. So if you don't want to come, I'll understand."

"I didn't say that! I wouldn't miss this picnic for anything."

That night, Luskell imagined a pretty girl just past childhood who laughed loudly and sang badly. When she slept, she found herself on the Other Side, and Luma was with her.

"You're not dead, are you?"

"No, I'm a wizard. Your mother is sorry she scolded you. She didn't want it to be the last thing you heard from her."

"I know. I'm sorry I made her cry."

"Would you have gone to your friend's house if she hadn't scolded you?"

"Yes, we had plans!"

"Then you didn't make her cry. The horse did." Horse. Something about a horse and Ketwyn ... Later. "And she doesn't care that you lost her bracelet."

"But I didn't lose it! I took it. I wanted it, so I hid it in my knitting basket. I wish I could give it back to her."

"And she wanted you to have it, when you were older."

"She did? Does that make it better or worse?"

"I don't know, it just is." Luskell thought a moment. "Do you have people here?"

"One of my grandmothers, and an aunt I never met before. Why?"

"I understand you can keep learning, maybe grow older here. And you can watch the people you care about."

"How do you know if you're not dead?"

"Because her brother is here." Ketwyn stood at Luskell's side as if he had been there all along. "Luskell, you know you shouldn't be here."

"No, I know someone doesn't want me here. There's a difference." She turned back to the girl. "Luma, this is my brother Ketwyn. He's been here his whole ... time. He grew up here."

"How awful! I'm sorry," Luma said.

"Don't be. I never knew anything else. Luskell?"

"I know, I know, but I need to ask you something. What was it?" About a horse? That made no sense. Dreams made no sense.

"No, you don't." Ketwyn was never so stern. "She'll have felt your presence by now. You need to go. Now."

He gave her a gentle shove, but a shove, nonetheless. Luskell fell and kept falling till ...

    ... she woke in her own bed. Now Knot and Ketwyn were both angry with her. She didn't understand and couldn't ask if she wasn't allowed on the Other Side. She would have to wait for them to explain.

    "Fine," she muttered. "But I won't wait forever."

Chapter 19

After another morning helping at Balsam's House, Luskell walked with Fandek and Shura to the Garden District for Daisy's picnic. The noon air was almost summer-warm, with a hint of fall coolness.

Cedar joined them a few blocks from Balsam's House, dressed as usual in shirt and trousers, similar to Luskell's travel clothes.

"I didn't greet you properly before." Cedar grinned and pulled Luskell into a tight hug. "Good to have you back."

"It's mostly good to be back."

"Hey, Sunshine!" Cedar shook hands with Fandek and slapped him on the back. "So she did invite you, after all."

"As a friend," he said, before Luskell could clarify.

Cedar and Shura exchanged a knowing smile. They

joined hands for the walk to Braffin's Garden. "Luskell, you still owe me the story about your eye."

"Oh, let me tell it!" Fandek said.

"I suppose you won't embarrass me any worse than I would myself. Go ahead."

"Have either of you been to Deep River?" Fandek began. "I hadn't either. Little tiny place in the middle of nowhere on the Dry Side. Anyway, Luskell went to stay with her grandmother there, and I went after her because I'd dreamed she was in danger."

"What kind of danger?" Cedar asked.

"The dream wasn't clear," he said.

"They rarely are," Luskell muttered.

"It was snowing pretty hard, but we were all safe and snug at the inn. Luskell taught me to mind talk to pass the time. She went out to see a friend, but then I heard her voice in my mind, saying to meet her at such-and-such a place — someone needed help. When I got there, she'd saved a local girl from ..." Fandek cleared his throat. "From the strangler."

Cedar and Shura gasped and grinned at each other. It did make a thrilling story, once it was all over.

Do they know who he is? Luskell was glad she had taught him to mind-talk that night. Better to ask privately than risk revealing his secret.

Fandek shook his head and continued his story. "He'd run away from the city and was hiding in disguise. He escaped out the window and we chased him. The storm had cleared enough that I could see him in the moonlight. I thought I could catch him, but I tripped and fell on my face in the snow. But you should have seen Luskell! She looked like a mighty wizard, cloak whipping in the wind, hands raised, all sparking and glowing. A bolt of lightning struck right where the strangler was running. If he hadn't fallen just before, it would have hit him. As it was, an old stump exploded. The strangler took enough splinters in his leg to keep him from running any more. Luskell got the worst of it, though. Splinters in her face, and a big one right in the eye."

"Luskell, you're a hero!" Cedar exclaimed.

"It sounds better the way he tells it," Luskell allowed. "What's more important, my injured eye has its own magic now. It can see how much life is in someone. That's why I'm working at Balsam's House again."

Luskell had worked up an appetite by the time they reached the entrance to the garden. Late roses perfumed the air. Maple leaves glowed golden and green in the afternoon sunlight. Oaks held mostly green leaves; some had bright red edges. She couldn't imagine a more perfect day for a picnic.

Luskell looked up at the statue of Good King Braffin as she passed. Did he resemble her father as much as people said? Or really, the other way around. He looked trustworthy, so they had that in common.

Her group met Daisy and Ambug between the statue and the fountain. They had spread a blanket on the grass, which was greening up again after the heat and drought of summer. They unpacked a lunch of cold roast chicken, apples, and fresh bread, with a jug of ale to wash it down.

"Daisy, this is my friend Fandek," Luskell said. "Shura and Cedar already know him, and I just found out Ambug does, too."

Ambug ran his hand through his pale hair and stood up to shake hands. "Little Fandek? How long has it been?"

"*Little*? I don't want to start a fight, but I think I'm taller than you now." Fandek stood next to Ambug. He was taller, but Ambug was much broader in the chest and shoulders. "But you haven't seen me in at least five years. I was shorter then."

"Five years." Ambug flopped back onto the blanket. "How's Baby Deklyn?"

"Good, though not a baby. He's a stableboy at the coach office now, and I'm working at Balsam's House."

"A healer? Good for you. No wonder you know these two." Ambug waved toward Cedar and Shura. "Is that how you met Luskell, too?"

Luskell laughed. "No, we met when he didn't show sufficient respect and I knocked him on his backside."

"True story," Fandek allowed. "I thought I was going to be a wizard, but healing suits my skills better."

"And he must have learned respect," Daisy said.

"She taught me that lesson, yes," Fandek replied with a laugh.

Luskell enjoyed the good food and good company of old friends and new. Fandek didn't say anything that would make her think less of him — far from how he'd been when they met, when he was trying to find his place in the world.

At the end of the picnic, Daisy and Ambug headed back to the Osprey, Ambug's mother's tavern. Fandek and Shura walked ahead, talking shop, but Luskell hung back with Cedar.

"So, are you on staff at Balsam's House, too?" Luskell asked.

"No, my practical skills are better suited to the neighborhood. Did you ever meet my granny? She was the neighborhood midwife when we were children."

"I don't think so. Any magic?"

"None that I ever saw. She used to take me along when she'd check on her mamas or deliver a baby, at first to watch the other children in the house and later to assist her. I went to Balsam's House for more training. If someone needs magic to cure them, I send them there. Or send for your mother, like the other night."

Luskell shivered. "That was a close one, even with her. Is Nalya all right now?"

"She should be fine. Stunned as he was, I wasn't sure how much to expect from her fellow, but he's taking good care of both of them."

"So you'll always bring the father in to help at the end?" Luskell asked.

"That might be taking things too far! But some of them are all right. What about you? Are you going to make a career of bringing people back to life?"

"I ... don't know about *career*." But in spite of Ketwyn's warnings, Luskell had added Crossing Over to her entry already. "If I'm there at the right moment, I'll do what I can."

"That's all any of us can do."

Luskell nodded toward the pair ahead of them. "I like Shura. I hope you're as good for her as she is for you."

"Me, too. I'm not the easiest to live with."

"And you're not even a wizard!"

Cedar laughed. "What about Fandek? Is he the one?"

"The one what?"

"The one who won't find you hard to live with."

"It's much too soon to say but ... well, I let him come along today. That's more than I would have done a few months ago. We can at least be friends."

A burly, baldheaded man stared at them from a doorway as they passed. Luskell gripped her staff and reached out with her senses, detecting nothing more menacing than a self-important man. She made eye contact to let him know she was fully aware of his presence and not intimidated.

The man snorted. "Can't tell the boys from the girls these days."

Cedar rolled her eyes but otherwise ignored him.

Fandek turned back with a laugh. "If you can't tell, there must be something wrong with your eyes. Not that any of us care what you think, but I'd be careful of the tall one if I were you."

Luskell lit her staff with illusion flame and brandished it, nowhere near the man. He flinched, then turned the movement into an almost-dignified retreat indoors.

Cedar laughed. "So you're going to make your reputation as the scary wizard girl."

"When the opportunity presents itself ..." Luskell let the illusion fire go. "As Balsam says, there's a place for some show."

"Men like him are exhausting," Cedar said. "I'm almost home. Do you three mind if I head inside?"

"Here, let me make you uninteresting before you go." Luskell cast a spell over Cedar to deflect attention. "There, no one else will bother you."

She walked on with Fandek and Shura until a movement in a narrow cross street caught her attention. A calico cat pounced on a mouse in the shadows. She was sure it was Rags but didn't see the cat's boy. She hoped that meant he'd taken Dadad's advice to wait for the cat to come home rather than following her. She sent the other two on and turned up the side street. She soon found Luma's house again. The front door stood open. The burial was over and the house was full of mourners, eating, drinking, crying, some even laughing. She found Luma's mother Palu in a knot of other women. Most of them recoiled from Luskell, and she couldn't blame them. Why was this stranger, this unusually tall girl with an eyepatch and a wizard's staff, intruding on their grief?

One of the women, older than Palu but with similar features, stepped in front of Palu as if to shield her. "What do you want? You don't belong here."

Palu gently moved the woman aside. "It's all right, cousin. Luskell is a friend." She held out a hand for Luskell to clasp. "I'm surprised to see you. Didn't think you'd actually come back, but you are welcome."

"I dreamed of Luma last night," Luskell said. "She wanted you to look in her knitting basket."

The other women exchanged startled glances. Palu gripped Luskell's arm and dragged her to a room at the back of the house. She dumped yarn and unfinished knitting onto the bed. Something metal tinked against the needles. A silver cuff bracelet, etched with intricate designs.

The woman gasped and picked it up.

"Is that it?" Luskell asked. "It's beautiful. No wonder you treasured it." *No wonder Luma wanted it.*

The woman thrust it into Luskell's hands. "Here, take it. As payment."

Luskell tried to return it. "I've barely done anything. And didn't you say it was an heirloom?"

"I can't have it here. It's ... cursed. Please take it. Sell it if you want."

"Cursed?" Luskell sensed for magic in the bracelet. There was ... something. Age, and more. But nothing evil.

"Not for you," Palu clarified. "Only for me."

"How about if I borrow it?" Luskell suggested. "I'd like to study it. I'll bring it back when I'm finished. You can decide then what to do with it."

Luma's mother nodded but didn't try to speak. Luskell slipped the bracelet into her pocket and left the house. Rather than going home or seeking more needs in the neighborhood, she went to the library. She found Terulo at his desk under the windows. The array of books and papers didn't seem much different from before. She set the bracelet in front of him.

He sat back and looked at her. "What brings you sneaking up?"

"Someone gave this to me. She said it was cursed. I couldn't sense anything, but ..."

Terulo picked it up and examined it. "Hmm. It's old, though. Look how part of the design is worn smooth."

"I thought I felt something, but not magic."

"You're sensitive to emotions, so you would. It's not exactly enchantment, but it's related. Wait, I was just reading something." He thumbed through a book until he found the passage. "'Ordinary objects can absorb strong emotion from the people using them, especially if the same person keeps the object close to them for an extended period. Over time, the emotion can affect the character of the object in subtle ways. One that has absorbed mostly positive feelings might give its wearer a sense of wellbeing, while one with mostly negative feelings, a sense of unease.'"

Luskell considered this. She had already observed how the trees outside Balsam's House held the feelings emitted by that place. It was easy to accept with something alive, but cold metal? But she had felt something like veiled sunshine in the medallion in Fandek's room, and traces of emotion in the paving stones at the site of one of the strangler's attacks. And what about her fiddle, made especially for her, or her green silk dress? Maybe it wasn't special only because it was beautiful, but because the fabric and stitches were infused with Tulia's fondness and gratitude. She was glad she would get to keep wearing part of it.

She slid the bracelet onto her wrist. It was cool at first but soon warmed. "A bracelet is worn next to the skin, and it's less ... ordinary than most clothing. Might it absorb more emotion than other things?"

"Yeah, good thought. Your eyepatch is probably the same way."

Luskell's hand went to the patch in a reflexive though not self-conscious way. "True, it is about more than hiding scars now. And Jagryn made it for me."

"He was in here the other day, updating his entry. I was surprised to see him with a girl who wasn't you." Terulo raised his eyebrows at Luskell.

"That was Ruvhonn. He was with her because he's her husband."

"Then we both know how it feels to have someone we liked marry someone else."

"I have two of those, but they're both better off," Luskell said. He'd never told her in words who his *someone* was, but it had been easy to guess. "I heard Virosh was back."

Terulo flinched. "So much for secrets. I suppose everyone knows."

"Not everyone is sensitive to emotion, and I haven't told anyone. Have you seen him?"

"Only to say hello. Not like I ever had a chance with him. He wasn't going to give me a silver bracelet or anything like that."

"So you're feeling it, too?" Luskell turned the bracelet on her wrist.

"Feeling what?"

"That it absorbed a lot of ... well, love, I guess."

"Not everyone is sensitive to emotion," he quoted her. "That's the kind of thing it *is*: a love gift. You didn't know that?"

"Why would I? I don't come from silver-bracelet kind of people. No offense to those who do."

"None taken." Terulo made a slight bow.

"It doesn't feel cursed at all, but that poor woman had

suffered a great loss," Luskell said. "Maybe it's better she's not wearing it right now."

"I wonder how old it is," Terulo said. "A silversmith might be able to tell."

"There's a silversmith on my street! I'll ask him."

"Can I come along? I need to get outside and move around."

As they crossed the square, Luskell remembered something else she'd meant to ask Terulo. "You read me something about the prison's walls being infused with suppression magic. When I visited, there didn't seem to be anything to stop me from sneaking in and freeing prisoners."

"The place was built a long time ago," Terulo said. "The magic might have worn off."

"And if it's forgotten magic, no one knows how to restore it." Luskell paused. "Is it forgotten? Dadad said you helped him find that book ..."

"Well, none of us learned about it from our masters. But maybe Master Crane can bring it back."

"Or fix the prison, anyway."

Luskell and Terulo passed near Wyll and Kiat's shop on the way to the silversmith's. Their son Wyllik emerged and began hanging fabrics for display. Luskell waved to him and he waved back.

Wyllik paused in his work as they crossed the street. "Who's your friend, Luskell?"

"This is Terulo. He's working on being a scholar-wizard."

The two young men shook hands. "Is there much call for that kind of work?" Wyllik asked.

"I don't know, but it interests me. There's no end of forgotten knowledge."

"It's lucky to get to do something you enjoy and are

good at, like our Luskell here. If any girl could be a wizard, she could." Wyllik, though shorter than Luskell, ruffled her hair like a proud big brother.

"How do you like the textile business?" Terulo asked.

"It's good. I have a head for business, my father says, and an eye for color and texture. And I meet a lot of different people. Not many wizards, though, besides the ones living upstairs."

"I'll have to stop by again; keep your wizard numbers up."

"Sure, I'd ... *we'd* be happy to see you."

They said their goodbyes and continued on their way to the silversmith's on the next block.

"Is he your new sweetheart?" Terulo asked. "Nice looking fellow."

"No, an old friend. Well, old in that I've known him my whole life. He's probably about your age. We rent rooms from his parents."

"Oh?" Terulo said. "Oh."

His smile had a private look about it. Luskell shielded herself from emotions that might leak out. It was easy enough to guess. She supported his interest, though she had once thought Wyllik might be interested in her. He had even given her a sloppy, awkward kiss on her last birthday. But now it seemed more like joking around with his sister's friend. And Fandek said Wyllik had been working out something personal.

They walked into the shop and Luskell set the bracelet on the counter. "Can you tell me anything about this?"

The smith turned, all his attention on the bracelet. "Let's have a look." He picked it up and examined it carefully. "Looking to sell it?"

"No, this is research. The woman who gave it to me said it was an heirloom."

"I'll say it is. Probably for ten or twelve generations."

"You can tell by looking?"

"It's this mark, here." He showed them the small mark, stamped or engraved on the inside. "This smith was a master craftsman. I've seen some of his pieces before, with similar designs. This is probably at least three hundred years old."

Terulo whistled softly. "Besides the age, is there anything special about it?" he asked. "Is it legendary or anything?"

"Not likely, but that doesn't mean it isn't special. In those days, something like this was often a wedding gift from a man to his bride. She'd wear it on special occasions, then hand it down to a daughter on her wedding day, or to her son to present to his bride. Lovely old tradition."

Luskell nodded. "And that's how it gets to be an heirloom. Thank you, it's helpful to know."

"Are you sure you won't sell it? I'd give gold for that silver."

"It's not mine to sell." She slipped it onto her wrist again and sensed for the emotions it held. Most were positive, but others mixed in — a touch of grief, a dash of disappointment, making the love more poignant. "I'll get to know it better, and then I'll return it."

Chapter 20

"Do you mind if I skip Balsam's House this morning?" Luskell asked her mother the next day. "I want to walk the neighborhood again." She had let Dadad go without her. She needed to learn to do it alone.

"It shouldn't do any harm if you skip a day, or stop in later," Mamam said, cleaning breakfast off Crett's face and hands.

Luskell hurried through her own breakfast and headed out. Her first experience walking the neighborhood had been disturbing but educational, and she thought she'd done some good. It would take practice, but it felt like the right way to use her abilities. She was passing the Wizards' Hall, planning where to begin, when a youthful voice called her name.

"Luskell! You're all right!"

"Hey, Lucky. Why wouldn't I be?"

Lucky ran his hands through his dark hair, leaving it more unruly than before. "No reason. Come here, you need to see this." He pointed toward the Wizards' Hall.

"What do I need to see?"

"The board."

"Oh?" She followed the boy into the entry and glanced over the notes pinned to the board. Then she took a closer look. "Oh. OH!"

She plucked notes off to read. Four were addressed to her by name, another four to "the Wizard Girl," and one to "Death's Friend."

"I heard people talking," Lucky said. "About how you saved a drowned baby and brought a message from someone's dead child. That kind of news spreads fast."

"So I see. Thanks for letting me know, I guess." She crushed the notes in her hand.

"Are ... are you really all right?" Lucky asked.

"Yeah," Luskell sighed. "I didn't expect to find notes addressed to me for weeks or months, and certainly not nine all at once."

The boy's face reddened. "No, what I mean is, I dreamed you were dead."

"Obviously I'm not." Luskell smiled to ease his worry.

"I know, but ... I dreamed *I* killed you. It seemed so real, I was worried you might have been hurt."

"*You* killed *me*?" Luskell asked. "How?"

"Remember that heavy wooden ball we used to practice repelling? I hit you in the head and you dropped. Then a tall, skinny woman in a raggy dress came and carried you away."

"What about that seemed real?" Luskell held up a hand. "You don't have to answer that. Just remember she can't hurt either of us in dreams."

"Right, it was only a dream. I'm glad you're not dead."

"Me, too." Luskell shuddered. It didn't matter whether Knot visited her dreams. Old Mother Bones was closing in, anyway, visiting people who knew Luskell. But she had no power in dreams. Luskell opened her hand to examine the wad of notes. She needed advice but didn't want to keep running back to her parents. They weren't her only mentors, though. "Is Bardin here, by any chance?"

"I haven't seen him yet, but it's early."

Luskell stepped outside and sank down on the front steps. Bardin had said he lived close by. She reached out with her mind and after a few misses, found his.

Master, I need your advice.

I'm making a slow start this morning. Why don't you come here?

He gave her the address, only three blocks away, and instructed her to knock at the side door. At least it wasn't the back door. As it turned out, she had passed the house hundreds of times on her way to Daisy's, across the street and two doors down. It was large, though not a mansion. Based on what Bardin had said, several generations of the family shared its three stories. She found the side door and knocked.

Bardin opened the door and flinched. "Sorry. Not used to the eyepatch yet. Please, come in." He ushered her into a snug sitting room where a low fire burned in the grate. A plate with crumbs hinted at a recently finished breakfast. Steam rose from a teapot. "I brewed a fresh pot after I heard from you."

While he filled two cups, Luskell studied him as well as she could without lifting the patch. He looked as exhausted as he had the day she'd come back to the city.

"Bad dreams again?" she asked.

"Not that I remember. I have been worrying about a friend who's ill, though. I'm at the age where my friends are all starting to die off." He forced a smile, though it didn't reach his eyes. "A good reason to make some younger friends. What can I help you with?"

Luskell dropped the heap of notes onto the table. "Word of my unique talent has gotten out. What do I do with all these?"

"You respond, if you can. Have you read them?"

"A quick glance. It's overwhelming!"

"It helps to take them one at a time. Weed out the unreasonable ones."

Luskell took a calming breath, sipped her tea, and unfolded the first note. "This one says his uncle hinted at treasure hidden in his house but died before he could reveal its location. He's offering to split it with me if I can get the uncle to tell where it is." She frowned. "He doesn't need me crossing over. He needs a good finder."

"Which you are. Will you help him?"

"You mean I get to choose? I don't *have* to do it?"

"You're expected to read the request and respond to the ones that suit your skills and make sense."

"This one feels ... greedy." Luskell's gift revealed the writer's emotions, absorbed by the note. "Like he expects me to be as greedy for the treasure as he is."

"You don't strike me as someone who chases after money," Bardin said. "Wizards rarely need it. You've probably noticed."

She nodded. "My parents will pay for a meal at the tavern, but Berdona usually throws in something extra. People Dadad helps will press a few coins on him, or something else useful. Someone gave me this bracelet, but I don't plan to keep it." She extended her arm to show it.

"My family has one of those," Bardin said. "I would have

given it to the girl I told you about, but it had already been handed down to my sister on her wedding day."

Luskell set the first note aside and picked up the next. "This one is too sad. A mother wants me to bring her baby back, but it died last winter. I might go talk to her, but I can't do what she wants." There was one more similarly impossible request to restore a dead child. The one after that wanted Grandma's secret honey-bun recipe, and the next two, some lost trinket, none of which seemed worth the risk of crossing over. Two wanted to be taken to the Other Side to visit departed loved ones, something Luskell didn't know how to do even if she thought it was safe. The last she picked up was the one addressed to Death's Friend.

Life for me is nothing but pain. Please help me.

The signature was not legible, but the address was written clearly. Luskell silently passed the note to Bardin. He read it and looked at her.

"What does she want from me?" Luskell asked.

"She wants you to help her with her pain."

"But why me?" Luskell could relieve pain, though not as easily as her mother; not as sweetly as Fandek, with his sunshine. "I guess I should at least talk to her. Maybe I can give her enough relief so she can go to Balsam's House. Or if she's dying, go with her to the Other Side." The way the note was addressed implied it might be what the person really wanted.

Out of the nine notes, she had rejected six and accepted three for further discussion. Maybe it wouldn't be so bad. But if there were this many each day ...

"You should consider teaching a few others to do what you do," Bardin said. "It might suit healers better than wizards, but you taught your friend Jagryn, didn't you?"

"I taught him to cross over in dreams, but that can be more dangerous than it is useful," she said. "Following someone who is dying — that would be a good skill for any healer. But right now, I don't know. They keep telling me it isn't safe. Something over there doesn't want me intruding."

"And we both know how much respect you have for prohibitions." Bardin kept a serious expression, but his eyes twinkled.

"I'm trying to be careful. I'll cross over if I think it will do some good, but I'm not ready to endanger anyone else."

After their meeting, Bardin walked with Luskell as far as the Wizards' Hall. She went on by herself to visit the first of the bereaved mothers, who lived only a few houses from Palu, Luma's mother. She had four living children under the age of twelve. A fifth, a daughter not yet two, had died in the wobbles outbreak the previous winter.

"I heard you brought a little one back to life. Could you maybe ...?"

"She wasn't quite gone. I'm sorry, I can't bring yours back." Luskell hoped her face didn't look as anxious as she felt. What was she doing here, with nothing to offer?

"Everyone's sorry!" the mother wailed. "No one can do anything. I thought another woman might understand, but you're really only a girl. My baby's gone and I can't have another!"

This was beyond Luskell's understanding, but she nodded sympathetically. "I ... I could watch for your child when I'm on the Other Side, if you'll tell me who to look for."

The mother wiped her eyes. "You don't mean it. Why would a wizard care?"

"She would have been about the same age as my baby brother," Luskell said. "I'd like to hear about her, whatever you feel like telling me."

Luskell listened until the woman ran out of words. She

didn't know what good it would do but reminded herself of Dadad's advice and kept quiet until she finished.

"She sounds like a delightful little girl," Luskell said. "I'm sorry I can't help you the way you want."

"It was good to talk about her. Most people don't want to listen anymore. They say I should be happy I still have the other four."

"You can be happy about them without forgetting your baby. But those four need their mother."

"I know." She sighed. "I wouldn't have expected a wizard to sit and listen to me go on and on."

"Some will and some won't. I'm learning from the ones who will."

Before leaving, Luskell looked at the four children with her wizard eye and reassured their mother they were all in good health. After that, she visited the home of a woman who had suffered three miscarriages before finally carrying a pregnancy to term. But something had gone wrong and the baby died within days of birth. The woman's husband treated her kindly, but gingerly, as if he feared she would break if he touched her.

"If we could have our baby back, maybe we could go on as we were. Be happy."

"I wish I could bring him back. Perhaps if I'd been here ..." Once again out of her depth, Luskell fell back on letting her talk. It had helped once. "Tell me all about him, so if I meet him, I'll know."

"No one else wants to hear about him. They say I should forget him and try again."

"Oh, don't forget! Your baby is on the Other Side as long as someone living remembers him," Luskell said. Finally, something she could be sure of. "He'll grow up there and watch over you. Try again if you want to, but don't forget."

It turned out the mother had detailed memories of those

few days, about tiny ears, little fingers and toes, the way her child startled when he sneezed. She wept while she talked but took heart from putting her memories into words. From being heard. She even smiled as she finished.

"I don't know if this will help. Let me tell you the story of another mother," Luskell said. "Her first baby died soon after birth, much like yours. It crushed her. She didn't think she would ever recover, but with help and remembering, she started living again. And eventually she had another child. That one lived and is sitting with you now."

"I don't know if I dare ..." the woman said, her eyes full of hope.

"That's between you and your husband. If you do happen to conceive, go to Balsam's House and ask for Healer Ketty. She'll be able to tell if there are any problems, and if they can be healed."

"I've heard of her! Why would such an important person want to help me?"

Luskell smiled, recalling Mamam cleaning porridge off Crett's face. "She's a mother, too. She wants babies to live, if they can. Tell her Luskell sent you."

Chapter 21

The whole morning had passed and Luskell had one note to take care of. She wanted to help the person, but not on an empty stomach. She was tired, too. Listening to people talk without doing anything for them was almost as much work as healing or levitation. She planned to eat lunch at Balsam's House but as she walked back, she changed her mind. She didn't like feeling unwelcome at the Wizards' Hall, but she couldn't expect it to change unless she made a point of stopping in as if there were no problem.

Bardin was leaving the dining room as she entered.

"Productive morning, Luskell?" he asked.

"I hope so. They mostly needed someone to talk to. I've saved the hardest one for after lunch."

"You'll be fine. Let me know how it goes."

Luskell filled a plate and found a seat at the table. The masters and most of the apprentices seated there pointedly ignored her. Dalmer, a boy she considered an ally, smiled at her, then turned away at a frown from his master. She had resigned herself to a silent, lonely lunch when Terulo came in.

"Just the wizard I wanted to see!" He quickly loaded a plate with food and sat across from Luskell. "I've found an important piece of that spell we were talking about. I'm ready for your help."

A few seats down, Master Larem snorted. "As if *she* could offer any real help."

Terulo glanced in his direction but otherwise ignored the comment. "Are you free after lunch?"

"Tell me more," Luskell said, happy for anything to take her mind off the icy welcome of the other wizards. "Did you finish it?"

"There's a chunk missing, but the first part is complete."

"What does the first part do?"

"It opens a doorway between where you are and another location you can see."

"See with your eyes?" Luskell asked.

"Right. There's a more complicated version that takes you to a place you know but can't physically see, but there's too much of it missing for me to be sure my guess is right."

"I have time now, if I'm the best person to help you." Luskell glanced meaningfully at Larem.

"It's for my quest. Any help has to come from wizards other than my master," Terulo explained. He raised his voice, as if to make sure the others would hear. "And you're the most powerful young wizard I know."

Luskell stifled a laugh. "You can count on me. Let's go."

Restored by the good food, Luskell and Terulo left the Wizards' Hall together and returned to his desk in the library.

"I don't think Master Larem approves of me helping you," Luskell said. "He has never liked me."

"If it makes you feel better, it's not only you." Terulo flipped through a book on his desk.

"Right, he doesn't like women in general."

"It's more than that. He's put off by ... bodies. Women's bodies especially, but really anything material — illness, blood and other fluids, birth, death."

"I didn't know. So what isn't he put off by?"

"His specialties are all about energy: fire, light, wind. And stars. He says they sing." Terulo paused on a page where fragments had been pieced together with a corner still held by the binding. "That's probably why he took me on as apprentice. I'm interested in stars, too." He gazed out the window. "And no one else wanted me."

"I didn't know that, either. I'm sorry," Luskell said. "You said you can't actually work spells. How did you learn you had power?"

"Dreams. I didn't think they meant anything, but my mother was sure I would have great power. She took me to the Wizards' Hall when I was twelve and insisted they test me."

"Good thinking. Were there wizards in her family?"

"A long time ago. The Wizards' Hall used to be the family mansion, before they moved to a better neighborhood. Anyway, they tested me but I couldn't do anything. Master Larem was the only one to notice or care that I could read and understand the books."

"When you've finished your quest, I could teach you to Listen to the stars."

"Maybe. Let's do this job first."

"Is that it?" She examined the pieced-together page. As he'd said, at least one piece was missing from the middle of the page but the lines above the hole appeared complete.

"The original is worn and faded, but I've copied it out," Terulo said. "Can you work with this?"

Luskell took the page and studied it. He had used spell ink, so random syllables rearranged themselves before her eyes into a sequence that made sense. They wouldn't do that for a person with no power. There was a gap in the middle of the page to correspond with the hole in the original. Terulo had guessed at what might fill the gap, using regular ink.

"All right," Luskell said, "so I look where I want to go, work the spell, step through, and I'm there? Sounds simple enough." She looked straight down the mezzanine. "There." She pointed to the next desk over, no more than five steps away — a safe target.

Luskell took a few deep breaths and focused her gaze on the spot by the desk. She drew on her power and spoke the words while tracing the shape of a doorway with her staff. A faintly glowing rectangle appeared before her, framing a view of her destination, which appeared closer than before. She stepped through. For a moment she fell through nothing. Her foot touched the floor and she was there. She had taken one step and covered five.

"It worked!" Terulo exulted quietly. "In one direction, at least. Can you come back the same way?"

Luskell turned around. The doorway was right behind her, and Terulo's desk on the other side. She stepped back through, experienced the falling sensation, and returned to her starting point.

"It's not a useful distance, but I think that was a successful test," she said. "Let's keep going." She looked out the window.

"But stay inside the library for now," Terulo cautioned. "If you're to be any help, you have to be unhurt."

They tried longer distances on the mezzanine, all successful as long as she could see her destination. She tried going to a spot on the other side of a tall bookcase, a place she could imagine but not see. The spell didn't work this time.

"You'd need the version I'm only guessing about," Terulo said. "I'm not ready to try it."

Luskell had seen enough of his guess to want to try it immediately, but this was not her quest. She would have to wait. "Then how about I try stepping from the mezzanine to the front door of the library?" she said.

"Only if you go down most of the steps first," Terulo said.

She thought he was being overly cautious but humored him. She descended to the second step from the bottom and worked the spell. When she stepped through, the falling sensation ended with a real drop to the floor.

"That's what I was afraid of," Terulo said from the steps. "I think we've done enough testing for today. Thanks for your help."

"Glad to!" Luskell said. "Let me know when you work out the other part, because that interests me even more."

Chapter 22

Luskell put her hand into her pocket as she left the library. The last note rustled against her fingers. It was time to respond to it, though she didn't know what would be required of her. If only she didn't have to work alone. If Jagryn would help her, or —

"Luskell," a cold voice said.

"Oh! I didn't see you, Larem." Luskell stepped out of his way.

He sniffed. "I don't think Terulo needs a woman distracting him from his quest."

"Was that a problem for you? You liked girls too much?"

"I have never *liked* anyone. Good day." He swept past her and into the library.

"Fine. I have more important things to do than talk to

you," Luskell muttered. She crossed to Balsam's House.

Mamam, may I borrow Fandek this afternoon? I'm visiting someone who might need sunshine.

Yes, where are you?

Tell him to meet me on the porch.

A few convalescent patients sat on the porch and enjoyed the fresh air and mellow sunshine of the fall afternoon. Luskell sat near them in one of the rocking chairs. It wasn't long before Fandek stepped out to join her.

"Where to?" he asked.

"Not far, but I should warn you — the person we're going to see is in great pain. They might be dying."

"I work with people in pain most days. I've never had one turn down sunshine."

They walked to the house indicated on the note and Luskell knocked on the door. The woman who answered gasped, taking a quick step back from the doorway. Luskell offered the note by way of introduction. "I'm Luskell. Sorry about the eyepatch, but it's better than the scars."

The woman read the note. "Can you give Mother the help she needs?"

"I need to talk with her before I'll know for sure. This is Fandek. He's training as a healer and might have some ideas, too."

The woman smiled sadly. "Yes, we've met. This way."

She ushered them to a quiet room at the back of the house. Heavy drapes covered the window. A single lamp provided dim light. A gaunt old woman wrapped in blankets huddled in a chair by the fire, though it was a warm day. She looked up when they entered and Luskell recognized Denna, the woman she'd seen leaving Balsam's House.

"Mother, this is Luskell; 'Death's Friend,' as you called

her."

"Why, she's only a child! And I must look like Old Mother Bones. But you may call me Denna. Please, sit by me."

Luskell lifted the patch for a quick look. This woman's body was failing but her mind was sharp — the opposite of Haleen, whose body was strong while her mind slipped away. Luskell sat next to the old woman on the only other chair.

Fandek made himself comfortable on the floor. "Denna, do you remember me?" he asked.

"Of course I remember you. It hasn't been that long, and I never forget a pretty face." She managed a smile and a wink.

Fandek blushed. "Luskell, your mother was treating her. She said there was nothing more she could do except ease the pain."

"So she told me."

"The sickness is in my bones and my blood," Denna said. "Healer Ketty offered to let me stay there, but even she couldn't take all of my pain away. They gave me drops to help me sleep."

"Did the drops help?" Luskell was familiar with the sedative, the same one partly responsible for her troubles with Jagryn the previous winter.

"The healers wouldn't give me enough to finish the job." Denna shifted in her seat and groaned. "They muddled my mind so I couldn't do anything but sleep. And then they'd wear off. That's no way to live. I'd rather die at home."

"Are you in pain now?"

"I'm always in pain." She looked hopefully at Fandek. "I recall the young man had a particularly good pain charm."

He placed his hands lightly on her head. She sighed as the pain charm and sunshine took the edge off her agony.

"This is good, but it isn't a cure," she said. "It isn't what I asked you here for."

"Then what is?" Luskell asked.

"Help me die."

Luskell bowed her head. "I ... would be honored to accompany you when it is time. Have your family send for me —"

"I mean now," Denna interrupted. "I want to go *today*."

Luskell gulped. She had given that kind of help once before, the night she sat with Mirion. Mirion had been afraid to die, in spite of her suffering. She didn't want the sleep charm Luskell offered her, and then gave without asking. Without meaning to, Luskell had helped her to die sooner than she might have, though it wouldn't have been long. Luskell didn't know if she could do it on purpose, or if she should. But Denna wanted to go, and Luskell was the one best equipped to take her.

Luskell met Denna's gaze and held her hand gently. "I want to help you if I can. I need to ... prepare. Fandek, will you stay in case she needs more sunshine?"

"I'll be right here."

Luskell left the room and reached out to her mother again.

Mamam, Fandek and I are with Denna. She wants me to help her die. Is it allowed?

Was it allowed when you did it before?

I don't know! That was an accident, but Mirion was nearly gone, anyway. Denna isn't as close, but she's ready.

How does her family feel about it?

I think they support her decision. I'll ask them.

Have her state her wishes in front of witnesses. If no one objects, you can do her this favor, but get it in writing in case anyone changes their mind later. You need to think about your reputation.

Reputation wasn't something Luskell had considered. She was developing one anyway, if all the notes and references to the Wizard Girl were any indication. Best to keep it a good one if she could.

Is there any ritual I have to perform?

Whatever you wish. You're the expert here, not me.

Luskell gathered all the family members in the house and had Denna repeat her wish to die sooner rather than later. There were some tears, but no one objected. Luskell wrote it out and had them all sign it.

"All right, then. We'll do it ... at sunset," Luskell improvised. She didn't want Denna to have to wait too long, and sunset was symbolic of ending without being grim. "Bring in flowers and good-smelling food. And as many candles as you can find to keep it bright as the sun goes down."

Fandek and a strong grandson moved Denna to her bed. Her daughter brought in some late roses and a loaf of fresh bread, warm from the oven. Fandek stayed near Denna and gave pain relief and sunshine whenever she seemed uncomfortable. The family gathered around and Denna told the story of her life while they waited for the sun to set. Luskell lifted the patch when everyone's attention was off her. The glow of Denna's life burned low. It would go out with only a little help.

Luskell parted the curtains slightly and watched at the window until the sun dipped below the horizon. She flung them open and lit all the candles at once with a thought. As Balsam said, there was a place for some show. She pulled a chair close to Denna's bedside and had her repeat her wish.

"I've had a good life. I'm ready for it to be over."

"Very well. Fandek, once more, please."

Luskell waited while he gave what relief he could. With Denna as comfortable as they could make her, Luskell sang

"Aku's Lullaby." Denna slipped into a shallow doze that deepened with each verse. Toward the end, Luskell added a sleep charm with extra power. Though Denna wasn't as near death as Mirion had been, she was near enough not to wake.

"Is she gone yet?" one of the family members whispered.

"Not yet," Luskell replied.

Denna's breathing and pulse slowed. Luskell followed her thoughts as they turned to dreams, and lifted her eyepatch for another look with the wizard eye. Barely a flicker remained. Fandek gave more sunshine so she wouldn't wake from pain. Luskell closed her eyes and followed the fading thoughts. When she opened them, she stood with Denna at the bottom of the long slope up to the bright, warm meadow. A faint sparkling thread stretched away from Luskell into the distance.

Denna sniffed. "Smells good here. Roses and bread."

"The smells are back in your room," Luskell said. "If you want to go back, it might not be too late."

"I'm finally free of pain. Why would I go back?" She glanced around at her family gathered around her bed and gave them a sad smile. "Oh, is this your handsome friend?"

"What do you ...?" Luskell stared. A bright form about her height hovered behind them, between the room and the Other Side. "Fandek?" It didn't answer but withdrew and vanished.

"What now? Up the hill?" Denna asked.

"That's right. I'd go with you, but my presence attracts the wrong sort of attention. There should be loved ones waiting at the top."

"I don't need an escort." Denna studied Luskell. "You're even more like a child without the eyepatch. Thank you for helping me over the hard part. You and your friend."

"I'll tell him. Goodbye, Denna."

Luskell watched Denna climb the hill until she disappeared over the top. That sparkling thread ... She was still bleeding power. She tried again to tie it off but the thread was too slippery. She tugged on it, meaning to break it. Her chest ached as if her heart would pop out and the thread would not break. She would have to find another way to stem the trickle that stole her power.

Luskell lifted her head, back in Denna's room. The body was still warm and appeared to be sleeping peacefully, but no spark of life remained. The family members were all crying and hugging each other, but there was more relief in the room than mourning. They insisted Luskell take a handful of coins, and the bread. Luskell accepted with as much grace as she could muster. She had earned them.

"How do you feel?" Fandek asked as they walked away together.

"Not too bad. Tired, but it's been a long day."

"I have sunshine to spare, if you want some," he offered. "You did go to the Other Side."

"I think you might have, too. Or your sunshine did."

His eyes widened. "I had a sense of ... something. I kept giving her sunshine until she was ... gone. I was in the room, but I could see you — blurred, like through a thin curtain."

"Bardin suggested I teach some other healers to cross over. I should teach you to avoid it, so you don't do it by accident." Luskell shuddered. "If the dead can sense me crossing over, they'll be drawn to your sunshine even more. They would drain you dry."

"I'd rather give it to you. You need it more."

"I barely crossed over." Luskell forced herself not to argue. It did cost her something every time she went there, even if she didn't stay long. Mamam said sunshine restored most of what she lost. "A little sunshine never hurt anything, though. I accept." Her spirits lifted as soon as he placed his hands on her head. "Mmm."

"I haven't started yet."

Before she could feel too embarrassed, the sunshine lifted her off her feet. Her mind went back to the time she'd kissed him in his room. Maybe they could —

"Will you be all right walking the rest of the way on your own?" Fandek asked. "I need to go back to work for a while."

Luskell returned to solid ground, half grateful to be saved from a decision she probably would have regretted. "I'll be fine. Thanks for coming along today."

Chapter 23

Luskell parted from Fandek at Balsam's House, buoyed by sunshine even as twilight deepened. Across the square, Larem left the Wizards' Hall. Rather than making herself uninteresting and hurrying toward home, Luskell approached him. She blamed the sunshine.

"Good evening, Wizard Larem."

He glanced at her, his lip curled. "*Wizard* Luskell."

She ignored the sarcasm and forced herself to be even more polite. Once again, the sunshine helped. "May I speak to you, sir?"

"No one is preventing you." Larem leaned on his staff and gazed at something over her left shoulder. He was shielding his thoughts, but emotion slipped through. The contempt she expected, but also ... fear?

"Thank you for allowing me to assist Terulo with his quest."

"He is allowed to seek help from anyone who is not family or his master," Larem said. "You don't need my permission, either to help or hinder the boy."

"I know, sir, but ..." Luskell searched for the right words. "... he holds you in high esteem. If you asked him to change his mind, he would at least consider it."

Larem turned fully toward her, hands on hips. "If you plan to back out of your agreement, you'll not have the satisfaction of blaming me." He shook his head and muttered, "Fickle woman."

"You misunderstand," Luskell said, tamping down her irritation. "I am honored to assist and excited about the project. Terulo is a brilliant wizard, in his own way."

Larem looked at her with a touch more respect. "Yes, he is. Anyone literate who has even a little power can read magic script, but Terulo *understands* it on another level. And he has a knack for turning up forgotten knowledge."

"Why is so much forgotten?" Luskell mused. "I mean, I understand with lore that was never set down in writing, but everything he's finding in the library must have been recorded so it *wouldn't* be forgotten."

Larem sighed. "The library is old. Writings have been piling up for centuries, and if they weren't organized properly .... And think about how wizards usually are."

Luskell nodded. "Difficult to live with."

"Related to that. We're solitary and secretive. We teach our apprentices separately, and only what we know. Other wisdom might fall away over time."

Luskell gasped. "And that's why Bardin organized those group lessons with the other young apprentices! That's why he wants an actual school!"

"You needn't shout. I'm right here." Larem rubbed his

ear. "But yes, Wizard Bardin has been angling for a school for years. And he may get one, at least for the younger boys. Apprentices, I mean."

Luskell thought back to her brief apprenticeship. She had not enjoyed everything about group lessons, but they had been effective and mostly suited her. Not only did the whole group work together, but they all had the benefit of learning from each others' masters, who had different specialties.

"I'm trying to learn to work alone," she said, "but I miss the teamwork I enjoyed at Balsam's House or with my friends. Combining strengths."

Larem smiled, an expression Luskell had not seen before, and some of the fear dissipated. "No wonder Bardin took a chance on you. He loves collaboration."

"Terulo told me you were the only one willing to give him a chance." Luskell breathed deep to steady her nerves. Although the conversation had thawed, the man still intimidated her. But perhaps he wasn't as hard and mean as he appeared. "I know how that feels, and what a risk it must have been. I ... admire your courage. Sir."

"The girl who speaks with the dead admires *my* courage?" Larem made a little bow that may or may not have been sincere.

Luskell remembered Terulo's words. *He's put off by bodies ... by death.* "It's not like I'm chatting with corpses. Souls feel more like energy, but with the appearance of the person as they were in life and health."

"Even so, I was only contending with the opinion of some well-fed wizards."

"Reputation counts for a lot," Luskell said. "But I think you chose well. I hope to continue working with *Wizard Terulo.*"

"I'm still not sure he needs a woman distracting him."

"No worries there." It wasn't Luskell's place to say more on the subject. "I might teach him to Listen to the song of the stars."

It was difficult to read Larem's expression in the fading light, but his voice was urgent with interest. "You've heard it, too?"

"I don't understand it, but I like knowing it's there."

"Like the song of the sun, always there under everything," Larem said.

Luskell gasped. The song of the *sun*? She'd never paid attention, filtering out the constant low hum, but of course that's what it was.

Before she could say anything, Larem continued. "Not as loud, of course. But that's what stars are."

"Little suns? Really?"

"*Distant* suns," Larem corrected.

"Are there other worlds, then?" Luskell had never considered there might be other worlds besides the one for the living and the one for the dead. "With people in them?"

"Yes, some close enough to see from here — the worlds, not the people." He pointed to a bright star in the sky. "See the one that doesn't twinkle? I've gazed on it with my glass, it and a few others. Not a star. A world. There must be many more."

"Thank you," Luskell breathed.

"For what?"

"For showing me that. For stopping to talk. For choosing Terulo. For reminding me there's more to you — to everyone — than I know."

"Likewise, Wizard Luskell. Good evening." Larem inclined his head slightly and swept away into the darkness.

Luskell stood alone in the square after he was out of sight. If she could have a civil conversation with Wizard

Larem as equals, anything was possible. Perhaps even something more than friendship with Fandek. She toyed with the idea of returning to Balsam's House to tell him, but her stomach growled. That was not a conversation to have on an empty stomach. Tomorrow, though. Tomorrow for sure.

Luskell's parents were both home before her and happy to see the fresh bread.

"From Denna's daughter." She added the coins to the family cashbox. "Denna passed peacefully, and the family seemed relieved. But I got it in writing, like you said."

Mamam smiled. "I'm glad you could help, but I hope such requests are few."

"You and me both."

"A letter came for you," Dadad said. "From Deep River."

Luskell grabbed it from him and read eagerly:

Dear Luskell,

I was so relieved to hear you got down from the Mountain safely. What an adventure, though! I wish I had gotten to visit Knot's Valley even once. I want to make a story of your time there, which is the next best thing. You'll have to write and tell me all the details.

I suppose you've seen Jagryn and Ruvhonn by now. The whole town is working on a surprise for them. They'll need a bigger house sooner or later, so all the strong, skilled folk are adding a room. They've already finished a barn for Ruvhonn's horse and the cow Ruvhonn's papa promised them. Grynni and Greelit are tending a clutch of chicks until the coop and run are finished. Now, not a word!

Knot did visit my dreams a few times, but I haven't seen him in weeks. Something about not wanting to draw attention to me. He also told me to avoid stories of Old Mother Bones. I don't tell them often, so that's no great loss. Do you know what any of this means? He seemed worried about you.

I don't expect I'll see you before next summer, but I'll be thinking of you! Write soon!

Love,
Klamamam

So Knot was keeping away from both of them? Luskell was relieved to learn he wasn't angry with her, but his worry seemed overdone. Old Mother Bones had shown up in a few dreams but had no power there to cause harm. As long as Luskell was careful about her visits to the Other Side, there shouldn't be any real danger.

"Klamamam wants to make a story about me and Aku."

"Before you know it, you'll be as legendary as your grandfather," Dadad teased.

She faked a smile. She didn't want to reveal how Knot was keeping away because of worry over a different legend. She changed the subject to share about her day. Her parents agreed with Bardin that she should train a few healers in the art of crossing over, as long as it was safe. Was it? She was confident she could keep herself safe, but anyone new to crossing over was another matter.

"I might start with Fandek. Or maybe with you?" She looked at her mother, the healer who could do anything. Of course she could learn to cross over.

Mamam shook her head. "I don't trust myself to come back. The one time I was there and saw my mother ..."

"Dreams are better," Luskell agreed.

Luskell sat in Klamamam's rocking chair in front of a cozy fire. Her grandmother chatted from the kitchen, though Luskell couldn't understand the words. It was like Listening to the stars; she didn't need to understand. How nice to be in Deep River again. Now she could tell Klamamam all about her time on the Mountain without writing it in a letter. Strange that she didn't remember the journey. She must have slept the whole way.

She held a red-haired infant on her lap. He looked at her with bright blue eyes and transformed into her tall brother Ketwyn, standing before her. She understood: a dream.

"This is nice, but why did you come as a baby?" she asked.

"I don't want to attract Old Mother Bones' attention. A baby's no threat."

"I thought you were angry with me and wouldn't come anymore."

"We only want to keep you safe."

"I remembered the question I wanted to ask you. Are there animals on the Other Side? And why is there a city?"

Ketwyn nodded. "That's two questions. The city is there because enough souls think it should be."

"They build it themselves?"

"It's made of ideas. Anyone who likes the idea of having their own space can think it up, and there it is."

"Do you live there?" Luskell asked.

"Grandma Lukett brought me to live with her as soon as I arrived. She added a room just for me, and we added one for Knot so he can be with us sometimes."

"Not always?"

"He's often away by himself."

Still a wizard: solitary and secretive. "What about Old Mother Bones?" Luskell asked. "Does she live in the city?"

"She lives by herself in a cave away from the city. The dead are warned about her when they arrive, so we don't wake her."

In a cave, just like the stories. But now she was awake, anyway, Luskell thought. Had she done that?

"As for animals," Ketwyn continued, "there are a few. Wild creatures don't stay long; no one remembers them as individuals. But I've seen dogs and horses whose old owners must remember them. A few cats, too. And this one magpie."

"I know which horse it was!" Luskell exclaimed.

"What horse, where?"

"I crossed over, before the time you found me with Luma," she admitted. "I went farther than I should have, but a horse came and gave me a ride back to the border. I'm sure it was a mare called Aunt Rosie. Uncle Jagree sat me on her once when I was tiny. And I've heard him tell of a magpie friend he had as a boy. That man loves his animals more than he does most people, so I'm sure any animal of his would persist on the Other Side."

Ketwyn grinned. "I know who you mean. He tends my grave."

Luskell's heart twinged at the reminder, but before she could say anything, Ketwyn smacked his forehead with an open palm.

"But that's not why I'm here. I have a message for you. Knot's been poking around. He found out Old Mother Bones is watching for the strangler to be hanged. She wants to be the first to welcome him so she can take him to her cave and turn him into a monster."

"What do you mean? He isn't bad enough?"

"Under normal circumstances, he'd become better rather than worse. Like Trenn, he might try to make up for the harm he did in life. But she wants to teach him to invade the dreams of wizards and other magic users and give them nightmares so terrible, he becomes an immortal legend like her. A real monster she can use to feel powerful over the living. Do you know when he is to be executed?"

"Fandek said at the end of the month." The date had seemed distant when he mentioned it, but ... "That's only a week away!"

"We need more time to figure out how to fight her. Can you get it delayed?"

"Me? I don't have that kind of power. Although ... I might know someone who does."

Chapter 24

"How do I get in to talk to Governor Klanya?"

For a change, Dadad had gone out early and Mamam was home. Luskell ate breakfast with her and Crett, who spooned porridge mostly into his mouth.

"You submit a written request for an appointment and wait for approval," Mamam said.

"Wait how long?"

"I don't know. What's so urgent?"

"Something ... some*one* is stirring on the Other Side. An ancient legend who thinks I'm ... I don't know what. A threat or a rival. It wants to use the strangler, Kerf, when he gets there." The explanation sounded ridiculous to Luskell as soon as she'd said it, but Mamam didn't laugh or dismiss her worry.

"Use him for ...?"

"Nightmares, but worse than merely bad dreams. He could terrorize any magic user."

Mamam nodded slowly. "That could be dangerous, if he chose someone fragile or already on a dark path."

"Right. I need to keep Kerf alive while I figure out what to do."

"I tell my dream!" Crett announced.

"Don't interrupt, Crett," Luskell said. "It's not polite."

"Laki say I tell!"

"It's true," Mamam said. "He's supposed to describe every dream he remembers so we can help him understand which are only dreams and which are visions of the future. Go ahead, Crett, before you forget."

He stuck his arms out to the side. "I fly in the blue sky like a bird does!"

Luskell and her mother exchanged a glance. "That sounds nice," Luskell said. "Maybe someday you will."

"Like you do! I wanna!"

"Did you dream anything else? Anything that ... troubled you?"

"Just flyin'." He flapped his arms.

"That's good." Luskell took a moment to enjoy the thought of someday teaching her brother to transform and fly. With a sigh, she picked up the previous conversation. "I need to ask the governor to delay Kerf's execution. Maybe she'll see me because of what I did to stop Governor Snowabi."

"She's a busy woman. Do you think she'll remember you after three years?"

"I have to try."

Her request was too peculiar to try to describe in writing. It would be much easier to explain in person. But there was the added peculiarity of her appearance. The Governor might not recognize her. With Mamam's advice, she cast the illusion of two long braids over her short hair, the way she had worn it three years ago. She added an intact blue eye over her scars. She put on the sober gray dress again, tucked the eyepatch in her pocket, and set out for the Governor's Mansion.

The morning was sunny but cool, and Luskell walked quickly to keep warm. She'd left in such a hurry, she was almost to Fortress Street before she remembered her staff, leaning against the wall at home. She hesitated, then went on. She hadn't carried a staff yet when Klanya last saw her.

At the mansion, Luskell approached the guards at the front door. One stood erect while the other leaned against a pillar.

"Good morning. My name is Luskell and I need to talk to the governor. It's urgent."

The leaning guard pushed himself upright with effort. "A little girl with braids has an urgent message for the governor? Hmph."

"Yes, I do." With her patch off, she couldn't help noticing how his light burned lower than his partner's.

"You may submit a written request to the Chief Usher and the governor's staff will review it."

"How long will that take?"

"Usually about two weeks," the healthy guard said. "This way."

"I don't have two weeks! If I could explain it to her — "

"That is the procedure." The sickly guard peered at her. "What's wrong with your eye? It just stares straight ahead."

Luskell dropped the illusions, since they weren't helping. The guards recoiled at the sight of her scars. Now that she thought about it, her hair hadn't been in braids the night she met Governor Klanya, anyway. It had been all loose and tangled after transformation. She turned and with no care for who might be watching, changed to an eagle and flew home.

Mamam greeted her with a paper-wrapped parcel in her arms. "You just missed Daisy, delivering your new dress."

"Oh, that's nice." Luskell took it from her without much interest.

"Well, let's see!" Mamam urged. "How did it turn out?"

Luskell removed the wrappings. The striped wool and lustrous green silk were the same she'd admired in Tulia's shop, but it was hard to care about a new dress now.

"Go ahead, try it on."

"Maybe later," Luskell said. "I should probably —"

"Look, 'uskell! Look, look, look!" Crett ran to her with a carved bear in one hand, a broom straw in the other. "Mamam Bear gots a magic staff. She's a wizard bear!"

Luskell couldn't help smiling. "What kind of magic does she do?"

"Flies, and puts out fires! Keeps baby bears safe." He turned and flew the bear back to her cubs.

Luskell gazed at Crett, then at the dress in her arms, and finally at her staff leaning against the wall.

"What is it?" Mamam asked.

"I'm going to try again," Luskell said. "This dress may be exactly what I need. This and a few other things."

This was not the time to look like a girl of fourteen, or even seventeen. Her new dress would do more to help her appear adult and respectable than illusion hair. She put the eyepatch back on. In some ways it was now more a part of her than her hair. She slid Luma's bracelet onto her wrist to test whether it gave her a sense of well being and confidence. Staff ... bracelet ... dress ... Dress!

After Luskell and her friends had traveled to the city to foil the former governor's corrupt plot, Klanya, a tall woman, had given Luskell three of her own old dresses so Luskell would have something to wear besides her boyish travel clothes. She had kept them, though they were no longer quite long enough for her. She unpacked the brown one and wrapped it up in the paper her new dress had been delivered in.

Although Luskell couldn't wait two weeks for a decision, they were going to require a written request. She wrote a carefully worded note:

To the Honorable Governor Klanya

> *I send you this dress in hopes you will remember the occasion when we met on the roof of your mansion, three years ago. In return for what I did for our country that night, I beg for your immediate attention to an urgent matter. I must see you at once. I would not bother you if it were not of gravest importance.*
>
> *Thank you for considering my request. Wizard Luskell (daughter of Wizard Crane and Healer Ketty)*

When she had done everything she could think of to improve her chances, Luskell returned to the Governor's Mansion. The morning was still cool enough that she appreciated her warm woolen dress. And as she got into the Government District, she saw a few women dressed in the same fashionable style.

She presented herself at the front door. The guards did not appear to recognize her and gave the same speech as before. This time, she agreed to submit her request to the Chief Usher.

Luskell paused and whispered to the sickly guard. "As soon as you get off work, go to Balsam's House. Ask for Healer Ketty. Tell her Luskell sent you."

The door swung open to a broad corridor with a patterned carpet on the floor. Just inside, a well-dressed man sat at a high desk. A uniformed boy no older than Luskell stood at his side. When Luskell stepped over the threshold, her skin prickled. She had passed through some kind of magical barrier, similar to what they used at Balsam's House. When she sensed for it, her own power seemed trapped inside her. They were using suppression spells. She didn't care for how it felt but approved of the idea. This was not magic worked into the walls, but something freshly cast. The governor must have had a wizard on staff to renew them regularly.

Luskell stepped up to the chief usher's desk. "I need to speak to the governor on an urgent matter."

"Submit your request in writing and her staff will review it."

"This can't wait. Governor Klanya knows me. If she sees what's in this parcel, I believe she'll want to talk to me." She placed her note and parcel on the desk.

It didn't take magic to see the usher was inclined to dismiss her, but she hadn't given him any reason to. She was playing by the rules, even if her request seemed strange.

"Wait over there. Page, please take this package to the governor's office and bring back her reply."

Luskell exhaled with relief and took a seat along the wall to wait. The page returned empty-handed and spoke too low to the usher for Luskell to hear, but his startled expression told her what she needed.

The man got down from his high seat. "She says she will see you. I'm to escort you myself."

"Thank you."

She followed him to the end of the passage, up a flight of stairs, and through a set of double doors with two guards outside. A young woman met them inside. She was dressed similarly to Luskell, in gray with black accents.

"You are Wizard Luskell? Please have a seat. Governor Klanya will see you next."

"It looks like there's someone ahead of me." An older woman with thinning gray hair sat waiting. Her clothing, though shabby, was clean and carefully mended.

"The governor wants to see you next. That is all I know. Please take a seat."

Luskell sat near the old woman. "I'm sorry. What are you here about?"

"Justice." When it seemed that was all she'd say, she continued. "My son worked for the last governor. He was promised great things. Now he's dead, my no-good brother is in prison, and I'm taking in laundry and mending to survive."

"I'm sorry for your loss." The story sounded familiar, though. "Excuse me, but are you Trenn's mother by any chance?"

"How do you know that?"

"I ... met him near the end of his life. We spoke a few times." She didn't feel it necessary to add that most of these conversations took place after Trenn's death. "I'll put in a word for you with Governor Klanya. I wish I could do more, but ... Did you say you take in mending? So you're good with a needle?"

"Yes, why?"

"I know a dressmaker in Old Town, Tulia, who needs an assistant. That might support you better than what you're doing now."

"I appreciate it. But why help me?"

"You shouldn't suffer for what Trenn and Snowabi did." This was the sort of thing her father had talked about and that she had begun to practice: notice a need, help the person fix it, often without magic. She was a wizard, after all.

"Wizard Luskell, the governor will see you now." Luskell followed the assistant into the office, an elegant, high-ceilinged room with sky-blue walls and large windows of many small panes. A side table held a teapot with dainty matching cups and a plate of small pastries.

The governor stood and came around her big desk to meet Luskell. If she noticed the eyepatch, she didn't show it. She was nearly as tall as Luskell, with silver hair in an elegant twist. "So you're a wizard now? I've often wondered what happened to the daring girl I met that night." She poured tea into two cups and offered one to Luskell. "Do try one of the pastries. They're particularly good today. Apricot or blackberry?"

"Oh, um ..." Luskell accepted the tea and forced down her impatience at these niceties. Although she was dressed for it, this was not her world. "Apricot, please. Thank you." She tried a nibble to be polite. The flaky, buttery crust was warm, the fruity filling tart and sweet. "Oh! That is good!" It was gone in three bites.

The governor smiled. "Have another."

Luskell helped herself to a blackberry one, which was even better than the apricot. At the governor's invitation, she sat in one of the armchairs in front of the desk. Klanya did not return to her desk but turned the other armchair to face Luskell.

"Thank you for seeing me," Luskell said. "I have a strange request."

"Wizards always do. We'll get to that, but first we should catch up."

"I wouldn't want to take up too much of your time," Luskell said. "You must have more important business."

Governor Klanya smiled. "It is important that I know my people *as people*. Relax, and let's chat. Your family left the city soon after we met, didn't you?"

"We went back to Deep River, my father's hometown, until after my brother was born."

"I had no idea!" Klanya clapped her hands. "Congratulations to all of you. Will he be a wizard, too?"

"He'll be something. We're actually worried, how his power revealed itself so early."

"I can't imagine a better place for him than with your mother and father. But you must have come back here for your training."

"Yes, I went to Balsam's House first, to learn healing," Luskell said. "It doesn't exactly suit me, but it's good, practical training. Last winter, I talked Wizard Bardin into taking me on as his apprentice. I left town to do my quest and bad luck threw the strangler into my path." She touched her eyepatch.

Klanya gave her a sympathetic smile. "Or good luck, from my point of view. But I'm sorry you were injured."

"I'm making the best of it." Luskell waited while Klanya refilled their cups. "May I make my request now?"

"Go ahead."

"I understand the strangler is due to be hanged at the end of the month."

The governor's lips tightened into a line. "Good riddance to him."

"Yes, I completely agree. But ... I need you to delay his execution. The reason will sound insane."

"I'll be the judge of that." The governor tilted her head for Luskell to continue.

"All right. You need to understand, I ... speak with the

dead. I've learned a legendary spirit has plans to use Kerf to terrorize the magical community. I need time to figure out how to keep her from doing that."

"A strange request, indeed. You're asking for a delay, correct? Not that he never be executed."

"I tried to kill him myself once." Honesty had worked so far. "I prefer a delay, but if that's not possible, I might have to break him out of prison."

"I doubt even your wizardry is equal to the wards worked into the stones of Fortress Prison."

"It shouldn't be," Luskell said. "But I have already entered and left the prison without the guard's knowledge. It seems those spells have worn off or were never correctly placed."

The governor sat back in her chair, clearly shocked. "That will need to be rectified. I have a wizard on my staff who is good with light suppression."

"I noticed." When she paid attention, Luskell was aware of her power, bound within her. "My father is studying suppression spells. He might be able to help."

"Thank you. So, this delay ..."

"I just need to keep Kerf away from Old Mother Bones."

Governor Klanya raised an eyebrow. "Fair enough. How long do you need?"

"I don't know. Can I contact you when it's safe to go ahead?"

"Keep me apprised. Consider the hanging delayed."

"Thank you. You won't be sorry." What else? "Oh, your next meeting — she was promised things by the previous governor that never happened. She's suffering through no fault of her own."

"I'll take that under consideration. Good day, Wizard Luskell. Keep in touch."

Luskell felt the moment when her power was unbound. She was tempted to transform simply because she could. But there was no reason to put on a show, and no reason to hurry. A mature wizard would walk home like anyone else. The morning, nearly spent, was sunny and warmer than it had been earlier — a lovely day for a walk, even for wizards.

Luskell shuddered as she passed the prison, the least lovely part of her route. She had no fondness for Kerf, who had attacked two of her friends and killed many other women. She did care for his brother, though. Instead of going straight home, she took a detour to Balsam's House and reached for Fandek's mind.

Can you meet me out front? I need to tell you something.

I'm listening — just tell me.

She could have done that. It would be easier in some ways. But this wasn't the time for easy. *I think it's better if we speak face to face.*

All right, give me a moment.

Luskell deliberately put her natural impatience aside and tried to enjoy the pleasant sunshine. Fandek was working. She couldn't expect him to drop everything instantly for her. She strolled into the maple grove and Listened. What did she know but didn't know she knew? When Bardin had tested her, she hadn't known Balsam was ill, probably dying. She hadn't known she was bleeding power. She hadn't known Crett —

"There you are!" Fandek said. "I almost didn't recognize you. Why are you dressed like that?"

"I had ... an important meeting." She couldn't get over

how the sight of him lifted her spirits. Was she only remembering sunshine? It felt like more than that, but now that she was here, she couldn't bring herself to tell him.

"You have something on your face. May I?" He lifted a corner of his apron. At her nod, he wiped next to the corner of her mouth. "Got it. Did you have jam on your face all through your important meeting?"

Luskell tamped down the thrill she felt at his touch. "It happened at the meeting. The governor serves delicious pastries."

Fandek's eyes widened and he took a step back. "The governor?"

"I spoke to her just now. She agreed to delay Kerf's hanging."

"Why, though? When he's ready — eager, even — to go?"

"I dreamed of my brother Ketwyn," Luskell said. "He told me something disturbing and asked me to delay the execution while he and Knot learn more."

"Learn more about what?"

"You know how any dead soul can learn to visit magic users' dreams."

"Well, yours, anyway," Fandek said. "You seem to enjoy those dreams."

"Maybe I remember better than most." She paused to consider. What was she, to have such a close relationship to the dead? But she had experienced dream visits only from those who cared about her, not from anyone intent on striking terror.

Or had she? A looming bony face ...

She shook off the unease. "But here's where it gets bad: Old Mother Bones wants to grab Kerf as soon as he arrives on the Other Side, to teach him to visit dreams the way she wants him to. As a monster."

Fandek frowned. "But he wants to be done with that.

When he dies, the monster dies with him."

"Yes, but it might not be his choice. As the strangler, he terrorized the city for years, right? If he lingers as a nightmare after his hanging, he'll become legendary. People will tell stories and he'll persist on the Other Side long after the real Kerf is forgotten."

"Is that what happened with Old Mother Bones?"

Luskell stared at Fandek, lost for words. She'd been wondering how a character from stories had made her way into a place for the souls of the dead. But it must have been the other way around — a real person died, but stories kept her in people's minds. So who was she?

"Here's another thought," Fandek said. "What's to stop Old Mother Bones from collecting other evil souls and making dream monsters out of them?"

Luskell imagined it: wizards tortured by nightmares, telling stories, driven mad ...

"It isn't enough to delay Kerf's execution." She gripped her staff to support herself. "I need to defeat Old Mother Bones."

Chapter 25

Maple leaves rustled in a gentle breeze. Luskell shivered, though the dappled sunshine was warm. She had just set herself an impossible quest.

"I don't think I can help with that." Fandek rubbed the back of his neck. "Are you planning to work here today?"

"I'll come back with Mamam this afternoon, after I've changed clothes and eaten lunch."

Luskell walked home, her thoughts swirling with half-formed ideas about how to deal with Old Mother Bones. Who was she? What did she want? What did she have against Luskell? These thoughts fled when she walked through the door. Jagryn and Ruvhonn sat at the table with Mamam, Crett on Jagryn's lap.

"What are ... I mean, I didn't expect to see you here.

Hello." Luskell wondered if she would ever see them when she was expecting it.

"I asked them to watch Crett this afternoon," Mamam said. "I wasn't sure when you'd be back and I figured you had other things to do, anyway."

"I could if you need me." She didn't know why she was offering, when she'd resented the expectation to babysit. But she had been trying not to make trouble for others.

"No, we're looking forward to it, aren't we, little buddy?" Jagryn ruffled Crett's hair.

Crett giggled. "'uskell, I gonna play with Uncle Jag'yn and Auntie 'vhonn!"

"After your nap," Mamam reminded him.

"No nap." He rubbed his eyes.

Ruvhonn's brow furrowed. "Luskell, why are you wearing a uniform?"

Luskell held her arms out. "Apparently this is what all the fashionable women are wearing. I needed all the help I could get this morning."

"It looks good on you," Ruvhonn said. Luskell waited for a "but" that never came. "Thank you. If you'll be in town long enough, maybe you could have Tulia make you something nice."

Ruvhonn blushed. "Oh, I could never —"

"That's a good idea," Jagryn interrupted. "You didn't even have a new dress to get married in."

Ruvhonn swatted him playfully. "My best dress isn't even a year old. But a city dress might be nice. Not like Luskell's, but something ..."

Luskell changed into an everyday dress and joined the others for lunch. She found the ordinary conversation hopeful — she hadn't spoiled everything. Jagryn was still her friend, and maybe now Ruvhonn was, too.

After the meal, she walked with Mamam to Balsam's

House.

"I know a secret," Mamam said with sparkling eyes.

"Ruvhonn's pregnant?"

"So not much of a secret."

"Does *she* know?"

"She hasn't said anything, and it didn't feel right to reveal it before she suspects."

"I wish I could see Jagryn's face when he finds out," Luskell said. "He'll be thrilled. As long as Crett doesn't give them too hard a time. And what about you? Not even one day off?"

"I don't know how Balsam kept up with it all — healing, teaching, running everything. But it's good to have a new challenge at my age."

"I'm not sure what age has to do with it. You're good at everything."

"A compliment from my daughter? Thank you. How was your important meeting? Did you get in?"

"The governor agreed to meet with me and she said she'll delay the execution. It's lucky Klanya is willing to take me seriously."

"Wizards have that effect on people."

As soon as they walked through the door, someone needed Mamam's advice. Luskell put on an apron and got busy with her own duties. She cast protection over herself and entered the contagious ward. Protective magic in the doorway brushed her gently. She smiled at the touch of sunshine in it; Fandek must have refreshed it last. While she scanned the small number of patients, Luskell refreshed the protection on each of them. Her scan revealed no change for the worse from her previous visit.

"Why do you stand in the corner and peek at us?" a child's voice rasped. "Are you a ghost?"

Luskell had thought them all asleep, but a boy,

recovering from a rash and a sore throat, lay awake, watching her. She moved closer to his bed so they could speak softly.

"What's this about ghosts?"

"You caught what I had. They put you in that bed." He pointed to an empty bed closer to the door. "A giant skeleton came to get you, so I thought you died. But here you are."

"I am so tired of that giant skeleton," Luskell muttered. "First Lucky, now you …"

"You've seen it, too?"

"I have, but visiting the dreams of sick children is low, even for her." And she was getting more skilled at the dream visits, controlling the setting and the action. She was *learning*. Luskell shook off her unease and put on a smile for her patient. "She can't hurt you here, but don't follow her."

"So are you a ghost?"

"No. I have a special eye," she said. "It shows whether you're getting better or worse. It doesn't look very nice, though, so I stand out of the way where it won't bother anyone." She felt his forehead, which confirmed his fever was gone. "You're getting better, by the way."

"I hope so, I'm tired of this. Why do you have a stick? None of the others have a stick."

"You ask a lot of questions, don't you?"

"Sorry. Mama says I ask too many."

"No, it's fine. You notice things and you're curious, and that's how you learn." Luskell held her staff in front of her. Back when she was working at Balsam's House, the necessary work of keeping up protection on herself and the patients had been tiring. It was easier now. "I have a stick because I'm a wizard. If you dreamed about that giant skeleton, maybe you will be, too."

"Ooh! I hope so!" He bounced against his pillow. "I'm Garnid. I'm almost ten."

Luskell grinned at his enthusiasm. "Glad to meet you, Garnid. I'm Luskell. My staff helps me control my power and makes difficult magic easier."

"Shouldn't they all have one, then?" the boy asked, his pale, rashy face serious again.

"That is an excellent question. I don't know the answer, but now I wonder, too."

Luskell made sure Garnid was comfortable, then left the contagious ward. When she passed back through the doorway, the protection there felt a little thin. She renewed it, relishing the comparative ease of working healing magic. If she'd had a staff when she was working as a healer, she might have stayed; but in that case, she never would have earned the staff. Why shouldn't healers carry something like a staff, though? The blue apron was a symbol but not magical in itself. She would have to ask —

Mamam stepped out of one of the examination rooms and beckoned her over.

"What did I do now?" Luskell asked.

"Soon after we got here, a guard from the Governor's Mansion staggered in half dead, asking for me by name." Mamam studied Luskell. "He said he was sent by a girl with an eyepatch and a big stick."

"I saw him this morning. He looked unwell." Luskell tapped her eyepatch. "I thought maybe you could help him, so I sent him here. Was I wrong?"

"No, you did right. We should be able to heal him," Mamam said. "I'm proud of you, doing your work while on your own errand. A day longer and it might have been too late to help him."

"That's a relief. I thought you were angry."

"Not angry. I was worried you'd already brought him

back once, but I don't see that kind of loss. You're still bleeding power, but not as much. Come in, he wants to thank you."

In the examination room, Fandek was settling an ashen man into a wheeled chair. Fandek glanced around at Luskell, then quickly away.

The sick man gave her a smile and held out his hand. Without his tall hat and uniform tunic, the guard looked smaller and older than he had in the morning. "They say I've got a bad ticker, but maybe they can fix it."

Luskell gave his hand a gentle squeeze. "I didn't realize you were so badly off, but I'm glad I sent you here."

"Maybe it's the short hair, but you look a bit like the redhead."

"I'll take that as a compliment."

She followed them to the chronic ward, where protection in the doorway kept contagion out. Fandek had cast that one, too. She enjoyed watching him work, patient and capable as he helped the man into bed. She smiled at him, but he left without meeting her gaze.

She couldn't waste time wondering about that when there was work to do. She moved off to scan other patients. An old man flickered like a guttering candle. Luskell sat beside him. She didn't expect any response, but he turned his head and smiled at her.

"How are you feeling?" she asked.

"I think I'm about done here."

"You ... may be right. Is there anyone you'd like with you?"

"My son, if it's not too much trouble." He told where the son would likely be found.

Mamam, there's a patient here who won't last much longer. Can you send for his son?

I know who you mean. I'll send Fandek to get him.

"All right, we'll bring him to you. I'll stay with you until he gets here." Luskell paused, unsure how to offer her specialty. "When the time comes, I could cross over with you. If you want."

"That won't be necessary. My dear wife will be there to meet me. I've been dreaming of her."

Luskell didn't know whether to be disappointed or relieved. "It sounds like you're ready. I'm curious, though. Are you a wizard?"

He laughed weakly. "Nothing so grand." He glanced at her staff. "I had some minor skill at finding."

"It's not minor to the people who lost something."

He laughed again, more of a gurgling sigh. "The last one ... wasn't satisfied. His uncle's treasure ... wasn't gold or gems. It was ... the house, with the names of all his loved ones written on the beams. He didn't believe me."

Luskell smiled. She'd been right, it wasn't worth the risk to cross over for that greedy request.

The man dozed off. Luskell stayed there until his son arrived. Fandek escorted him in and waited by the door. He glanced at Luskell and looked like he wanted to say something, but this wasn't the time. He was shielding his thoughts well enough, but a hint of emotion slipped through. Disappointment? Over what? She was sure they'd parted on good terms in the morning.

"Papa?"

The sick man opened his eyes. He smiled and held out his arms. "My boy."

The younger man fell into his embrace. The old man patted his back once. He released a breath and didn't inhale again. His arms went slack.

His son looked at Luskell. "Is that it? He's gone?"

"Yes, he's gone."

"I thought it would be more ... profound. A struggle or ...

I don't know." He blinked back tears. A mix of sorrow and hope washed off him.

"Sometimes there is a struggle, but your father was ready to go," Luskell said. "He waited for you. He wanted you to be with him. That seems profound to me."

Other healers came in to take over. Luskell left the chronic ward, planning to seek needs in the neighborhood. Fandek joined her outside the examination room and walked with her to the front door, quiet and subdued. She respected his imperfect shield and waited for him to speak, but he couldn't get started. She paused on the porch and turned to face him.

"Out with it. What's wrong?"

"Nothing. Well, not nothing, but ... where'd you get that bracelet? Did Terulo give it to you?"

"Terulo? No, why do you ask?"

"He could afford something like that, and Shura saw you walking together, so ..." Another wisp of disappointment escaped his shield.

"Terulo's helping me learn about it, and we're working together on a project, but he's not interested in me. Nor I in him," Luskell explained. "So you know what a bracelet like this means?"

"Sure, it's what a fellow gives his sweetheart, if his family's rich or used to be." Fandek frowned. "So who did give it to you?"

"No one." *But I wish you had,* she thought. That was the sunshine talking. At least she hadn't said it aloud.

"You don't have to lie to me," he said, quiet but intense. "You say we're friends, you invite me to the picnic, you raise my hopes but when it seems like maybe ..." Hurt and anger washed off him, but mostly hurt.

Luskell threw her shield up, too late not to feel it. "We are friends and I'm telling the truth. I'm only borrowing it."

"Sure you are. I —"

Before he could finish, Luskell heard Mamam's voice in her mind.

Balsam wants you. Fandek, too.

Luskell hurried upstairs with Fandek on her heels, their argument set aside for later. Two deaths in one day wasn't uncommon at Balsam's House, but she hadn't expected this one so soon. When she reached Balsam's apartment, she found the old woman dressed and sitting up in a wheeled chair. Luskell's wizard eye showed no improvement from her last visit, but Balsam herself seemed energized.

"I feel like getting out. Fandek, be a dear and fetch my buggy. I want you two to come with me to Braffin's Garden."

"If you're sure you're up to it," Luskell said. "It's a beautiful day, and the Garden is greening up again."

While they waited for Fandek, Luskell made sure Balsam was wrapped in a warm shawl and chatted with her about this and that — nothing serious or worrying.

Balsam watched her, a smile playing about her lips. "Fandek holds you in high regard."

Luskell shrugged. "We're friends. And he admires my parents."

"It's more than that. And you're in love with him, too."

"So everyone tells me, but how would I know with his stupid sunshine leaking out along with whatever he's doing?"

"It did that in the early days," Balsam said. "Not anymore. He's learned to control it quite precisely. He never gives it without permission, though who would turn it down?"

I would, Luskell thought. But if what Balsam said was true, he hadn't sneaked sunshine into the meeting with Laki and Tatakla, or given it to Luskell except when asked. So what she felt ... was what she felt. She cleared her throat. "I guess I misunderstood."

When Fandek returned, he wheeled Balsam to the top of the stairs, then picked her up as if she weighed nothing and carried her to the bottom. Luskell followed with the chair. The horse and buggy stood outside the front door. Fandek settled Balsam on the seat and strapped the chair on behind. It seemed like he'd done this before. He climbed up on the driver's seat and Luskell joined Balsam.

"Now I wish I'd left my good dress on," Luskell said. "We could pretend we're fine folks out for a ride."

"We are fine folks," Balsam said. "Well, I am, and you're with me ..." She paused for breath. "... so you must be, too."

Luskell's parents rarely rode when they could walk. It put them closer to people in need and cost nothing. Luskell expected she'd be the same way in her wizard life, but she enjoyed the comfortable ride for a change. She lifted the patch a few times but didn't see anything disturbing. Balsam's flicker didn't change, and the fall breeze brought color to her cheeks.

When they reached Braffin's Garden, Fandek set the wheeled chair on the ground and helped Balsam into it.

"Where to, ma'am?"

"Oh, the fountain! It was always my favorite spot."

Fandek pushed the chair and Luskell walked alongside down the broad pathway to the grassy lawn around the fountain. Children ran and played, shouting to each other and laughing.

Fandek parked Balsam's chair next to a bench. Luskell

sat beside her, and Fandek sat next to Luskell. She could almost believe there was no tension between them, but when she dropped her shield to check, it was still simmering.

"Thank you both for this," Balsam said. "What a day! If I could, I'd run races with those children. And climb the tallest tree."

"You sound like me!" Luskell said.

"I was like you. Well, you can do more than I ever could."

"I can't turn my family home into a place of healing. You're a gift to this city. I hope you know that."

"I've tried to do right. I feel better now that your mother is running the place. I've told her to move your family into my apartment. There's more space, especially if you open some of the other rooms. And it's much more convenient."

"How generous! That will be nice when the time comes."

"The time ... has come."

Fandek jumped up. "We need to get you back home right now."

"Sit down, young man. I am home, or nearly. Luskell, you said you'd go with me."

"It ... it would be an honor." Luskell lifted the patch for another look. Balsam's light was fading quickly. She knew.

Balsam closed her eyes as if going to sleep. Luskell held Balsam's hand and reached for her thoughts. A jumble of memories in no particular order, some of this place, some of the gracious mansion in which she grew up and later worked, and many others. There were people Luskell didn't know, and a few she did: her wizard master, Bardin, but as a young man; Jagryn's great-grandmother Elika; a child who must have been Jagryn's grandmother Sudi. The memories grew blurred and muddled. When Luskell opened her eyes, she was with Balsam at the base of the long slope. The trail of sparkles led over the top of the hill.

"Is this it? The Other Side?"

"It is. But are you sure? We could still go back." Luskell glanced back at their bodies on the bench, Fandek standing over them protectively.

"My work is finished and I'm worn out," Balsam said. "Though not so worn out I couldn't climb this little hill."

Luskell smiled through her sadness. "There'll be loved ones waiting at the top."

"Let's run!"

Balsam ran as easily as a child. Luskell kept pace with her, her long legs giving her no advantage for a change. Elika and a crowd of others waited at the top to greet Balsam. Luskell didn't get to enjoy the joyous reunion, though. Looming behind them was a skeletal figure in rags, much taller than Luskell. So that hadn't been a dream, or not only a dream. Luskell ducked down to hide herself in the crowd of souls.

"I'm coming for you, wizard girl!"

"You'll have to go through me, then," Balsam said.

"And me," Elika added. The two healers crossed their arms and stared up at the legend.

"I'll haunt your children with nightmares."

"I have no children," Balsam declared. "You don't scare me."

"You do have a house full of healers. So convenient for me to haunt their dreams, how they all sleep in the same dormitory."

Luskell stepped in front of Balsam and Elika. "You leave them alone. I'm the one you want. What's this about?"

"You come and go as if crossing over means nothing. My domain is not for the living."

"Your domain? Who do you think you are?"

"I am Old Mother Bones. I have always been here." She

stooped to the ground. When she stood upright again, she held a sparkling ribbon in her bony hand. "You should go and not come back. Unless you want to stay?" She jerked on the ribbon.

Luskell stumbled forward a step, her chest aching. "I'll go, but not because you say so. And I'll come back when there is a need." She grasped the ribbon of her power where it connected to her and yanked hard enough to break it off in spite of the pain. She half-expected all her power to gush out and be lost but felt only the ache of emptiness. This was a place she could visit but it was not her place.

Luskell wanted to run but turned and stalked away with what she hoped came across as dignity. She opened her eyes in the peaceful garden by the fountain.

"Is she gone?" Fandek resumed his seat on the bench.

"She didn't need my help, but I'm glad I got to be there." Luskell turned toward him. "And I'm glad you were here, too."

"For the sunshine, right? Because you don't look so good."

"I need it if you'll give it, but that's not the reason."

"What happened?"

Luskell shivered. "I met a monster who says she's always been there. I'm glad I'm not alone." Was now the time to tell him how she felt? No, if she did, it might draw the attention of the legend. Old Mother Bones had left Fandek alone up till now, perhaps because he had never slept in the dormitory at Balsam's House. She might find him eventually but there was no need to hurry that outcome.

Sunshine, though. Luskell could accept sunshine. When Fandek rested his hand on her head, a sense wellbeing flowed through her. The bracelet warmed. She held it out for him to see. "I really am borrowing this, from a woman I helped. It's hundreds of years old and has absorbed a lot of emotion in that time. Can you feel it?"

Fandek touched the bracelet and gasped, then smiled. "Is that what my sunshine feels like?"

"Kind of. This is weaker but steadier, I think."

"It reminds me of … something." He frowned in thought but had let his anger go.

"Come on, let's take Balsam home," Luskell said. "Then I need to learn everything I can about Old Mother Bones."

Chapter 26

On the ride back, Luskell embraced the body of her beloved mentor and friend. Balsam was still warm. Anyone who didn't know would think she was sleeping.

Mamam, we're bringing Balsam back now.

Did something happen?

Mamam could always tell. *Yes, the thing she'd planned all along. We're bringing her body back.*

We'll be ready to welcome her.

All the healers waited in the entrance hall when they arrived, even those who weren't on duty. Some stood dry-eyed and solemn, others let tears run down their faces, a few bowed their heads in grief. Hanny and Shura stepped forward to help Luskell and Fandek bear the body. Balsam weighed so little, Luskell could have carried her upstairs herself, but this was more dignified. They laid her out in her room with the view of the Mountain. Mamam and the other healers lined up to pay their respects.

"The Mountain's out," Luskell whispered, and kissed Balsam's forehead. If it still hurt to look at Aku, Luskell couldn't tell. This new loss was fresher. Luskell turned to her mother. "I already said goodbye. I have something important I need to do."

Luskell left Balsam's House and went to the library. She'd hoped Terulo might help her find something about Old Mother Bones that she could use, but for once, he was not seated at the table under the windows. Luskell was on her own. She went to the shelf with collections of folk tales and chose a book with pictures. She flipped through, glancing at the block printed illustrations until she came to one of a skeletal old hag dressed in rags, eerily similar to the figure she had seen on the Other Side. The story that went with it was more of a warning than a tale. Children who stayed out after dark or disobeyed their parents risked drawing the attention of Old Mother Bones, who would carry them away to the Other Side whether they were dead or alive. Luskell knew the story. Everyone did. It didn't reveal who she had been or how long ago she might have lived.

The library would close soon and Luskell was hungry. She returned the book to the shelf, no wiser than when she'd gone in. She headed home for supper with the family. She arrived ahead of her parents. Jagryn and Ruvhonn were still there with Crett, who was sprawled asleep on his trundle bed.

"He never goes to bed this early! Is he sick?" Luskell gently felt his forehead, but he didn't have a fever.

"He wouldn't nap. We took him out to play instead,"

Jagryn explained. "He was worn out after that, so he napped after instead of before. And he didn't fight it."

"Funny boy." Luskell smiled fondly at her sleeping brother, then remembered the main event of the day. "Jagryn, you should know: Balsam died this afternoon. She's laid out at the House if you want to pay your respects."

"I should. I didn't know her well, but she was Grammy's cousin. Was it ... peaceful?"

"Very. Fandek and I took her to Braffin's Garden so she could pass from her favorite spot."

Soon after they left, Luskell heard her parents' voices on the stairs. They brought supper from the tavern again and set it out on the table. Crett stirred but didn't wake.

"That's what happens when you skip a nap," Mamam told his snoozing form. "You miss supper. But he must have needed the sleep. I wonder if he's coming down with something." She felt his forehead, just as Luskell had. "He'll probably be taller by morning." She put a diaper on him in case he didn't wake in time. "He'll wake all of us in the middle of the night, I'll bet. Little rascal."

A face loomed over Luskell, skin stretched tight over the skull. No matter where she turned, she couldn't escape.

"My domain is no place for the living. Stay out or stay forever!"

Luskell didn't want to stay forever, but she was trapped. And she couldn't fight with her arms full. She held a red-haired infant. It gazed up at her with light blue eyes, and then she knew.

"This is my dream and you have no power here. Who are you?"

"Myself. Old Mother Bones."

"When did you die?"

"I didn't."

But Luskell heard the briefest hesitation. "Go away!"

Old Mother Bones vanished. Ketwyn reverted to his grown self, laughing.

"Thank you, brother. I didn't like that dream."

"She knows who you are now. No point in staying away."

"She knows who I am, but I don't think she remembers who she is. Or was. But she must have been a regular person before she became a legend."

"Another legend might know."

Before Luskell could ask what he meant, Ketwyn vanished and the dream shifted. Luskell was back in Braffin's Garden, on a bench near the statue of Good King Braffin. Knot sat beside her.

"Finally!" She embraced him, then sat back to look at him. A warm smile lit his dark face, framed by white hair as curly as hers. She gazed into his deep blue eyes. "I thought I'd never see you again. Are you the legend Ketwyn talked about?"

"I'm not nearly old or famous enough."

"Then who ...?"

The bronze king turned and stepped down from his pedestal. "How may I be of service?"

Even in a dream, Luskell hadn't expected that. "You ... look just like your statue."

"Because that is how my people remember me. If there is a problem in the land of Eukard, I will help if I can."

"Even though we got rid of kings?" Luskell asked.

Braffin smiled. "That was my idea. I worked with a team of trusted advisors so they could replace me with something better when the time came. Why do you think I left no legitimate heir?" He tapped the side of his head. "Deliberate plan."

"All ... all right. I've never had two of these dreams one right after the other."

"Ketwyn sent us to help you," Knot said.

"Thank you. I hope we can figure it out before I wake up." Luskell looked around the empty garden, not busy and lively as it had been when she brought Balsam. "My understanding of the Other Side is the souls of the dead stay only as long as they are remembered by the living. So most of us will fade away after a couple of generations. But those with stories about them persist longer. Because the living ... feel like they know them?"

"That sounds right," Knot said. "But with no one left who knew them in life, it appears legendary people take on the form of the legend. So the king here looks like his statue, and because he was remembered for being kind and trustworthy, he maintains those aspects."

"Old Mother Bones looks exactly like an illustration in an old book," Luskell said. "She says she's always been there. I think she must have been an ordinary person who died like anyone else, but stories grew up around her, so she was remembered as a monster. Either she has forgotten who she used to be, or she prefers the monster and won't tell."

"Why does it matter who she was?" Braffin asked in a ringing voice.

"This is a wizard hunch, but I believe if I knew who she used to be, it might help me figure out how to stop her. She's threatening to give nightmares to healers and wizards. She wants to teach the souls of murderers to do that, too. Turn them into legendary monsters."

"But if she doesn't know ..." Knot frowned.

"Even knowing when she died would be a clue. How long has she been on the Other Side?"

King Braffin nodded solemnly. "Longer than I have; I

was warned when I arrived not to wake her. That's over two hundred years."

"It's a place to start. Thank you both."

Luskell managed to hug Knot once more before the dream faded.

Luskell rose early the next morning and put on her good dress and Luma's bracelet for Balsam's funeral. Mamam was up and dressed, too. Crett was still sleeping.

"If we eat breakfast at Balsam's House, we can go now and not disturb him," Luskell said.

"I don't know." Mamam cast a worried glance at the sleeping child. "It's early, but he's had a long sleep. Maybe I should stay behind in case he really is ill."

"I'll stay with him," Dadad said. "It's important that you be there."

The funeral ritual was held in the entrance hall, with chairs carried in from every other room and the body in repose at the foot of the stairs. There were some formal words, but most of it was taken up with people telling stories. Balsam had touched many lives as a teacher and healer. Bardin had known her the longest and spoke at length, but with great warmth and humor. It dawned on Luskell that Balsam was the girl he'd loved long ago. She'd guessed it, after seeing him in Balsam's last thoughts, but there'd been no chance to ask. She was glad now they'd made up and been friends for so long.

It took a long time to tell all the stories, and then there was a feast. Finally, Balsam's body was loaded onto a wagon for the ride to the graveyard. Most of the crowd processed with it, but Luskell broke away at the library.

Braffin's words had reminded her of something in the *Registry of Practitioners*. There was one other person besides Luskell who had listed the specialty Crossing Over. That didn't mean no one else could do it, but no one else had publicly claimed it. And that person had lived around three hundred years ago. She would have died before Braffin.

Luskell opened the curtained alcove and approached the great book, open to the page she had signed. "Show me Crossing Over."

Two glittering ribbons of light emerged from the pages. Luskell flipped to the one far in the past. Serana, witch. Could she have become Old Mother Bones?

Luskell flipped back to her own page and carefully closed the curtains so the book wouldn't be damaged by daylight. The clue was there but the answer had to be elsewhere. Maybe in another book, but which one? Luskell knew how to read but she was no researcher. She was relieved to find Terulo back at his desk by the windows.

"I need your help again."

"Well, since you introduced me to your friend Wyllik … Something enchanted, or something forgotten?"

"Forgotten, in more ways than one. My specialty of Crossing Over seems to be a forgotten skill. The last person to claim it lived three hundred years ago. She is herself forgotten. Now I'm dealing with a legend who doesn't remember who she used to be, but I wonder if they're the same. How do I find out more about a witch from that long ago?"

Terulo rose from his seat. "Where have you already looked?"

"Folktales about the legendary figure, but they weren't much help."

"You want history or lives of prominent magical folk."

He walked around to another tall shelf opposite the collection of folklore. He pulled down a large volume and placed it in her arms. "This looks like the oldest. A reasonable place to start."

Luskell sagged under the heavy tome, appalled. "Can I ask it what I need?"

"No, it's not like the *Registry*. But these are organized by date. That should give a general idea of where to look."

She thanked Terulo and lugged the book to another desk. She opened to a random page, found a date (too early), and flipped ahead to a more likely spot, skimming the pages for the name. The old-fashioned script was difficult to read, and she had to battle her own impatience. Most of the entries concerned hero wizards and their great deeds, but here and there, a skilled healer or witch got a mention. Luskell kept turning pages until the dates were too late to be helpful. She paged back. The book flopped open to a torn fragment stuck between two pages. As she plucked it out, her glance fell on the words *the Other Side.* Heart racing, she gave the scrap to Terulo and turned back one more page to find the beginning of the entry.

The witch Serana was renowned for her skills as a healer, her love of children, and her sharp tongue. She claimed to have the ability to travel to the Other Side and fetch the soul back. Whether true or not, she saved many lives, sometimes when all hope seemed lost. Her own death was shrouded in mystery. She was caring for a patient who had fallen unconscious and could not be roused. As he slipped away, she announced she would go after him. She fell into a stupor and after many days, passed from this life, though she had been in perfect health. Most mourned, but some fearful souls told dark tales and celebrated the witch's passing.

Luskell shuddered. When she accompanied the dying to the Other Side, she fell into a trance. A stupor. And those dark tales? Luskell thought of Larem's fear of her ability to visit the dead. Easy enough for a frightened, hostile person to twist that ability into the Old Mother Bones legend of dragging a living soul to the Other Side and holding it there till it perished. But if Old Mother Bones had once been Serana, she crossed over at the risk of her own life, not anyone else's. Luskell had thought she understood the danger. Crossing over frequently or staying too long cost something, a little of herself, a debt she assumed she would pay at the end of her life. This story implied a more immediate peril. A chill ran up her back as she thought how close she might have come to being trapped on the Other Side. If not for Uncle Jagree's horse ...

Luskell pictured the healer Serana desperately following the departing soul to bring it back, refusing to give up, eventually unable to return. She didn't die in the ordinary way, but she died, all the same. But she didn't remember how or when. No one else remembered anything but the frightening, twisted anecdote, told and retold until it was all that was left of Serana. She became Old Mother Bones.

And now that legend threatened to haunt magical folk with nightmares, all because she envied Luskell's ability to do what she had done. She wanted to turn Kerf into a monster. Imagine if the strangler appeared in Hanny's dreams! She was one of the few to escape his attack; she did not deserve any more nightmares than she already had. And could these nightmare monsters draw the dreamer from the safety of the dream over to the Other Side?

But why would a healer who loved children give nightmares to Lucky and Garnid? Maybe in some twisted way she was still drawn to youngsters. A new thought struck Luskell. They'd been concerned Crett was too young to tell visions of the future from regular dreams. And it followed, if he was having visions, he must have power when he was too young to understand or control it, so it might need to be suppressed. But if he had power ...

Chapter 27

Luskell flew down the spiral stairs, barely feeling the steps under her feet. The librarian shushed her as she ran through the reading room. She ignored him and flung open the door to the outside. Good to know she could run in her good dress, but that wasn't fast enough. Even transformation to a falcon was too slow.

She imagined the building where her family lived — the base of the stairs up to their rooms, since she was at street level. She traced a doorway with her staff and spoke Terulo's guess at the spell. Framed in the doorway, she saw home. She stepped through, closed the doorway behind her without even looking, and raced up the stairs.

She burst in without pausing for breath. "Crett's in danger!"

Dadad looked up from the book he'd been reading, the one about suppression of power. "No, he doesn't even have a fever."

"But he's still sleeping. That's not normal." Luskell examined her brother with her wizard eye. He glowed with health. Relieved on that count, she replaced her eyepatch and knelt beside the trundle bed. She laid her hand on Crett's forehead. He was warm but not feverish. His eyes flicked back and forth under closed lids. She shook him gently. "Come on, Crett. Time to wake up." He didn't rouse. It reminded her of when she'd found Jagryn in a drugged sleep, lost on the Other Side. "I'm going after him."

Dadad stood up. "After him where? Surely you don't think — "

"That he can cross over? Not without help. And he needs my help to come back."

Luskell closed her eyes and reached out for Crett's dream thought. As she'd feared, she found him in the bright meadow with no sun. He sat in the grass next to Old Mother Bones, who towered over both of them. Her tattered black dress did little to hide her sallow skin on a skeletal frame.

"'uskell!" Crett grinned and stood up to run to her. He managed two steps before he fell back as if yanked. A sparkling ribbon of light wrapped around his waist.

The monster held the other end. "It's not time for you to go yet." Her voice was grating and hollow, bone on rock.

"How ... how are you holding him?" Luskell asked.

Old Mother Bones showed her teeth in a mirthless grin. "Don't you recognize it? You left it here."

"My power," Luskell murmured. Her chest ached, a ghost of the pain she'd felt when she broke the connection.

"I've collected it for my own use," Old Mother Bones said. "It gives me strength, but this is the last of it."

"What happens when it's gone?" Luskell's voice trembled, though she wanted to be strong and steady for Crett's sake.

Old Mother Bones stared at her but didn't answer.

"Dis Grammy Bo! I play at her house."

"That's nice." Luskell fought to keep her voice calm. He had mentioned Grammy Bo before. It was so obvious now, too late. "Have you come here before?"

"Dissa first time. She in-vit-ed me." Crett puffed out his chest, proud he could pronounce a big word.

He seemed fine. Old Mother Bones wasn't touching him, which would drain his life. The place itself would drain him eventually if he stayed too long, but she wasn't speeding the process. If she was who Luskell suspected, she might remember at some level her love of children. But if she didn't intend to hold him until his body perished, what did it mean? He was ... a plaything?

"Thank you for inviting him. Crett needs to come home with me now." Luskell stepped closer.

Old Mother Bones tightened her grip on the leash. Was it shorter? "What if he wants to stay with me?"

"He doesn't know what he wants."

"You could trade places with him."

So not a plaything. A hostage. "Why should I?"

"You like it here so much, you should stay. It isn't right to go back and forth. Choose a side." Old Mother Bones grinned, which made her look even more skull-like. "You could still visit the little one's dreams."

As if Luskell would stay and send Crett back alone. He hadn't done this before; he didn't know the way. If she stayed, they'd both be lost. "I'm going and I'm taking Crett with me."

"Aw, do you love your baby?"

"He's my brother. I don't have children yet." Luskell

grabbed for the leash.

"And you never will!" Lightning quick, Old Mother Bones jabbed a bony finger into Luskell's abdomen. Freezing pain doubled her over, while Old Mother Bones glowed with renewed vitality. Luskell cried out ...

... and jerked alert, back in the room where Crett slept. She had not brought him back.

The door opened and Mamam walked in. "Oh no, still sleeping? Is he ill?"

"No." Luskell blinked back tears and swallowed hard. "He followed Grammy Bo. She's holding him hostage."

"Slow down, you're not making sense. Who is?"

Luskell took a deep breath to calm herself, but her voice shook. "The dead can enter his dreams. He's been dreaming of someone he calls Grammy Bo, for I don't know how long. It's Old Mother Bones! She drew him to the Other Side and she's holding him there. I tried to bring him back, but I couldn't." Her voice broke at the end and a deep sob escaped her careful control.

"My poor baby."

Luskell thought Mamam meant Crett, but she reached to smooth Luskell's hair. She meant both of them. Under her tender touch, Luskell fought back tears. She was not a child anymore. She was a wizard now.

"What did she do to you?" Mamam sounded concerned and indignant. "You've lost ... something. More than usual."

"She touched me. It drained some of my life, but it hurt more than I've felt before."

"Where?" Mamam asked. Luskell pointed, and Mamam paled. "It might be nothing."

"She said I'd never have children. Is that possible?" Luskell hadn't been in any hurry for motherhood, but *never*?

"I don't know. We'll wait and see whether there's permanent damage." Mamam laid her hand on Luskell's head and looked directly into her eyes. "But you can't go back there. It's too dangerous."

Luskell pounded her fists against the floor. "I can't just leave Crett there!"

"We'll bring him back. Perhaps we need to do it from here." Mamam changed Crett's diaper, then picked him up. He flopped against her, a sleeping weight. "He's still strong and healthy. He hasn't been injured or poisoned. He's not in immediate danger."

"Unless Old Mother Bones or some other soul touches him and drains all the life out of him." Luskell shuddered at the thought, but when she looked at Crett with her wizard eye, he had all the bright bloom of perfect health.

"You said she hadn't touched him yet," Dadad said. "And I doubt she would allow another soul to get close. He's too valuable as bait."

"Bait, yes. For me."

He nodded. "If you don't rush back to challenge her, she might lose interest and let him go."

"She seems to have a lot of patience. It's not like she has anything else to do. And just being there will drain him eventually even if no one touches him."

"We might need Fandek's sunshine," Mamam said. "Can you think of anything we might do to help him return on his own?"

Luskell considered. "My staff anchors me, and other meaningful objects. Smells, too. Maybe sounds?"

"Yes, give him a toy to hold." Mamam smiled as if the problem were already solved. "And we could sing to him and tell him stories. Cook his favorite foods — the aroma might draw him back."

"It won't hurt, I guess." Crett's carved wooden bears lay

on the floor where he'd last played with them. Luskell picked up one of the baby bears and placed it in his hand. His fingers closed tightly around it. If Terulo was right, the beloved toy should be infused with positive and encouraging emotion. She looked to her mother again. "How long does he have, if he doesn't wake?"

"That depends." Mamam sat Crett up on her lap and put a cup of water to his lips, dribbling a little in as he opened his mouth. He swallowed and sipped more. "Good, he can swallow on his own." She laid him back in his bed. "This would be easier if he weren't already weaned. We'll have to baby him, but as long as he can eat and drink, we can outwait your legend."

For supper, they warmed up leftover chicken pie. Mamam mashed and strained some of it for Crett, as if he were a toothless infant again. He didn't wake but opened his mouth eagerly. It smelled almost as good as it had fresh but Luskell had no appetite. She ate a few bites, then got out her fiddle and played the rollicking tunes Crett liked best. He didn't respond other than to smile in his sleep. That was encouragement enough. They took turns telling stories and singing to him until bedtime.

Luskell reluctantly went to her own bed. She was exhausted and there was nothing to be gained from watching Crett sleep. But what if she dreamed herself to the Other Side by accident? If she crossed over, Old Mother Bones would know she was there. She might attack Luskell again, or worse, harm Crett. For now, at least, Luskell's power protected him. While that sparkling ribbon lasted, Old Mother Bones wouldn't touch him. There couldn't be much left, though, and having cut off the trickle, Luskell was determined not to start bleeding power again. It would only weaken her and strengthen her enemy.

In spite of that small protection, Luskell felt guilty that

Crett was on the Other Side at all. It hadn't occurred to her until too late that even a small amount of power meant the dead could visit his dreams. Was he afraid? Did he even understand what was going on? Knot or Ketwyn might help him, but she couldn't risk going there to ask.

Maybe one of them would visit her dreams. She couldn't control that, but it was her best hope. Luskell hummed "Aku's Lullaby" to herself. She was tired enough for it to relax her and she didn't resist. She drifted and dozed and began to dream.

She was back in the cabin in Misty Pass, and Ketwyn was there.

"I was afraid you wouldn't come! I need you to help Crett, but it isn't safe for me to cross over."

"I wish I could. I don't think she'll let me close enough to him, and I couldn't do more than tell him how to get home."

"I know, but you might keep him safe until we work out how to draw him back. Do you think you and Knot could gather everyone who cares about him? If we have a big enough group, they can block others from touching him and sapping his life."

"I'll help if I can. Who were you thinking?"

"Everyone! You, of course, and Knot. Balsam. Elika. Grandma Lukett. Jagryn's Grandpa Ohme. Elika's husband or whatever he was — Greelin? Uncle Jelf, Uncle Soorhi, Dadad's grandparents Stoli and Telna. Trenn would probably help. That girl, Luma. A woman, Denna, who arrived recently."

"I get the idea. I'll do everything I can. But ... what if he can't get away on his own?"

"Then I might have to come after him."

"Promise you'll be careful, little sister."

"Careful might not bring Crett home. I'll do what I have

to."

In the morning, there was no obvious change in Crett's condition. When Luskell examined him with her wizard eye, though, his light burned lower than it had. Not as if a dead soul had touched him, for which she was thankful, but being in that place was slowly draining his life. It was time to bring in more help.

Fandek, come quickly. Crett and I need your help.

On my way.

The brief contact with his mind lifted her spirits. It helped that he didn't waste time with questions. While they waited, Dadad scrambled some eggs, Crett's favorite for breakfast. Mamam blew on a spoonful to cool it, then held it to Crett's lips. He opened his mouth readily but pushed the food back out without swallowing.

"What's wrong? Why won't he eat?" Luskell asked.

Mamam did her best to hide her worry. "Sunshine might help."

Fandek arrived moments later. "What happened to him?"

Luskell explained as briefly as she could. "Sunshine should give him back what he's lost, or most of it. Buy us time to bring him home."

"Here you go, little fellow." Fandek laid his hand on Crett's head. Crett smiled but didn't open his eyes.

He had a stronger glow of life about him, but when Mamam tried to feed him again, he still wouldn't swallow. She held him close. "This changes things."

Luskell hated to hear the quaver in Mamam's voice.

They had grown used to Crett as a "big boy," his own person. Seeing him so helpless strengthened her resolve to deal with Old Mother Bones.

"I'll try again."

"Too dangerous," Mamam said. "She hurt you once already."

"But I'm the only one who can do it!" Luskell thought of her previous failure. "Except ... I can't."

"You can't do it *alone*," Dadad said. "What about with help?"

Help. What kind of help would do any good? With all the wizards and healers she knew, though, there must be a way.

A plan began to form. "All right. I'm going to need ... everyone."

She reached out to Jagryn first. *I need your help.*

It's yours, but ... we shouldn't speak this way. It's too ...

He didn't need to finish. She understood and agreed. Mind-talking not only allowed secret communication, it was intimate in and of itself. Especially for Luskell and Jagryn, who had learned it together, and had literally shared a dream.

You're right. I'll come down and we can talk in person.

Right now? Yes, all right, as long as you don't stay long.

She hurried down the back stairs and knocked at the door. Jagryn came outside and closed the door behind him.

"I'm here alone. The neighbors might talk if you come inside."

That explained his hesitancy, though not which of them he didn't trust.

"All right. Where is everyone?"

"Ruvhonn's having a dress fitted. Kiat went along. Wyllik said he was meeting a friend at the library."

"At the library?" Luskell allowed herself a smile at that

interesting development. "I'll be brief. Crett's in trouble and I need you to help me rescue him."

"You need me, specifically?"

"I need someone with experience crossing over. Since you're the only one I've had a chance to train, you're it."

"I don't know if that's a good idea," Jagryn said. "I told you we shouldn't do magic together. And us, on the Other Side? Even worse. How does that help Crett?"

"He's there already, but he's alive. For now."

"What do you need me for? You cross over like it's nothing," Jagryn said. "Why haven't *you* tried to bring him back?"

"I did try, and I failed." Luskell's insides ached where Old Mother Bones had touched her. "I can't do this alone." The tears she had held back before now spilled over.

"It's all right." Jagryn drew her into an embrace. "He'll be all right. I don't know how much help I'll be, but I'll do what I can."

"Thank you." Held in his warm arms, she remembered how close they had once been, close enough to share a dream in which they were fully together. That time was past, and he was right about the neighbors. She could still count on him, though, and she loved him for it. She pushed back from him and dried her tears. "I'm asking a few others, too. Come upstairs and we can start planning."

"When Ruvhonn gets back. She comes with me."

"If that's what it takes, then fine with me. See you soon, I hope."

Luskell returned to her parents and Crett. "Jagryn will help. I should ask Laki, too." She wasn't sure what his job would be, but the three of them had been a team in the beginning. They worked well together, and Laki cared about Crett as much as Jagryn did. He'd had a vision of him before Crett was even conceived.

Laki, Crett's got bigger problems than visions of the future. I need your help.

And Tatakla's?

Of course. Come as soon as you can.

Who else? Fandek was already there. No question her parents would be part of this effort. Try to keep them away. But not all the helpers were alive. She hoped Ketwyn had managed to gather all the ancestors he could find.

Luskell paced up and down, clutching her staff. Jagryn and Ruvhonn arrived first. Luskell greeted them but put off explanations until Laki and Tatakla joined them. She had thought the room was crowded with a family of four, but that was nothing compared with how packed it was now with eight grown folks and one toddler.

"What's wrong with Crett?" Ruvhonn asked. "You don't mean he's been sleeping since we were here last! Oh, I'm so sorry!"

"It isn't your fault," Luskell hastened to reassure her. "He's shown signs of power, but none of us thought it might mean danger from the Other Side."

"What is happening?" Laki gazed intently at Crett and squeezed Tatakla's hand.

"A legendary spirit, Old Mother Bones, took his soul to the Other Side."

"We all know those stories," Ruvhonn objected. "It doesn't really work that way, does it?"

"I thought she was only a story, too. But she's real, and jealous because I can cross over." Luskell paused in her pacing and leaned on her staff. "I believe she used to be human long ago, with the same ability I have, but she stayed too long on the Other Side. Her body perished but she was already there, so she hasn't accepted that she's dead. Or doesn't remember; it's about the same. She became a cautionary tale over something she did that was misunderstood. Even though it wasn't true, she was remembered beyond the normal span and became a legend." Luskell remembered Mamam's warning to protect her own reputation if she planned to act as death's midwife. Neither of them had considered the danger of becoming a legendary monster after death. "So now she doesn't even remember who she was, but she remembers enough to feel threatened by me. She wants to be some kind of nightmare queen. She couldn't lure me over, so she's holding Crett hostage. His body is alive here but his soul is on the Other Side. I can't bring him back alone."

Laki and Jagryn exchanged skeptical glances, though they had agreed to help. Fandek leaped to his feet. "How do I help?"

"Thank you, Fandek." Luskell glared at Jagryn and Laki. "Your sunshine will be necessary. You can restore most of what I lose on the Other Side. Can you control it well enough to give me a small, steady amount? Or periodic, regular doses would work, too."

"I think I could manage either, as long as it doesn't take too much time. More for Crett, too?"

"Yes, Crett too. Jagryn, I can't even start unless you're part of this."

Jagryn stepped forward. "If Fandek's up for it, I'll help, too."

"What's my job?" Laki asked.

"I'm not sure. But you have a lot in common with Crett. He may need you when he comes back."

"*If* we bring him back," Jagryn said. "What am I supposed to do?"

"I need you to cross over with me, but stay hidden and bring Crett back as soon as he's free. Then I'll face Old Mother Bones."

"I won't let you do it alone!" Jagryn objected.

Jagryn, you have to. I didn't want to tell you like this, but ... Ruvhonn's pregnant. You must stay safe.

She's ... but she hasn't said ... are you sure?

More to the point, Mamam's sure. I need your help, but you must promise to stay safe.

I promise. Jagryn glanced a Ruvhonn, a dazed smile on his face.

"I won't be alone," Luskell said. She hoped no one had noticed the pause. "Ketwyn will help us, too."

Chapter 28

By the time they'd made their plan, the morning had passed. Food was the last thing Luskell wanted, though she hadn't finished her breakfast.

"I don't like what you're doing, but you'll need all your strength." Mamam glanced down at Crett, limp in her arms.

Luskell forced herself to eat the soup in front of her. She couldn't bear to see her brother that way, or her mother. After her bowl was empty, she changed clothes. Her new dress had given her confidence for her meeting with Governor Klanya. Maybe it would help with Old Mother Bones, too. The overtunic would be too warm, but she put on the blouse and skirt. She associated the green silk with controlling her power, and the whole outfit with authority, not to mention Tulia's affection. She slid Luma's bracelet onto her wrist, too. Its centuries of positive emotion could only help. She returned to the front room and found the rest of Crett's wooden bears. The largest — Mamam Bear, Wizard Bear — went into her skirt pocket.

"I have something for you," Fandek said. "It might help." He reached into his pocket and placed an object in her hand.

It was the medallion she'd seen hanging on his wall, now polished so the old silver shone. It was scalloped around the edge and decorated with etched designs, similar to Luma's bracelet. A small ring pierced one scallop, a leather thong laced through it and knotted. The metal was warm from Fandek's pocket and held echoes of emotion.

"It's like the bracelet, but for poor folks," Fandek explained. "This was my gram's. Mom showed it to me once when I was small, after I promised I wouldn't tell Pop. He thought it was lost. I've kept it safe since she died."

It was his treasure; his only treasure, the only thing he had from his mother or her family. "And you want me to ...?"

"If you wear it, it might help keep you safe over there. Don't worry, I won't take it as a promise or anything."

She slipped it over her head and tucked it inside her blouse, where it could rest against her skin. "Thank you."

Dadad answered a knock at the door. "Oh, Shura! Hello, Cedar. What can we — "

"Fandek told me Crett was in trouble," Shura said. "We want to help if we can."

"We do, too." Daisy and Ambug crowded in behind Shura and Cedar. Ambug carried a large basket of fruit and bread.

The place had already been packed, but with twelve

adults, one of them large enough for two, there was barely room to turn around. Everyone meant well, though, and they were united in their affection for her little brother. Rather than turn them away, Luskell quickly summarized her plan. "You probably won't have to do anything, but I'm glad you're here."

There weren't close to enough chairs for everyone. They made do with standing against the wall or sitting on the floor.

"Jagryn, I want to try something new," Luskell said. "This should get us there without her feeling it, the way she does when I cross over the usual way. It might give us an advantage."

Jagryn gave her a worried smile. "You know I hate when you say *should* and *might*. What's this new way?"

"Terulo discovered a forgotten spell for stepping from one spot to another instantly. We've tested the version that takes you somewhere you can see. The other version takes you to a place you know but can't see."

"And you haven't tested that one yet?" The smile left Jagryn's face while the worry remained.

"I tried it on my own. Terulo's guess is sound," Luskell said. "Once the doorway is open, I'll be able to see whether it goes to the right place."

Dadad frowned. "You'll be crossing over in your bodies?"

"I won't know till we try, but I doubt it. There's a good chance our bodies will fall into a trance when we step through. You should be ready to catch me. Ambug, you can catch Jagryn."

"Lay them on the bed, where they'll be safe," Mamam said. She glanced down at Crett, limp in her arms.

Luskell stood next to Jagryn, with Dadad and Ambug ready to prevent them falling. She spoke the doorways spell. She pictured where she wanted to emerge and traced the doorway with her staff. It opened onto the familiar hillside on the Other Side, below the place where Old Mother Bones held Crett captive. The hill was steep enough to hide their arrival.

"I'll go through first and you follow." She lifted her foot to step through.

Behind her, the real door burst open. "Stop!" Terulo shouted.

Luskell turned. "But look, your guess worked!"

"No, there's an error." Terulo paused to catch his breath. "I walked Wyllik home and his mother told us what you were trying to do."

"What made you think I'd try the doorways spell?"

"I know you well enough to worry," Terulo said. "That piece you gave me before filled most of the gap. Not enough to finish the spell, but enough to show what was missing from my guess."

Luskell gazed through the doorway, opening where she wanted to go. "I don't understand. What's missing?"

"A way back."

Luskell leaned on her staff and her father to steady herself. When she'd used the doorway to come home from the library, she hadn't been concerned about going back. If she'd opened a one-way door to a place farther away, it would be inconvenient, but she could open a new doorway or return by a conventional method. But to the Other Side? There was no guarantee she'd be able to return the way she normally did. She couldn't work magic there, so a new doorway was out of the question. She would be stuck over there, and Crett and Jagryn with her. She didn't *know* that's what would happen, but as Larem had said, Terulo didn't only *read* magical writing. He *understood*.

She closed the doorway. "We'll work on that one

another time. Sorry, Jagryn, we'll have to do this the hard way. Do you think you can follow Crett's thoughts the way I do? That way we can arrive at the same time."

"I've never done it except in dreams. And wouldn't that ruin the surprise, us arriving where he is?"

"You're right." Was the whole plan ruined before it began? It couldn't be. She sank down on the side of her parents' bed. "We'll do it this way: I'll put you to sleep, you'll dream your way in, and I'll follow your dream."

"I saw where you were headed with the doorway, so at least that work wasn't wasted." Jagryn's smile had a hint of his old untroubled self.

"Right, you don't want to arrive in the open meadow. That's the entry place, but the dead can't go down the long slope below the meadow."

"So we're safe until we go up where Crett is. How do we avoid the dead who might hurt us?"

"You shouldn't be in any danger. Stay out of sight, pop up when I give the signal, grab Crett, get out of there."

Jagryn frowned. "What about you?"

"Ketwyn's taking care of it. I asked him to gather our ancestors. They should be able to protect us."

"That's good thinking, I guess."

"I'll follow you there and make it look like I'm on my own," Luskell said. "But this time, I'm bringing my staff and a few other special objects. Bring your staff, too. It might help."

"What's the signal?"

"I'll say, 'Crett, it's time to go home now.' Keep it simple."

Luskell laid her staff on her parents' big bed, next to the wall. She stretched out beside it. Jagryn lay down beside her, his staff in his hand.

"Sorry," he muttered, his face red.

Before he could say more, Ruvhonn silenced him with a kiss. She reached across him and squeezed Luskell's hand. "Be safe. Both of you." She backed out of the way so Mamam could place Crett between them.

"Fandek, give Crett sunshine before we start," Luskell said. "He's been there more than a day already. Then give each of us a dose at regular intervals."

Fandek laid his hand on Crett's head and was rewarded with another smile.

"Ready, Jagryn?" Luskell asked.

"As I'll ever be." Jagryn settled back and closed his eyes.

Luskell laid her hand on his head and sang Aku's Lullaby to put him to sleep. She read his thoughts until he began to dream, then made herself comfortable and followed his dream to the Other Side.

She had never tried arriving below the entry place, but she had climbed from the bottom when she accompanied the dying. This time, she found Jagryn about three-quarters of the way up. He lay prone, keeping out of sight of anyone at the top. His hand gripped a sparkling nothing.

"I came in closer to the top," he whispered as she crawled up next to him. "I don't think anyone saw me, but there's a crowd gathering. Be careful."

"If Ketwyn did his job, the crowd is friendly." Luskell couldn't yet see the gathered souls, but if the gabble of conversation was any indication, it was a large group. Muffled whispering seemed closer to her ears, though Jagryn was the only one nearby. She recognized Tatakla's distinctive accent and smiled. They had a friendly crowd supporting them at home, too. Together, they belly-crawled up the slope to get closer. "Stay here. Time to find out if my guess is correct."

Luskell stood and walked the last few steps up to the level meadow. Across the way, the souls gathered. Knot was there, of course, and Elika. She recognized Grandma Lukett, Uncle Jelf, and Uncle Ohme. Many she didn't know, though they shared features with people she knew well. She couldn't even see Ketwyn, there were so many, but he had done his job better than she could have hoped. There were even some tall figures at the back who looked Aklaka. No one living remembered Knot's parents; it was unlikely his half-Aklaka mother or her ancestors were still here. These were probably Laki's grandparents. She was glad they were there, whoever they were.

Old Mother Bones waited as if she hadn't moved since Luskell's last visit, the same towering, skeletal figure in a tattered black dress. The glittering ribbon was shorter and now surrounded Crett's neck. Was that why he couldn't swallow? He smiled weakly at Luskell and sat too quietly. At least Old Mother Bones wasn't touching him. He gazed at something in his hand: the faint ghost of a toy bear. Luskell reached into her pocket and grasped the larger bear. She approached Crett cautiously, staying out of reach.

"I told you not to come back unless you were ready to stay."

"I only want to talk." Luskell ached where Old Mother Bones had touched her before. This was a bad plan. It wouldn't work. She and Crett would both be trapped.

The medallion over her heart warmed and a sense of well-being infused Luskell's soul. Sunshine. The plan had to work. It was all she had, and she wasn't alone.

She forced herself to meet the legend's gaze. "Tell me what you want."

"What I *want* is the respect that is my due." The hollow, grating voice filled Luskell's ears. "I want my domain to be *mine*, without little girls flouncing in as if they own the place."

If not for the sunshine, Luskell would have lost her

temper. If she had ever flounced in her life, she didn't now. But that word, *domain*, caught her attention. She had used it to describe Knot's Valley. It wasn't hers anymore and she had deliberately let it go. No easy task, and probably not yet complete. Old Mother Bones was wrong; the Other Side did not belong to her. But Luskell granted her a measure of sympathy.

She held her voice steady, her gaze on Crett. "Isn't it enough that I don't come for myself anymore?"

"What do you mean?"

"I only come to help people. To bring back those whose time hasn't come, or to escort those who are afraid to go alone. I only do what you did ... in life."

Old Mother Bone's eyes blazed in her skull-like face. "I have always been here."

"Let my brother go. You don't need him."

"Will you stay in his place, then?"

Before Luskell could answer, Old Mother Bones lunged toward her, her free hand outstretched. Luskell barely eluded her grasp. Jagryn sprang up from his hiding spot and stepped across the boundary, his ghost-staff raised like a weapon. As he swung it downward, Old Mother Bones spun toward him with inhuman speed and grabbed him where his neck met his shoulder.

"I thought I saw someone else. You're a couple of sneaks."

Jagryn fell to his knees and dropped his staff. Old Mother Bones grew brighter and more solid in appearance. Jagryn faded. Was she draining him that quickly? No, more likely his body was trying to preserve his life by waking. That might be the best thing — they'd lost the element of surprise. But Luskell didn't know how to save Crett by herself.

Out of the whispering close to her ear, she heard ...

singing? Yes, Laki's voice singing Aku's Lullaby. He was keeping Jagryn asleep. Another voice joined, higher, singing only the melody without the words. Jagryn sprang up, strengthened by more than sunshine, and shook off Old Mother Bones' grip. Luskell chanced a look down the slope into the crowded room, far away but perfectly clear. Ruvhonn lay next to Jagryn, holding him and singing into his ear a song she didn't know. She was risking her husband, the father of the child she didn't know about yet, to save Luskell's brother. Luskell's own determination hardened. Somehow, she would make this work.

Jagryn stepped beyond Old Mother Bones' reach. "Sorry, Luskell. We should have known better than to try to fool a legend." He picked up his ghost-staff and with an apologetic shrug, walked off down the slope and out of sight.

"A fine friend he is," Old Mother Bones grated. "Now what will you do?"

Luskell wasn't about to admit she didn't know. How could Jagryn have simply left her on her own? Yes, there wasn't much he could do now, but ...

A child toddled out of the crowd of souls. A child a little older than Crett, with redder hair and paler skin, but no freckles. Giggling, he trotted up to Crett and hugged him. Startled, Old Mother Bones took her eyes off Luskell. Luskell grabbed her chance and raised the ghost of her staff. She brought it down on the glittering ribbon, which scattered to nothing.

The other child grew into a young man. He ran with Crett in his arms. "Come, Crett, it's time to go home!"

Strange, that was the signal Luskell had arranged with ...

Jagryn popped up at the edge of the meadow. Ketwyn tossed Crett to him. He squealed, "I flyin'!" Jagryn caught him securely in both arms, like the wonderful father he was going to be.

Jagryn and Crett disappeared down the slope. Ketwyn kept running, around behind Luskell and back to the crowd of friendly souls. Old Mother Bones scowled after him. She couldn't harm him directly, but she could haunt the dreams of those he loved. She could train up nightmare monsters from the souls of criminals and madmen. What if she fed those dreams to sleepers with both power and evil intent? Crett was free but Luskell's work was not yet done.

"Then you choose to stay?" Bony fingers wrapped around Luskell's wrist. A chill ran through Luskell, though not as painful as the first time Old Mother Bones had touched her.

"No. You will let me go."

"Don't you know anything? I am Old Mother Bones. I can hold a living soul here until the body perishes."

"Th-that's what the stories say." A dose of sunshine drove the chill away. Old Mother Bones pulled her hand back as if burned or bitten. She stared at the bracelet. It was nearly invisible, the engraved design standing out in relief.

"What is this? I know it." Old Mother Bones frowned in deep thought and for a moment shrank to normal human size before becoming giant again.

"The stories aren't true." Luskell hid her surprise at the legend's reaction to the bracelet, which Luskell had expected only to help protect her. It was old enough, though. "Did you have a bracelet like this when you were *alive*?" Old Mother Bones' eyes blazed at the emphasis on the word. Luskell hurried on. "You were a powerful witch and healer. You pursued a dying man here." That was the end of what Luskell knew from the book. Now for her guess. "He wouldn't go back. You stayed, hoping he would change his mind, but he died. By then it was too late to return to your own body and you were trapped here."

"I ... have always been here." She sounded less certain now.

"You don't remember. People told stories about the powerful witch who could follow a soul to the Other Side, and then fearful, envious people changed the story to a powerful witch who could drag a soul to the Other Side. She became a skeletal old hag, a monster to frighten children. Now that's all anyone remembers, even you. No one remembers the skillful, caring healer. They don't remember what you did when you were ... Serana."

Old Mother Bones gripped Luskell's arm again, not taking anything this time. The bony hand trembled.

"You weren't always here, but you didn't die and arrive in the ordinary way," Luskell persisted. "Your body died, but your soul was already here. Is that why you don't remember? Or has it just been so long?"

"How ... long?" Old Mother Bones' voice sounded different. Lighter, and with a slight quaver.

"A long time. Around three hundred years. But you are not a monster. You are Serana."

"Serana." She was shorter than Luskell now, and plump, not bony. Her brown hair was streaked with gray. She might have been older than Mamam, but much younger than Balsam. "A healer-witch. Yes, I was. I was the best. Even death was not always the end."

"That's right. When you got there in time, you could bring them back. Except the last one."

"The last one. Yes. The last one ..." She frowned, seeking the distant memory. "It was a mystery, why a strong man would lapse into a stupor and not wake up. I went after him, but he wouldn't go back. Or *couldn't*." Serana eyed Luskell conspiratorially. "I wasn't sure at the time, but later

I suspected poison. Of course by then it was too late. I tried to tell them in dreams but no one was listening."

"That's the problem with dreams." Luskell knew she shouldn't stay much longer. How long had she even been there? But she had one more thing to do. "Come with me. I'd like you to meet some people."

She walked over to the crowd, Serana beside her. "Thank you all so much for your help."

"You know I'm always here for you," Knot said. "Even if we don't meet often."

A small old man beside him smiled up at Luskell. "So you're my Bardin's wizard girl. Tell him Ordahn's proud of him, will you? And of you. Well done."

"Th-thank you," Luskell stammered, stunned to finally meet the wizard who had been her master's master, as well as her grandfather's. She shook herself. Her work wasn't finished yet. "Friends, this is Serana. She was a great healer long ago. No one who knew her is still living, so I don't know what will happen with her now. People still tell stories about Old Mother Bones. She might persist. If she acts like a monster again, remind her who she is. Call her by her name."

Knot held out his hand and Serana grasped it. "Welcome, Serana. I have stories about me, too. If I start calling myself Yrae, you may remind me of my new name."

"This is my grandfather, Knot. He was a wizard."

Luma burst from the crowd. "You're wearing my mother's bracelet!"

"*My* bracelet," Serana corrected her. "I remember now. A young man presented it to me with a marriage proposal. I liked the bracelet and wore it for a time, but I didn't want to marry him, or anyone. I gave it back and he found someone who wanted both the bracelet and the husband."

"Then we should be friends," Luma said. "We're related

by bracelet."

Serana smiled, a gentle expression with none of the skull-like grimace. "I would like that."

Luskell introduced everyone else whose name she knew, until Knot and Ketwyn reminded her of the time she'd already spent. She hugged them, and Grandma Lukett.

"Oh!" Grandma cried in response to something over Luskell's shoulder. She released Luskell and hurried away.

Luskell turned to see what was so exciting. Grandma Lukett embraced a new arrival and brought him to join the crowd. Grandpa Eslo.

"Grandpa, no!" Luskell said. "What are you doing here?"

"Luskell!" He took her hand. "I could ask you the same thing. I suppose you're doing one of your wizard things, but I must be dead."

"You can't be! Not yet. Go back while there's still time!"

"My time has run out," he said. "No going back. But this is a gift, to see you one more time. Tell your mother, won't you?"

She nodded, unable to speak. She kissed Grandpa and turned to leave.

Serana grasped Luskell's hand. "It was nice to meet you. Who are you again?"

"Luskell. I'm ... well, a lot of things. Healer. Listener. Wizard."

"Witch, too?" Serana asked.

Luskell laughed at that. She had rejected that title at first, but it fit better over time. "Maybe. With your permission, Death's Midwife."

"You don't need my permission, dear. Not anymore."

"Thank you. And it was my ... pleasure to meet you, Serana."

Luskell opened her eyes and sprang to a sitting position. Both Mamam and Fandek started back to avoid knocking heads with her. They'd been hovering, and she could feel traces of their concern as it passed. She grabbed them both in a hug.

"Welcome back," Mamam said. "You were gone long enough, we were starting to worry. You had tears in your eyes."

"I got some bad news right at the end." Luskell looked her mother in the eyes. She deserved to know, but Luskell hated to spoil the joy of having Crett back.

Mamam sighed. "Your grandpa?"

Luskell nodded. "I'm sorry. I tried to get him to go back, but he said it was his time."

"Then it was. This news is ... not unexpected. Mama and Ketwyn were there to meet him?"

"*Everyone* was. It was a real crowd."

Mamam smiled. "He'll feel right at home."

"I'm glad you're all right," Fandek said. "I kept giving you sunshine even after Crett and Jagryn woke up."

"Thank you! It really helped. How is Crett?"

"See for yourself." Mamam stepped out of the way so Luskell had a view of the rest of the room. Crett sat at the table eating a huge lunch — soup and slices of bread and fruit from Ambug's basket. He chattered at Laki between bites. Both baby bears sat on the table in front of him. Apart from the rest of the group, Ruvhonn sat in Mamam's rocker and Jagryn knelt beside her. They were in their own world. Ruvhonn placed her hand on her belly and beamed. Luskell's belly twinged. She hadn't been that happy the one time she'd feared she was pregnant. Now she might not get the chance.

If I never have my own child, at least I have Crett back. That's all that matters.

"Grammy Bo take me to her place!" Crett said. "It pretty there but no fun."

"That is why we never go with people in dreams," Laki said. "It is no fun."

"She wouldn't let me go home with 'uskell." Crett frowned. "L-l-uskell. Luskell. I say it! Then a fren come to play, grow big, carry me! And I flied!"

"That was our brother Ketwyn." Luskell removed Mamam Bear from her pocket and set her on the table with her cubs.

Crett's big eyes widened even further. "We got a brother? Yay!"

Mamam brushed a tear from her eye. Luskell squeezed her shoulders. She'd nearly lost a second child, who, after two days on the Other Side, still knew nothing of death. He was excited to have a brother.

"Maybe he'll visit your dreams now, too. Or ..." Luskell shared an uncertain glance with their father.

"Even if I succeed in suppressing his power, I suspect the dreams will continue," Dadad said.

Luskell had first experienced dream visits from the dead before she was aware of her own power — when she was suppressing it. She recalled how the suppression spell at the Governor's Mansion had felt, her power tightly bound but still there. "All right, then. Crett, keep telling us your dreams."

"What happen to Grammy Bo?"

"I don't think she'll bother you anymore, Crett. I reminded her who she really is. If someone called Serana visits your dreams, you may talk with her, but don't follow her."

"I stay here?"

"You stay here for a long time."

Chapter 29

Crett was safe. The dreams he shared were mostly nonsense. Visions of the future were happy or at least harmless. Knot and Ketwyn visited one of his dreams after Dadad worked a spell to suppress his power, which seemed to prove their guess that the dreams would continue, regardless. He'd made the spell as conservative and gentle as possible.

"It ought to wear off by the time he's ten or twelve," Dadad told Luskell. "We won't make the same mistake we did with you, though. We'll make sure he knows well in advance."

After a full week with no dreams of Old Mother Bones, Luskell wrote the letter she had been putting off.

To the Honorable Klanya, Governor of Eukard:

Thank you for delaying the execution of the murderer Kerf. I believe the threat to the magical community has now been averted and the sentence may be carried out without harm to anyone but the criminal himself.

Sincerely,
Wizard Luskell

Soon, Kerf's hanging was back on the schedule. Because he was a notorious criminal who had terrorized the whole city and places beyond, the authorities declared it a public event. Broadsides were printed and posted all over the city.

"I should be there." Fandek stared at the notice posted outside the cheese shop.

Luskell heard the reluctance in his tone. "We both should. Finish what we started."

She was no more eager for the event than he was, but at least neither had to be alone. Before that, it was time to return the bracelet. She didn't want it tainted with the horror of an execution. Luskell went back to what she would always think of as Luma's house. She knocked on the door and waited.

Palu opened the door. "Yes? Oh, Wizard Luskell! What can we do for you?" A delicious aroma of fruit and spices wafted from another room. And … children's voices?

"It's what I can do for you. Thank you for letting me borrow your bracelet." Luskell held it out. "I learned a lot about it. It turned out to be useful in ways I didn't expect."

Palu hesitated, then took the bracelet. "Useful?"

"It protected me from harm and reminded someone who they really were. It isn't cursed at all. Quite the opposite."

Palu smiled sadly, rubbing the bracelet before slipping it onto her wrist. "I didn't mean it was literally cursed."

"I know. There are powers besides magic. It's been around a long time. It has absorbed centuries of love."

A girl ran up and grabbed Palu's hand. "Come back, Palu! We don't know how long to stir it!"

"Just a moment, Ryla." Palu turned back to Luskell. "This is my neighbor's girl, Ryla. Sometimes I borrow her and her sister Sery when it gets too quiet. We're making applesauce."

Luskell recognized Ryla as the eldest child of the woman who had lost her toddler in the wobbles epidemic. "Yes, we met once. How's your mother, Ryla?"

"Ooh, you're the wizard girl! I think she's better. She took the boys out to be measured for new boots. I dream about the baby sometimes, but she's bigger now."

Luskell smiled. "I would love to hear more about that another time."

"Go on back and help Sery stir," Palu said. "I'll be right with you."

"It looks like things are better for you, too," Luskell said when Ryla was gone.

Palu shrugged. "They're not Luma, but it's a comfort to have them over. It helps their mother, too. Children find you if you let them." She extended the arm with the bracelet. "You could keep it longer, if it's useful to you."

Luskell sensed Palu's reluctance to give it up again, in spite of her offer. "It will be more useful to you now, I think. And ... I have something like it." She still wore Fandek's medallion next to her skin.

The authorities had the gallows erected in an open square in the Government District at enough distance from the prison that Kerf would have to be transported in a cart. On the appointed day, crowds lined the streets to get a look at the monster before he met his doom. Although some in the crowd had put on their best clothes as if for a festival, Luskell wore her plain gray dress. She did not care to attract more attention than her staff and eyepatch already drew, and what was there to celebrate?

Luskell met Fandek at the prison gates. "How is he?" she asked.

"Scared. Sick." Fandek's shoulders sagged. "I offered to ride with him, but they won't let me."

"I have an idea."

Luskell threw concealment over both of them. When the cart came out, she pulled Fandek close to her and followed it. The cart moved slowly because of the crowds. She held the tailgate with her hand and whispered to Fandek. "Climb up and I'll follow."

Once they were in the cart, she dropped concealment.

"Get down from there!" a guard shouted.

"No." Luskell pointed her staff at him and he backed off.

"We mean no harm, but we're not getting down before the end."

Some in the crowd had brought rotten vegetables to throw. Luskell sympathized — she had called down lightning on Kerf — but he didn't pose a threat anymore. She cast a spell tent over the cart so Fandek could give comfort and sunshine to his brother at the end of his life.

"We're almost there," she announced when the gallows came in view. "We should get down before they drag us down. Kerf, do you want me to go to the Other Side with you?"

"I'd appreciate it. I still don't believe I won't be punished."

"You've been punished. You're being punished today. I don't know exactly what comes next for you, but it won't be more of that."

She hopped down from the cart and immediately concealed herself and Fandek to confuse the guards. They made their way to the front of the crowd.

"How can you go with him?" Fandek asked. "Don't you have to touch him? They'll never let you close enough."

"I know. I have ... most of a plan." To touch him with her hand, she'd have to be on the scaffold. Even concealed, she would risk bumping one or more of the officials, and would lose concealment when she crossed over. But what if she didn't use her hand? Her staff was part of her, too.

"I'm going to move closer," she said. "I'll stay concealed as long as I can."

"I'll be right next to you, ready to provide sunshine."

The guards were busy enough unloading Kerf from the cart to have forgotten about Fandek. Luskell crept up to the front of the platform where they were arranging the noose around Kerf's neck. She almost broke concealment when he spoke.

"I am getting what I deserve. Thank you."

Luskell stretched out her staff to touch his bound hands. He twitched, then grasped the end of the invisible stick. An official read words Luskell didn't pay attention to. She focused on following Kerf's thoughts. They were as strange as ever, but muted. By the events of the day or by the staff? Whichever, she was right there with him when the trapdoor opened and he dropped ...

... onto the slope to the Other Side.

"Well, that was sudden. I'm glad they made a neat job of it." Kerf stood up straight. "The monster is gone!" His smile beamed with more joy than Luskell had imagined he could feel.

Luskell gestured with her staff toward the top of the hill. "Shall we see who's waiting for you?"

He sobered. "I'd rather not."

Luskell gave him an encouraging shove. "No choice. Come on, I'll go with you to make sure someone remembers who she is."

They climbed slowly to the top, Kerf setting the pace. Luskell was relieved not to see Old Mother Bones. A crowd of women waited, all angry except one, who looked sad and disappointed. Who looked like Fandek.

"I'm sorry, Mom. I'm so sorry." Kerf fell to his knees.

The woman embraced him. "I know. I blame your pop."

"Is he here?"

"Somewhere. Hiding. Ashamed. We've had some long talks since he got here."

"Did it help?"

"Some. You'll be having some talks of your own." She looked up at the crowd of his victims.

"Maybe later. I've already had a bad day."

"That's not for me to decide," Fanlyn said. "Or for you. You gave each of them the worst possible day. Take it up with them."

"Let me say goodbye to my wizard friend." Kerf turned to Luskell. "I guess I'm on my own from here. Thanks for your help."

"Thank me by becoming something other than a monster."

"I'll see to it," his mother said.

As Luskell turned to go, she found Serana waiting behind her, still in the form of a capable healer.

"Thank you for returning me to myself," she said. "I'm remembering more of my life every day, though it was so long ago. I don't think I will forget again."

"I hope you're right," Luskell said. "I wish you had living people to help you remember. Or loved ones here."

"Don't worry about that. Luma and her grandmother have adopted me. They made a room for me in the city."

"And the cave?"

"Gone, as if it never was."

"I'm glad." Luskell paused, weighing her next words. "How would it be if I tried to teach other healers to cross over? I don't know how many will be able to do it, but ..."

"It's a good idea. You taught your friend, didn't you? And you can't be everywhere."

"That's what I thought. I didn't want to be disrespectful."

"You don't need my permission but thank you for asking." Serana smiled.

Encouraged, Luskell asked a more difficult question. "When you were ... in that other form, you took something from me. Can you give it back?"

Serana bowed her head. "It was wrong to hurt you. But what's done is done. I'm sorry."

"I understand how the touch of a dead soul can shorten or even end my life. You did something different."

"I have been dead a long time," Serana replied. "And I gained strength from the power you left here. We were linked. It allowed me to hurt you in a way I couldn't hurt another."

"But why like that?"

"I wasn't myself, so I can't say for sure. I loved children when I was alive, but I never had any of my own. So maybe I was ... making you more like me. Can you forgive me?"

"I ... will try."

Luskell emerged from her trance at the foot of the scaffold. She had crumpled to her knees but still gripped her staff. Fandek held her. She welcomed the warmth of his arms, and the sunshine. They were both visible, but no one bothered them as the crowd dispersed.

Luskell got to her feet and brushed herself off. The medallion hung visible outside her dress. She didn't put it back. "Your mother was there."

"You saw her?" Fandek covered his face with his hands for a moment, then met Luskell's gaze. "I didn't dare hope. How is she?"

"Ready to keep Kerf out of trouble. He has work ahead of him."

"Good. What about Pop?"

"I didn't see him, but she mentioned him. He hasn't finished his work yet."

"Thank you for coming with me today."

Luskell turned and pulled Fandek into an embrace. "It was the least I could do. You were there when I needed help with my brother, so ..."

"That was an easy choice. Your brother is the opposite of

a monster."

"Oh, he has his moments. Maybe we all have a bit of a monster in us."

"Probably. Kerf's was worse than most, though. I would have understood if you didn't want to help him."

"He wanted to be better. And you *are* better."

"You did it ... for me?"

"I did it because I have a strange gift I'm only beginning to understand. But yes, you were a big part of it." Luskell touched the medallion, turning it in her fingers. "I'd like to keep this, if you'll let me."

"I wouldn't tell you no. But some people might know what it means."

"I know what it means. Maybe ... we can learn to work together."

"I'd like that, I think. But only *work* together?"

"For now. Anything more wouldn't be appropriate, as long as you're Mamam's apprentice."

He smiled. "That's all right, then! She promoted me a week ago. Didn't she tell you?"

"No, I would remember. We've all had other things to think about, though." Luskell's whole being tingled with something like her power, his sunshine, but stronger. It felt so good, so right, she was tempted to keep her secret. She sighed. Her time on the Mountain was supposed to have made her more considerate. "In that case ... you need to know something. When Old Mother Bones touched me, she took more than just a little of my life."

"Do you need more sunshine?"

She shook her head. "Sunshine can't fix this. I ... can't have children. And I know you want to be a father."

"Is that all?" He pulled her close and held her tight. "If you want children, they'll find you one way or another. I'll take my chances with you. As long as it's not all work."

"Oh, there's much more to life than work." She slid her hand into his. "There's music, and stories, and magic. And love. Let's see what we can find."

THE END

About the Author

Karen Eisenbrey lives in Seattle, WA, where she leads a quiet, orderly life and invents stories to make up for it. Although she intended to be a writer from an early age, until her mid-30s she had nothing to say. A little bit of free time and a vivid dream about a wizard changed all that. Karen writes fantasy and science fiction novels, as well as short fiction in a variety of genres and the occasional song or poem if it insists. She also sings in a church choir and plays drums in a garage band. She shares her life with her husband, two young adult sons, and one elderly cat. Find more info on Karen's books and short fiction, follow her band-name blog, and sign up for her quarterly newsletter at kareneisenbreywriter.com

Special Thanks

... to Benjamin Gorman for starting a publishing company that so perfectly fits my writing; and to Viveca Shearin for her astute editing.

... to the whole Not A Pipe family of authors for their support, encouragement, and example.

...to Michaela Thorn for the beautiful, powerful cover art.

... to Angelika, James, Nan, and Yvonne, my invaluable beta readers.

... to Amy and Tim, my writing group that willingly listens to chapters out of order, some of them more than once.

... to Steve Scribner for help with the map of Eukard.

... to Karen Finneyfrock, who helped unstick this project during a 15-minute one-on-one at Write Here, Write Now in 2016. Old Mother Bones emerged from that meeting.

... to Keith Eisenbrey, my example for doing the creative work that needs to be done in spite of everything else. He has read countless drafts (of this and other projects), listened to me fuss over ideas, welcomed the host of fictional people who live in my head, and kept a roof over our heads all these years. I couldn't do any of it without him.

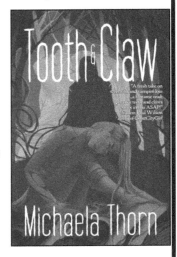

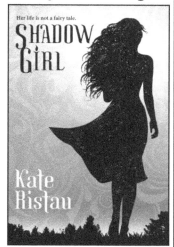

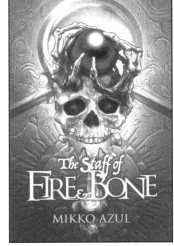

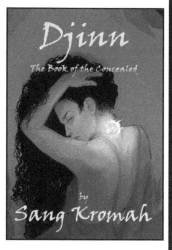